Come out of our grave, the woman said. Her heart was flying. Bells rang. The beech trees tried to blow away. She pointed at the boy. Good enough for you, she said, they crucified you. They were collecting the dustbins of the world but the gale drowned everything. She had a bunch of roses from other people's gardens. She could not give the flowers to the boy because his eyes were closed. He was asleep and she could not wake him. People wakened from sleep had terrible thoughts, she knew. They woke from a dream and the dream might not go away.

If anyone else had found him but this woman they would have known the story. They would have known who the boy was because everyone in the town knew him.

The woman was brighter than the dawn, whiter than the sky. Her white hair, her white mac, her tennis shoes. She dazzled. She shook the flowers at the grave until the heads snapped. Then she walked away towards the priest's house across the road.

Mrs Pearse told the priest there was a boy in her grave.

They crucified him, she said.

The priest put his hand on her arm and said she should say a little prayer, he found it was a great consolation to offer it up. She said she brought flowers for her son but there was a strange boy. She was concentrating hard but other things kept getting in the way. She had her voices but they all got along well enough now, they had a good relationship. There was always a good story. She was trying not to listen so she could speak. She explained it again. The priest was thinking that he should be in the vestry. And what about those old beeches? What if there was a gale from the north and one blew down on the church? They could all be killed. But he couldn't bring himself to call in a tree surgeon. The men collecting the dustbins were all Latvians. Nobody in Ireland wanted to collect rubbish anymore; it was a national characteristic. The Poles were good Catholics but the priest wasn't so sure about some of the others, after all it's not so long ago they were communists. Anyway, they were cheerful. Now Mrs Pearse, the priest said as severely as he could.

Mrs Pearse gave him the roses. The heads were snapped but he didn't say anything.

The priest watched her go.

In the May morning's dawning, idly staring out the window, laptop open at another blank page, the thought comes to me to set up a writers' group. An online writers' group. It seems like an uncomplicated idea, something to keep my head occupied because, as with many writers, nothing else is happening in there since the crisis began. The idea comes to me in the vacant space between one irrational thought and another. The place where ideas for books come from. Normally I see phrases, sentences, or the shapes of characters emerge from that primitive darkness to assume an earthly shape on the page. But this time it is a practical thought that will – or should – have consequences in the real world. An online writers' group.

And to give it an extra twist, it will be entirely anonymous.

I'm pleased with that idea. An anonymous online writers' group. For beginners.

A masterclass in prose composition.

I discuss it with my wife, Catherine, who is too well aware that I have been kicking my heels in frustration for two months and more, that the book I had begun in good spirits in January ran out of energy as the pandemic closed in, the numbers began to rise, international travel came to a stop and publishers and agents went into semi-hibernation. She thinks it is an excellent idea, though the idea of a 'master' class in prose (air quote gesture plus cynical laughter) might be better left out. Musicians are giving free live concerts, she tells me, sopranos are singing '*Un Bel Dì, Vedremo*' to their neighbours from their balconies whether the neighbours want it or not, impromptu jam sessions are happening on Facebook and elsewhere, people are phoning random strangers, librarians taking books to the housebound. The manifest of human kindness. The idea of doing something that might help others to survive the lockdown is in the air. The world has discovered solidarity.

An advertisement on social media. I set up anonymous accounts on Twitter, Facebook and Instagram, screen-shot a piece of text and attach it as an advertisement, and the ad is picked up by book bloggers, influencers, other writers, agents and publishers – all of us sitting at home, desperately trying to avoid facing the blank page. Within twenty-four hours it has been retweeted over fifteen times on Twitter alone.

Writers Anonymous: Call for Unpublished Writers
An Irish author of five novels and a book of non-fiction who wishes to remain anonymous will give free work-shops for five unpublished prose-writers (English language only). Application must be anonymous. Applicants will submit a sample of one thousand words. The selected five will remain strictly anony-mous throughout the entire period of six months. Any information which might identify the applicant will incur immediate disqualification. Email applica-tions to: writers.anonymous2020@outlook.com. The sending email address must also be anonymous. Offer closes Tuesday May 5th.

The email address has been specifically set up for the group. I choose May the fifth, only three days away, because it was the date on which I was originally due to fly to Rome for a festival. Rome is my city of escape. Cancelling that, way back in early March when it was clear travel would grind to a halt, was particularly painful. But I also want to keep the applications to a minimum. Three days is enough. I don't want it to become a full-time job.

By evening I have seven applications. On checking my emails the following morning I find that the number has risen to nineteen. I begin to panic. What if I receive a hundred applications? That would be a hundred thousand words. Would I have to read every one? If not, perhaps I would miss the one genius, the one true writer in the group. I watch as the applications come in over the next days. Catherine offers to help and we begin to read. By Tuesday we have a grand total of twenty-six applicants. We begin making longlists and then shortlists and eventually we narrow it down to ten anonymous writers. Most of the rest of it is utter junk, easily dismissed. (You forget how you started, Catherine admonishes me, you can be an arrogant prick you know.)

We argue for some time over how to reduce the number from ten. Each of us has our favourite. We agree on one (Tom). My favourite is from someone called Emily, a prose piece about Italy and the film *Roman Holiday* (Strolling on Via Margutta one is assailed by memories that are not memories because one has lived them only at second hand. The actual experiences belonged to Audrey Hepburn and Gregory Peck or Crown Princess Ann and Joe Bradley …) I spent two years studying for a master's in the University of Rome, 'La Sapienza', two of the best years of my life, and I devour anything related to that country. Catherine's choice is from someone calling herself Deirdre. I read it but there is something about it that unnerves me. It opens with a descriptive paragraph:

> The trawlers are resting quietly against the pier. Detritus collects between the stone and the boat, both flotsam and jetsam. The sea breathes slowly in and out and the world hurtles through space like a cannon ball. Here on the stone pier the motion is imperceptible, but on the deck of a boat the world is full of uncertainty. The smell of diesel oil and sour nets and holds and salt and something chemical from the ice plant. Mattie walks out to the breakwater past the bags of nets, the net-boxes, the fish-boxes, the floats and shackles and chains and ropes and buoys, the otter boards like giant rusted razors, the lobster pots, the yellow-painted button-shaped bollards, the bowlines and springs and stern-lines. Someone has written a sum in felt pen on a net-bag. Mattie notices the numbers, 78, 78, 156, 174, 186. All even. Total 672. The appearance of order.

There is more in the same vein, a story that doesn't much interest me, but I feel I know the location. I can almost walk the pier. I can hear the voices that she conjures, of the fishermen and the buyers and the harbour master. The thing is, it reminds me of home, the little fishing town of Rally where I grew up and which I fled with such haste and determination the moment the opportunity presented. Small-town Ireland where everybody knows everybody and their business, where nothing is private and everyone

– including me – has secrets. In my case a secret I have never revealed to anybody, including my wife. The secret of why I ran away. The nasty virus of my past waiting to irrupt and contaminate everything.

I am conscious of a residual guilt about that, the people I left behind me, the friends, that atavism that afflicts every Irish writer – about ancestry and the meaning of place, the dead generations. Even though I rejected all that, there is still that pole and its attraction like an alignment of molecules or a sequence in the genetic code. I notice it when I hear certain songs, especially in Irish. The magnet of the stony hills and the sea. I remember the otter boards that were used to keep the mouths of trawl nets open as they were towed and the jumble of nets exactly as she describes it. I was even at school with someone called Mattie, a relatively unusual name in the small-town Ireland of the time. The whole thing feels intrusive, an encroachment on my own material, an invasion on my private psychological terrain, an invisible boundary crossed. I never read books that have settings like my own. People come up to me and say, You should read such and such, it's very like one of yours. And I nod my head politely and mentally mark it down as not for me.

Catherine does not want to let it go and she fights as only she can.

The woman can write (if she is a woman) and what else do I need? The style is interesting, a kind of naive clear-sightedness, a crossover between first and third person. Something like Joyce's style in *Ulysses*, whatever it's called. Close third-person narrative maybe. The movement between the third and first person without any boundary. I'm rejecting it solely out of a desire to protect my own material, or possibly out of jealousy that this Deirdre can write so well about things I too have written about. I am being stubborn, unreasonable, fragile, defensive.

For fuck's sake, I say, don't you think I can separate my critical judgement from my personal preferences?

She gives me that sly, amused look that drives me crazy.

Quite frankly, no, she says.

It's eleven o'clock at night and I'm tired. I am familiar with Catherine's mood. Often she takes a position opposite to mine simply for the sake of the argument, and when she does she is trenchant and unrelenting. I'm faced with a senior lecturer on track for a chair when the present incumbent kicks the bucket or retires (the former being the more likely if cirrhosis of the liver can still be relied upon as in days of yore) and I know from experience that resistance is futile. My feeble attempt at argument will be pared to a core by Occam's razor. I will see its broken and bleeding corpse on the ground, skinned alive and carved into morsels before we finish. Besides, I would like to sleep tonight.

I concede.

We need two more and we can't see how to choose. None of them seems very promising, though they are competent. I suggest we cut at three but Catherine points out that the three we choose will know they're not five. They'll wonder why, and some will conclude (correctly) that I'm lazy and others that the standard was too low and they were picked by default.

I prefer the idea of selecting nobody. They would all assume that five other people got it, nobody will ever know it's not happening. I think that's a clever idea. I chuckle to myself about it. Catherine watches me cynically. Before I have even finished proposing it I know it will die a death.

It's too late to back out, she says. Even though I can see you're already regretting your generosity.

It's never too late to lie.

This time her look is not so amused. That's interesting, she says.

No one will ever know, that's the beauty of it. Everyone will assume the workshop is going ahead in cyber-space, hidden from view. It will be the perfect virtual workshop. Something with no reality. Just a thing of my imagination and theirs. It's like something Donald Trump would come up with, the greatest workshop ever, truly magnificent. As Debord said, in a topsy-turvy world, the true is an instance of the false. Or words to that effect. I could even write an article about it, five fictional writers of fiction. I could invent their names and their backstories. Now that I think about it, it even sounds like a good novel.

Truth is an instance of falsehood, she snorts. You're out of your depth citing Guy Debord. Better stick to something banal. It's more your territory.

Eventually she comes up with the suggestion that we use random selection: we assign a value to each letter according to its position in the alphabet – a = 1, b = 2, etc – count the letters in the first word of each manuscript and pick the two with the largest count. As it happens, one manuscript begins with the indefinite article A and another with the personal pronoun I – eliminated. We do our calculations for the remainder and quickly select two – Walter and Judy.

Afterwards we pour ourselves the last glass of wine in the bottle and toast our ingenuity. It's random, but it's fair, we tell ourselves. We think it is hilarious. Clink.

Before going to bed, I email the five successful applicants to let them know. *Dear X, I am delighted to tell you that you have been selected as one of the five participants in this workshop. I look forward to working with you in the coming months.* I sign it WA for Writers Anonymous. And when I log on next morning there are three replies thanking me for my kindness. One of those to reply is Deirdre. She thanks me for taking time off from my schedule to help some would-be writers. It's very generous of me considering how busy I must be.

That evening we have a family Zoom call with our kids. Son, Marcus, is in London, lecturing in philosophy at King's College (like mother like son); daughter, Aoife, works at the Irish embassy in Rome. She's a third secretary but is hoping to get the promotion to second soon. She has inherited my love of Italian but also speaks French and German fluently and is currently learning Chinese. I'm envious of her Zoom background – she's sitting on her tiny internal terrace, barely big enough for a table and two chairs and some pot plants, but high overhead is the unbroken blue of the Roman sky. Marcus, on the other hand, is in an anonymous-looking flat in north-east London. He hasn't done the washing up – I can see it stacked on the draining board behind him.

We tell them about the workshop plan and they both think it is a great idea. The unspoken relief. Something to keep Dad off the streets.

Have you thought about geographic spread and gender balance? Aoife asks.

And of course, I haven't, nor is there any way of knowing without undermining their anonymity.

Marcus wonders if I would bring a masculine bias to the reading of the texts. The two of them chuckle over my protests.

Don't forget to ask them for their pronouns, Marcus says just before signing off, and good luck with the pastoral care side. Writers are so needy.

And then he's gone.

You shouldn't let him irritate you, Catherine tells me later. You know he's doing it on purpose.

It's just cabin fever, I say.

The silent road beyond the garden normally busy with traffic for the city, for the university and various shopping centres – twenty years in this house and it has been this quiet only on Christmas Day. Nothing is happening and everything is happening. No one is working except in hospitals and there people are drowning and every ward is code red. If you could travel over the world on a magic carpet it would seem like a dystopian novel. The empty streets, the frantic dying. The soundtrack would be the steady hiss and thump of a respirator or someone gasping for air – 'I can't breathe' in all its various and frightening iterations from the streets of Minneapolis to Wuhan.

These days, quarantined at home, we are both obsessed by the idea of plague, reading everything we can find, buying books we see reviewed or hear about. It's counter-intuitive, but the history is consoling. Plagues have come and gone throughout time. The first well-recorded one (discounting the Bible, which is a bit inventive about plagues) occurred in Athens at the time of Socrates, or so Catherine informs me. The mortality rate was about twenty-five per cent and nowadays historians speculate that it may have been Ebola. One of my consolations is that plagues tend to be self-limiting. Either by killing people, or in modern times by vaccination or treatment, they tend to run out of hosts. Sooner or later these things pass.

Did you read that article about the idiot Robert Kennedy, Catherine asks me as we drink our mid-morning coffee.

You mean Kennedy the anti-vaxxer? What a bastard. Apparently Anthony Fauci and Bill Gates set up the pandemic so as to make money out of vaccines. And on the other hand the Covid is caused by 5G.

We shake our heads.

I'll take any vaccine, I say. They can use me as an experiment. All I want is to be able to have a pint in a bar. I don't even care if I'm the only one there.

You know, she says, in the plague of 1630 the city council of Florence really followed the science. These conspiracy theorists claiming that lockdowns have never happened before, I just feel like laughing. It's easy to make pronouncements about history if you haven't read any. Florence had a scientific commission studying it and they were in constant communication with other scientific colleagues. They were watching the pestilence moving across Northern Italy. They locked down fast and fed the people to make sure they stayed locked down.

French and German troops brought it, according to Manzoni, I say.

As it happens, for once I know what I'm talking about. I'm reviewing a new translation of Manzoni's *The Betrothed*. The book gives a brilliantly researched account of the pestilence in Milan. And not so long ago I read Daniel Kehlmann's *Tyll*. Also, coincidentally, about the same plague, but told from the German point of view.

Yes, mercenaries. They arrived as part of France's claim to the Duchy of Mantua, which had been left without a male heir.

When she says 'male heir' she deepens her voice to comic effect. Masculinity and all the shit about bloodlines and primogeniture amuse her.

The first signs of plague seem to have been noted at Monferrato. You remember Monferrato?

We both smile at the memory.

Barbera wines, I say, I remember it well. The bend of the Po river, the old fort. And not far away is Barolo country. We had a dinner of truffles there once. With Aldo and Meri. I had an email from Aldo the other day. He's about to retire.

And that vineyard. Remember the guy with the broken arm? I remember him telling us that some wine was missing its nose.

I remember.

I miss travel, she says.

We're silent for a time. A robin is lurking nearby, hoping for a saucer of crumbs. Sometimes he comes within a metre of me. I rub a piece of scone into tiny pieces and he perches on the edge of the saucer, bows twice, watching me sideways, and then eats, pausing every now and then to check that I'm still where I should be. He flies away with the biggest piece and lands in the hedge. We assume he's feeding his mate or their children.

You should read *The Betrothed*, I tell her. It's particularly good on the conspiracy theories. And the bishops urging prayer. Processing relics through the city, carrying the plague with them. All the churches flooding with people praying for salvation until they realise that the churches themselves are spreading the plague. Then, empty churches and furious bishops.

I'm not surprised. They weren't that different to us. Protecting the economy was uppermost in their minds too and that's what allowed the disease to do so much damage. Milan lost forty-six per cent of its population. By contrast, Florence only lost about twelve.

Twelve per cent? How did they manage that?

First of all, they were convinced from experience that the plague would come no matter what precautions they took and no matter how many masses were offered up or how many saints or relics were paraded around the town.

Now she is in lecture mode. I can see her marshalling her facts. Where do they come from? Her memory is phenomenal. When did she read this stuff? Years ago when she first studied Machiavelli? We met when she was already teaching, at a lecture on Italian political philosophy, and fell in love over a glass of wine afterwards. Or at least that is our agreed story. The reality was a little more complex and protracted.

And she's perfectly capable of remembering the minutiae from her undergraduate days. Teaching helps, she always tells me, it keeps detail and ideas fresh. I have attended her classes from time to time and I notice how her students hang on her words. Some of the boys fall in love with her, I think, some of the girls too perhaps. And in truth I find that authoritative side of her sexy. She's doing it now, I can almost see her shuffling her notes or firing up a PowerPoint. In fact, later this morning she has a Zoom meeting. Only the top half of her will be visible, so she's wearing a crisp white linen shirt. She'll look cool and professional. Below the waist it's beach shorts.

Tell me, I say, teasing her into further lecturing, what did Florence do that was so successful? I mean they had no idea what caused the plague. In fact, I think the jury is out scientifically on it still. I've seen suggestions that it couldn't have been passed by fleas on rats.

So they established the commission, which carried out an audit of the living conditions of the city. Because their theory of disease was that it was caused by miasma, by foul smells in effect, they repaired all the septic tanks, painted the houses of the poorest, and carried out remedial works in many parts of the city. Whatever about the plague it made the place healthier. And they closed the second-hand clothes market, which turned out to be really important because of the fleas.

A coincidence of bad science and good effect?

It wasn't bad science. You can't look at 1630 through the lens of 21st-century science. It was the best science they had at the time and, as it happened, it was a damn sight better than prayer and fasting. Or hydroxychloroquine and bleach for that matter. By the time the plague came to the city the *signoria* had already established an isolation hospital – a *lazaretto* – a contact tracing system and the legal instruments needed to impose lockdown, together with a means of supplying food to people confined to their houses.

In Manzoni, the only people who come out well from it are the monks who ran the *lazaretti*.

That was Milan though, and Milan was devastated. It was a chicken vendor from across the border in Emilia-Romagna that brought the plague to Florence, she says. He went through the mountains to avoid the border posts on all the roads. Contact tracers eventually found him and all his contacts, as well as his family. Imagine, they even had contact tracing then.

But by then too many people had been infected?

Exactly. Then during the period of the plague the city council fed the poor in much the same way that governments in the developed world today have paid workers to remain at home, and so effective was the strategy that the poor of Florence were better nourished after the plague than before!

She hands me her coffee cup.

Will you wash that for me? My meeting is in two minutes.

And she disappears into her office.

I wash her cup and top my own up with the gritty end of the cafetière. I'm thinking about the fact that the best two accounts of plague I know are from Defoe and Manzoni, and both accounts are based on research, whereas those who actually lived through it tended to be silent or to write little. Bocaccio, for example, gives a very short chapter on it in the *Decameron* and devotes the rest of the book to a riot of smutty laughter. I don't count Camus because his plague is really fascism and though he lived through *that* he never experienced an outbreak of actual plague. I can't see myself writing about this plague year any time soon, and probably never. There's something about living through a catastrophe that strangles the muse. I've heard other writers say the same. The creative impulse choked off and dying of asphyxiation.

I'm about to put down these thoughts when an email comes in from Deirdre. I see the notification and decide to let it sit. The review is to be what is called essay length; in other words, it's to be long and thorough and I have delayed too long. And I am slightly irritated that Deirdre has jumped the gun. I had planned to circulate a writing task to everyone, give them a week to prepare it and then call it in the following Monday, by which time I would have sent in my review. It should have been a further eight days before I would need to think about them.

But now curiosity gets the better of me. I open the email.

From: der-driu101@hotmail.com
To: writers.anonymous2020@outlook.com
Subject: Novel

Dear WA,

I've been writing feverishly since I heard from you – I am so excited to be part of this, you have no idea – It's a dream come true literally.

I'm enclosing the opening, at least I think it's the opening, of what I'm desperately hoping will be a novel, I do hope you like it – Before this all I ever wrote was short stories but the chance of having your advice and a deadline of six months just energised and excited me, I might also say that it has given me confidence – Up till now I didn't think I had the staying power for a whole novel, I'm thinking of calling it *Lonely Rock Light*, What do you think?

Yours sincerely,
Deirdre

From: writers.anonymous2020@outlook.com
To: der-driu101@hotmail.com
Subject: Novel

Dear Deirdre,

I'm delighted my little idea has given you such confidence and energy.

I really like the title.

I'm up to my ears in work right now, but I'll read it later. It will be a pleasure. And I'll reply once I've done that.

Kind regards,
WA

My suspicion is confirmed. Lonely Rock is a passable translation of the Irish name for Fastnet – *Carraig Aonair*. We could see the rock and its light from Rally. A local, no doubt about it. And something English in it too. I *do* hope you like it.

This power to communicate instantly across hundreds of miles is a miracle that we seem to have lost sight of. It has become routine, but it never ceases to surprise and excite me when I reply to an email and the other person's reply pings back to me a few seconds later. Here am I in my study in Ireland and there, at her desk or table or sitting up in bed or on the couch, is Deirdre in her home in some other place, some other country or continent, and we can communicate as readily as if we were children passing notes in class.

But what I find most interesting is that she can have no idea who I am yet she believes in me. It is the idea of a writer that she is energised by, some sort of imagined figure of literary power and authority and possibly reputation – for all she knows I might be a Nobel Prize-winner, although, of course, our most recent Irish Nobel laureate, the late great famous Seamus, has passed on to Parnassus, may the earth rest lightly on him. He was one of those presences whose passing left a shadow that no new sun can erase.

(Having thought of this image I decide it is too good to lose and make a note of it.) She can have no concept of the egotistical fragility with which I face the empty page, a contradictory mixture of paralysing fear and absolute conviction that I have something to say if only I can find it. No doubt she believes I work with certainties, whereas the reality is I never know what I'm doing or whether it will work, and indeed it frequently doesn't. I have a computer hard drive full of what were brilliant ideas up to about ten or fifteen thousand words (and a few that lasted until forty thousand or more) and which turned to ashes one fine morning when, with a clearer head, I looked back over what I had written. Why? Sometimes a character has nowhere to go. Sometimes the voice just falls silent in my head. Sometimes the plot seems clever until I realise it's not clever, or it was brilliantly clever in someone else's hands, or it's clever but it's missing some ingredient that would make it credible. And sometimes there's no plot and I reach a point where I have no interest in the ideas or the characters or what they get up to and quite frankly I couldn't be arsed continuing. A frequent question at readings is 'Where do your ideas come from?' But a better line would be 'Where do all those brilliant ideas go? Why do they fail?' And my reply? I don't know. Or sometimes I know and sometimes I don't. Sometimes the problem is not the story, it's me. Sometimes I literally feel that it's beyond me, out of my grasp or just not my story to tell. And sometimes the energy runs out – in me rather than the story. It's always disheartening, often frightening, always unsettling.

I return to my review but now I can't concentrate. Instead I browse the newspapers. In Minneapolis respectable opinion is outraged that their poorest neighbours would loot from multinational corporations and small-time capitalists as if capitalism had not taught the message that consumption is a public good. Black lives matter, it seems, as long as they behave themselves as if they were white and rich, or at least comfortably off. At least they burned the third precinct. Some good I mean to do despite of mine own nature, as Shakespeare put it. There's a link to a video of it burning and the sight of a police station in flames awakes something buried in me. I almost punch the air.

And, as if to say you ain't seen nothing yet, Ebola is back in the Congo in earnest.

One plague is enough to cope with this particular morning, I think. I close my browser.

Deirdre's file sits in my email download folder. I know she can write despite the fact that she was Catherine's choice (it's a grudging admission, I know). She has a fully developed style, quirky and unsettling but sustained and attractive. I decide the review can wait. I'm halfway through it anyway and the deadline is several days away.

I will read just the opening paragraph, no more. Discipline is important – as every one of us ever interviewed comes round to saying whether we're asked to or not. We all sit down to our page or screen every morning, day in, day out, including on holidays and feast days, and we stay at it all day or for whatever part of the day constitutes each writer's defined work period. This is so ubiquitous a trope that none other than Roland Barthes remarked upon it in an essay in his book *Mythologies*. The writer, he notes with his characteristic irony, is a false worker because he works even when he is on vacation. He is both proletarian (because he takes holidays) and the prey of some god who makes demands of his medium without bothering his head about whether it's a working day or not. What he does not remark upon is that this continuous work is the product not of some blessed relationship with the muse but of a deep-seated anxiety that, in fact, we are imposters, charlatans, snake-oil salesmen with nothing to say, or nothing that has not been said better before. And we therefore present ourselves at the factory door, every morning without fail, in the hope that today there will be real work to be done. Mostly the door rests slightly ajar, an invitation to enquire within. We are like those middle-aged workers whose jobs are on the line and who know they will never get work again if the job closes. Except that we have been like that from the start. From our youth. From the first time we put pen to paper. Our egos, like the famous banks of systemic importance about which we heard so much during the late crash, are too big to fail. We have to keep trying.

Come out of our grave, the woman said. Her heart was flying. Bells rang. The beech trees tried to blow away. She pointed at the boy. Good enough for you, she said, they crucified you. They were collecting the dustbins of the world but the gale drowned everything. She had a bunch of roses from other people's gardens. She could not give the flowers to the boy because his eyes were closed. He was asleep and she could not wake him. People wakened from sleep had terrible thoughts, she knew. They woke from a dream and the dream might not go away.

If anyone else had found him but this woman they would have known the story. They would have known who the boy was because everyone in the town knew him …

I stare at the opening in shock. I realise after a time that my heart is racing. I can feel it rattling in my chest like a car whose clutch is gone. I try to slow my breathing, calm my pulse. I recognise this scene, or at least I think I do. There was no Mrs Pearse, of course. That's a narrative trick, an observer who is incapable of understanding and therefore represents the reader's bafflement. The boy's name was Mattie Lantry and I knew him because we were in school together; he was found spreadeagled in a grave in the churchyard, his skull resting tenderly against a piece of broken headstone that had the word 'lies' inscribed on it.

Mattie and I were friends of a sort, though how much of the friendship was a need for mutual protection I don't know. Like everyone else I had avoided him for a long time, but it slowly became clear to me that I was an outsider because I was bookish and he was an outsider for a thousand different reasons. I recall falling into step beside him one day after school and telling him that I noticed he and I followed the same route home. And I remember him replying without any preamble that his grandfather had bought half of the *Encyclopaedia Britannica* at an auction and it was brilliant. After that we left school together every day, Mattie happily doing most of the talking. I remember him telling me he had started at the letter 'A' and was working through it. He was taken by the oddest things: *Abaris*, for example, some sort of priest of Apollo who travelled around Greece on a golden arrow and saved Sparta from a plague. Mattie didn't know where Sparta was and they didn't have the 'S' volume. He was especially intrigued by the golden arrow. We would walk to the foot of Union Street together and part ways. In my memory it was always raining. Mattie's wet hair – he never had a cap or a hood – his wet face pale, pierced by dark brown eyes. His full, broad mouth. He fished all summer but never got a tan. He was taller than me and had the powerful shoulders of a swimmer. He was beautiful.

The police never found his killers and came to the conclusion that it was 'drug-related', which is police code for 'haven't a clue'. They let it be known that they thought the boy was killed as a punishment or a warning, that he was most likely a low-level pusher. We all knew it was complete nonsense. Anybody could have told them that

Mattie Lantry had never touched an illegal substance in his life. I knew because I was one of those who had and I knew all the boys who messed with weed and other substances. But Mattie came from Connolly Road, and the guards knew all about Connolly Road.

In fact, Mattie was a brilliant innocent, one of those kids whose intelligence got in the way of understanding the world. He was, in some ways, the butt of everyone's jokes, but none of us would have wished him dead, not even his worst enemy, and certainly not in that way.

The piece has hooked me, of course, the corpse, the strange circumstances, the character of Mrs Pearse as the uncomprehending observer, the suggestion of a strong plot. And I think it might hook a publisher and a reader. But what does she know about Mattie Lantry? More importantly, how does she know? Who is this 'Deirdre'? She must come from Rally or nearby. Or perhaps she researched the story. Or heard about it from someone else. An unsolved murder in a beautiful remote place.

I have never mentioned Lantry's death to Catherine. It was too painful, too private a pain, and already, by the time we met, too old a story to be worth the telling. Perhaps I should have – though in my experience, a trouble shared is never a trouble halved as the old saying has it. It's just a cloud in someone else's life, not quite as large or as dark as the cloud in your own, but something to trouble the other person too. Better kept to yourself.

Catherine is in her office. She never uses a headset if I'm not working, so I can hear the drone of a presentation. End-of-term meetings – everyone living vicariously, watching their YouTube videos, TikTok videos, sharing their living rooms or bedrooms or studies or just snooping. Work is invading homes, time recalibrating itself. It's hard to believe things will ever return to normal, but I have a feeling that our old habits will reassert themselves once the key is turned in the lock again. We humans are less adaptable than we like to think. I pour myself a sizeable glass of whiskey and take it out to the garden. A pair of buzzards is circling over the field behind our house and a blackbird is agitated about something, rapping out that staccato whistling that indicates danger. Otherwise nothing moves. The grass, I notice, is parched and beginning to burn in places. A patch of moss that had invaded the lawn in the shade of one of our trees looks like it's dying. It is after five and the heat is still intense. The fine days continue uninterrupted. We joke that if the price of a climate like the French Riviera is a pandemic then it might be worth paying.

I swallow a mouthful of whiskey and wait for it to take effect. I feel my pulse slowly return to normal.

I hear Catherine sign off on her meeting and then the toilet flushing and finally she comes out with a beer.

How was the meeting?

The usual, nobody knows whether we'll have in-person classes or not next year, it's a mess. Bit early for the hard stuff, isn't it? How is your review going?

Fine, no problems.

That's good. Are you cooking or am I?

Our first meeting on Zoom. Six anonymous images including mine, which is a still of Jacques Tati in *Jour de Fête*, the gormless, moustachioed postman with the permanently suspicious look. I love the film. In front of me, arranged in a comic strip along the top of the screen, I have (1) part of what I take to be *Blue Nude* by Picasso (Emily), (2) a bucolic countryside scene, possibly an actual photograph (Tom), (3) a black rectangle (Walter), (4) a rose (Deirdre) and (5) a sailing ship (Judy). I call on each of them in turn to read the new piece they sent me for the meeting. Emily is North American, possibly Canadian to judge by her accent. She jokes that if we're to be Writers Anonymous shouldn't we have The Twelve Steps. The first step is to admit powerlessness, I reply. I tell her that I think this is the opposite of what a writing course should be saying.

She reads the opening of what, in her email, she called her magnum opus (followed by a series of wry looking emojis to indicate that she was joking). A butterfly has no internal source of body heat (she reads)

but needs actual sunlight to quicken his muscles: hence butterflies rarely pass through shadow but take their uneven course from one bright place to another. A man is both more adaptable and less fortunate, troubled by darkness but unable to tolerate the light forever. It is an experience to walk out of the warm sun, sit on a bench in – for Rome – an unprepossessing little church by way of catching one's breath and resting one's feet, and find oneself gazing for several minutes, in mute astonishment and without recognising it, on a statue made by Michelangelo. Fate conspires with the well-disposed traveller to send him the very things he is bound to love.

I ask for comments.

Silence.

They need to unmute their microphones to be heard and either they don't know that or they don't want to speak. I decide to wait it out and my silence is rewarded after about a minute by Deirdre unmuting.

That's really lovely, she says. I love that about the butterflies. I didn't know that.

English accent, not London, further south. Hampshire? Devon? And yet there was a touch of something else to it.

What I'd like to know is, she goes on, where is it going? And I suppose that's a good thing, isn't it? I mean I already want to know what happens next.

Tom sends a message. Sorry my mic is not working, but I really liked the description of Rome.

Thank you all so much, Emily says.

She begins to explain her story. It would be about a retired English civil servant, very conservative, a bachelor, giving himself the treat of a long holiday in Rome for his retirement and finding himself drawn into unexpected events.

I'll stop you there Emily, I say. That much we'll be able to gather from the blurb. But I'm sure you all know the rule of 'Show don't tell'. Well, I'm insisting on that here in relation to explanations. A general outline of your plan such as Emily has just given us, but no details, no spoilers, no twists. Your work will reveal itself as we go along. It will be slow, but it should be slow.

This is, in fact, how I work myself. I never talk about my work in advance because of a superstition that I will talk it out and not want to continue. I'm even reluctant to let my agent in on it in any detail. Too often I've talked up a book that I lost interest in immediately afterwards. It's an ego thing, I'm sure, this pleasure I take in the slow revelation, making the reader follow the twists and turns, making them wait.

Judy is active now.

Thank you for saying that, skipper, I'm not particularly sure where I'm going and I hope to find out as I go along. That's OK, isn't it?

Skipper. I could get used to being called that. Judy seems to be English but with something slightly Germanic in her pronunciation.

Theodore Roethke, 'The Waking', I say. I quote the poem from memory. You learn where to go by going there – that's you Judy. You'll learn by going where you have to go.

Could you spell that name?

Deirdre again.

I spell it for her and give her the title of the poem.

I'll google it later.

Emily, I say, do you have a working title?

I'm calling it *Salter's Art* because he likes art. He likes Caravaggio and that's one of the reasons he goes to Rome.

I am now staring at the black rectangle. Walter has said nothing. I wonder about calling on him. But Deirdre comes in again.

I'm just wondering why you chose a retired man to write about? I mean why not a retired woman? There are plenty of female civil servants now.

Silence.

Emily?

Silence.

Well, I should say, if there's any comment anyone doesn't feel like responding to or any question you don't want to answer, that's fine. This is not an interrogation. Maybe if we could arrange a signal for that. How about raising the hand. Do you see the hand icon here ... Ah I see Emily has raised her hand. That's fine. Thank you, Emily.

Emily's microphone goes live suddenly.

That's a totally woke question. I don't go there. Thank you.

Microphone closed again. Silence.

I am taken aback. And irritated. I decide to move things on.

Walter, can you read something for us? I know you didn't send anything in but maybe you have a piece ready.

Silence.

Then a sidebar text message: How do I turn the microphone on?

I explain about the microphone icon and after thirty seconds or so first his camera comes on then his microphone. He greets us all ceremoniously. My guess is he's a retired civil servant. He could be the model for Salter in Emily's story. Late sixties, a shock of white hair, blue eyes, American accent, New York possibly. Certainly East Coast.

Walter, the camera is meant to be off. We're an anonymous writers' group.

He mimes the palm-up helpless gesture.

What do I do?

I explain about the camera icon.

I just pressed every button, he says.

He leans towards the screen and I see that, in fact, the white hair is thinning on his scalp and there is what looks like a nasty cut on it. Then his camera turns off.

Steep learning curve as they say, he says. But hey, I gotta say, I love that stuff about Rome. You know? It really brings it alive. Anyhow, I'm sorry I don't have anything ready. I'm real sorry. I just couldn't get it together this time.

That's OK, Walter. Next time?

Sure. I'll have something, I guarantee you.

Then Emily goes live again and without any introduction begins to read the rest of her chapter in a voice quivering with irritation.

I breakfasted every morning at the hotel to which my apartment was an annex. At first I found it somewhat threatening to walk into a room full of Americans, Germans, Austrians, Italians even. I believed myself to be the centre of their disapproving attention, a common misconception among solitary people. The breakfast room – there was no dining room – was reached by a series of small stairways and corridors and was immediately preceded by a residents' lounge scattered with easy chairs and lined with prints of Rome in the eighteenth century. The walk through that space was agonising.

Nevertheless, one morning I was befriended by an elderly American lady. I had noticed that she arrived in the dining room rarely more than a few minutes later than me. She too always had a book, though not a notebook and pen. She spoke less Italian than I did but was possessed of the belief that loudness equals communication. The waitresses were a little frightened of her, perhaps believing, because she shouted a lot, that she was angry.

When she turned her attentions to me she did not mince words. 'Excuse me, sir,' she said, smiling and tilting her head slightly. 'I noticed that the book you're reading is in English.'

Her face seemed to be stretched taut by invisible stays which gave the skin around her cheekbones and eye-cavities a diaphanous appearance, as though the structure of the skull were about to break through. Her hair, tied back, was dyed black and added to the austere stretched look. She wore the obligatory American polo-neck shirt and a pair of high-waisted, slender slacks.

'Yes. I speak English,' I replied in a surprised voice.

'Are you British?' she said suspiciously. 'You sound kind of British. I'm from New York.' She held out her hand and grasped mine firmly. 'Vivienne Tampier. Pleased to meet you.'

We exchanged pleasantries about the hotel, the city, her travels – she had come down from Paris by night train a week before. At some point she moved her cereal bowl, containing a sizeable mound of some kind of brown cardboard parings, onto my table and sat down beside me. From that moment it was dangerous to put either of my hands on the table because she was continually touching things and was inclined to squeeze my wrist and forearm to emphasise a point. She held very firm views on many things.

I take a deep breath.

Are you all familiar with the concept of a loaded tag, I say. There is no response. So, I continue, a loaded tag is when you say something like 'she said suspiciously'. The 'she said' part is fine. But the suspicious is best covered by the 'show don't tell' rule. If her suspicion is important, and I don't think it is, I think you could suggest it by ending the sentence at the question mark, for example, but if it is important, then you should make her do something that indicates her suspicion. In other words, don't *tell* us she was suspicious, give us a word picture of her suspicion. Does that make sense to everyone? It's considered bad style nowadays. It would be better just to say 'she said' and leave it at that. There are a few examples in Emily's passage. Another one I remember is where he says 'I replied in a surprised voice.' In fact, in that particular instance there was probably no need to say who was replying because the question of whether or not he spoke English had already been asked. The sentence 'Yes. I speak English' could only have been spoken by Mr Salter. So in that case, it would be better style to leave the tag out completely.

Emily's microphone goes live again. Her voice exudes irritation.

Thank you for sharing that, she says. We used to call them adverbs.

Had it been part of Emily's story she would have written: 'Thank you for sharing that, she interjected irritably.'

And Stephen King said the road to perdition is paved with adverbs. Deirdre?

Deirdre comes in too fast. It's as if she wants to rescue us from a fight.

It's a morning scene, her character is leaving the house by the back door because …

No explanations, I say. Let the text speak for itself. She begins to read immediately.

Mattie Lantry exited by the back door on hearing the sound of a knock at the front door in the perfect certainty that the hand knocking was a Garda on truancy duty. In any case, he never came and went by Connolly Road these days because of the business with old Mr Morrish. Mr Morrish came out one day with his walking stick and had it in for Mattie. In fact it looked like he was lying in ambush for Mattie to go by on his way home from school. The old fart took a swing but overbalanced.

You little fucker, he said, even though Mattie was bigger than him, keep away from my apples.

Mattie had not, as a matter of fact, touched his apples that season yet. Mattie had to help him up and when he had got him standing again the old bugger flaked him with the walking stick across the back of his legs. Mattie's grandfather, old Jack Lantry, said the old man was irrational and even before he was irrational, if there ever was such a time, he was a nasty bastard, give him a wide berth Sunny Jim.

As he cleared the back fence it was raining softly and dawn was very late. Between the winter solstice and the vernal equinox everybody waiting for the light.

Here's Willy Morrish's dog Comic. Willy Morrish was old Mr Morrish's son. Willy was fishing the *Susan Deane*. Mattie whistled softly and Comic pricked up his ears and trotted across the field. He stepped dainty in the barley stubble. Mattie caught his head. How are we, Comic? He tickled behind his ear and Comic leaned into his hand. His eyes glazed over.

I'm on the run from the guards myself. But what are you doing out in the rain at this hour of the morning, Mattie asked.

The dog thought but did not say that he was out for a piss and a look around the neighbours' places, that he had always taken security as his solemn duty, and that Mattie Lantry was a poor orphan bastard that badly needed a dog. He followed Mattie to the bottom of the stubble field. Everything that was black was becoming grey. There were hedge sparrows, blue tits, blackbirds. Soon there would be finches at the last haws, and thrushes and pigeons. Daylight invested the gloomy hillside ...

Three more Zoom workshops at the rate of one per week. The dynamic has already been set. Emily's wounded passive aggression dominates. Tom stays out of it as much as he can, but every once in a while he tells her to get a grip. She rarely responds; perhaps she doesn't understand his Northern Irish accent. He is from Derry, he tells me. Walter is much given to reminiscence. He is a retired high school teacher who worked in public schools in relatively poor neighbourhoods. He is Irish-American and is fond of recounting times when he came to Ireland on holidays and things his students said to him. Emily is impatient with his stories and her impatience makes me want to defend him. Storytelling is what it's all about, I tell her, and Walter tells a good one. Her passive-aggressive strategy is to activate her microphone just long enough to cut him off – Zoom brings active mics to the front – then deactivate it again. It's the technological equivalent of sighing or shuffling papers. In the course of an exchange between them I discover that Emily is a realtor and a hesitant Trump supporter (I guess he is what he is, she said, I can't say I like the man, but he's the only one fighting the good fight right now. When I suggest that her encomium is a version of Roosevelt's 'he's a son of a bitch but he's our son of a bitch' she does not reply). She could learn from how Walter pitches his reminiscences, I tell her. He has a natural instinct for a well-told tale.

Later she emails me to ask me to avoid using curse words.

Judy is not going to make it, I think. She is writing a modern *Hound of The Baskervilles* set in Brittany. It is utterly derivative and very badly written. In essence what she's writing is fan fiction, and low-level stuff at that, and there are online magazines for that kind of thing. I try to explain the concept but she doesn't see the point.

Judy: So fan fiction is stuff people write to copy real writers?

Me: Well, it's fiction that makes use of characters in other people's fiction.

Judy: But my characters are new. It's not actually Sherlock Holmes.

Me: But the plot is almost the same as the Sherlock Holmes story …

Judy: There's no Sherlock Holmes though.

Me: But there's a howling dog and a male private detective and his best friend …

Judy: But his name is Yves Bellacroix ….

Me: But he smokes opium …

Deirdre has been sending material at a steady rate. Everything she writes is good but seeing Mattie named still comes as a shock to me – even though I had already guessed from the opening description of the graveyard. The rawness of it. Perhaps I hoped that it was something she had imagined and the details just happened to be similar. Or that she would fictionalise the names and facts. I wonder what brought her to this particular story and how far her research has gone?

Her next piece brings with it another ghost from the past.

Ash Reck nodded to Lantry when the bell rang. They slung their bags over their shoulders and headed out without uttering a word. It was as if they had always been doing this. If she was with Lantry, Ash Reck knew, Longy would leave her alone. She thought Lantry knew that too, but she couldn't be sure. Lantry was strange but in a good way. They walked out the front gate and turned left. They were headed down the hill. Lantry was talking about an article he'd found in an old National Geographic about a type of small pig called Sus andamanensis which is to be found in the Andaman Islands. He didn't know where the Andaman Islands were because there were three pages missing from the article. He would have to consult the letter 'A' in his grandfather's *Encyclopaedia Britannica* tomorrow. Or just ask his grandad. His grandad had sailed the seven seas. He might know.

Will we swap tapes, Ash Reck said. Have anything good?

Mattie Lantry shook his head. No tape recorder, he said, no tapes.

Ash Reck stared at him. No tape recorder?

Mattie nodded. He was wondering if the pig looked like an ordinary pig and what did he eat. The picture pages were missing.

Cat Stevens is amazing, Ash Reck said.

Mattie gave her one of his looks.

Whose cat?

Sometimes Ash Reck thought Mattie wasn't all there. Like not the full shilling. But ask him about the French Revolution and he could name everyone who was in the Bastille and why they were there.

Tea for the Tillerman, Ash Reck said.

Which tillerman?

It's an album. I got the tape last Saturday. I can bring the tape recorder over to your house. If you want to listen to it?

Mattie thought it would be a good idea.

I have the lyrics too, Ash Reck said, I wrote them out. I'm thinking I might try writing songs. Like Leonard Cohen is a poet too.

I like poetry, Mattie said. I'm a poetry lover.

Ash Reck laughed. You're not, you never even ask a question in English.

All in one breath Mattie recited: Owildwestwind thoubreathofautumn'dbeing thou fromwhoseunseen presencetheleavesdeadaredriven like ghosts from anenchanterfleeingyellow,andblack,andpale,and hecticredpestilence-strickenmultitudeso thou who chariotesttotheirdark wintrybed the winged seeds, where they liecoldandloweachlikeacorpsewithinits graveuntilthineazuresisteroftheSpringshallblow …

Jesus stop, Mattie! Fuck it, do you know the whole thing by heart?

I do. Percy Bysshe Shelley, 1792 to 1822. Died in a shipwreck. Drowned. Body burned on the beach. Remains buried in Rome.

Can you do the Leaving for me?

I have to do it for myself, otherwise I would.

Ash smiled at Mattie. You're such a dote, she said.

Mattie blushed.

They parted ways at the foot of Union Street.

Ash Reck came to our school in sixth year and almost immediately she and Longy Long were talked about. But that changed after the fight. In a way I think Ash Reck was looking for someone to rescue, a shipwrecked sailor or a wounded soldier. You see that sometimes, the wounded nurse the wounded, the blind lead the blind. Mattie became that for her. In fact, he was the obvious candidate. Even we could see that he was a bit shipwrecked.

The fight was a simple matter, the kind of ritual that happens among schoolboys. The bully chooses his victim with care. The point of the ritual is not to avenge some stupid insult or whatever the pretext is, but to assert the bully's dominance. To that end, there is much petty harassment of younger boys, but the ritual requires a victim who at least appears to be able to defend himself. Mattie was taller than Longy but leaner, lacking Longy's bruising bulk, and also completely incapable of reading the situation, of understanding Longy's motives or even identifying the threat. As a complete outsider whom even the teachers rejected, he was the perfect scapegoat who could be sacrificed with impunity.

One day Longy waited for Mattie after school. There was some pretence about Mattie insulting Longy or stealing something from him – unlikely, since Mattie was painfully honest. Mattie denied everything. It was obvious he didn't understand what was happening. Lying was pretty much outside his experience and he tended to take people's words at face value. Longy lost patience with the argument and lashed out a sidewinder that left Mattie with a split lip. Mattie was so surprised he allowed Longy to get a second fist in. Then a one-sided fight developed. Mattie ended up with a black eye as well as the split lip. Longy would have continued to pound him except that his friends intervened. This too is part of the famous ritual. I had to be dragged off him boys, only for the lads I would have killed the spa.

Longy boasted about it for weeks until Mattie came back and had his revenge. In the meantime, it seems, he had some lessons from his grandfather and next time round he could actually box. In fact, he broke Longy's nose. He told me later that his grandfather had been Fleet Boxing Champion 1937 on the China Station.

But that first time, I was there, along with everybody else – schoolboys love a fight – and I saw that Ash was shocked. I don't know if she had noticed Mattie up until that point. Longy claimed she was his girlfriend, he was dating her, or, in the parlance of the time, he was shifting her. But it was she who took Mattie away at the end. And significantly, she gave Mattie her handkerchief and walked him home to make sure he was all right. I can still see Longy's face as he watched the two of them going down past the graveyard. What I saw in it was bewilderment. How was it that he, the king of the castle, was watching his queen walk off with the peasant he had just tortured? It was a social inversion that was outside of Longy's experience. And I remember thinking that Ash was complicated. I remember wondering how all this would shake out in the coming weeks.

I sometimes think that was what really wounded Longy, that turned his desire for dominance into a vendetta. Ash

Reck was his and in his moment of triumph she left him. The fury of the dominant male. Elephants have a similar hierarchy, according to a documentary I saw, but female elephants live apart from the males except for mating. They have their own world, their matriarchs and their social bonds. Their need for males is strictly limited to the exigencies of species reproduction.

From that day onwards Ash went home with Mattie. Sometimes I tagged along, but I felt like a spare wheel. And Longy never forgave Mattie for taking her away from him.

And so the workshops continue. Week after week Walter sends me a section of descriptive prose scattered with fragments of stilted dialogue full of loaded tags and past participles. His text is a coming-of-age story that isn't coming of age. In fact, it's going nowhere. His ability to tell a tale does not translate into writing and I do my best to inject some urgency into the narrative, to pare back the redundancies, to get him to see how turgid it is and how directionless – without, of course, using those words. And he fails to see what I'm saying. As for Emily, her retired civil servant has become embroiled in some unlikely radical politics and has fallen in love with a student he met at a protest. It will end badly, no doubt about it, but it's already going badly. As it happens I know a little about such protests from the inside and Emily does not understand the politics. She is, in fact, extrapolating from a white American civil society context where people believe that peaceful protests are a demonstration of the power of the engaged citizen to effect a change in well-intentioned public policy, whereas Italian protest movements start from the point that the state is redundant, corrupt or oppressive and that only anarchism or communism can change anything. Let's say the text of the American protest movement is Dr Martin Luther King's 'I have a dream' or Kennedy's 'Ask not what your country can do for you', whereas that of the Italian protest will be Marx or Bifo Berardi or even Tony Negri.

Who would believe in this repressed English bachelor falling hook line and sinker for what is beginning to look like the modern equivalent of the Red Brigades? I tried dissuading her from this line but she simply retreated into silence and a week later sent me a new and even more unlikely instalment in which poor old Salter is handed an automatic pistol (this is an American story so naturally we know that it is an Italian police issue Beretta 92 together with nine 19mm Parabellum rounds – if it had been a car we would know the make, name and year). I suspect she thinks me overbearing. I know from something she said that she has never read any of my work, but neither has she read any of the books I suggested she look at – Banville's *The Sea*, for the elderly repressed character Max Morden, Ian McEwan's *On Chesil Beach*. Elizabeth Bowen. John le Carré when none of the others took. I even suggested she watch the film of *The Constant Gardener*.

And now I suspect Deirdre has been writing the story of Mattie Lantry for some time and what I am seeing is close to the final draft. Her supposed feeling that there 'was something in it that she had been trying for' in one of her first emails is a lie intended to mislead me into thinking that she is writing it day by day. In another context I would say she was curating her image very carefully. I can't help feeling uneasy about the subterfuge. What game is she playing? One night recently I dreamed about her. I had arranged to meet her in some sort of waiting room. When I walked into the room I found myself waiting for me. The other me was wearing flared jeans and an Aran jumper. I woke in a cold sweat.

Today she sends a new piece. Mattie had a weekend job painting and varnishing at Eddie Ross' boatyard. It was the kind of job that suited him. He was meticulous in everything. His geometry notebook, for instance, was a model of precision. His drawings for physics were beautiful. I imagine he must have been one of those children who from the very beginning coloured precisely within the lines. Deirdre is giving us a classical character description here. It's nice work.

Young Mattie Lantry to do the brightwork of a Saturday in Eddie Ross' boatyard. Funny youngster, but a dinger with a paintbrush. Boatyards need four things: a marine engineer, a carpenter, a rigger, a painter. The rest can be dawfaked. Mattie boy I'll give you a fiver an hour, how does that sound? By the looks of the grin on him it sounded good enough. And the owners were all happy. Give him a bit of broken glass and he'll strip varnish off a topside before you can say snap. Give him a paintbrush and a pot of varnish. Give him a mug of coffee twice a day and he'll go from dawn till dark like a machine. Eddie Ross was well satisfied with him.

Johnny Kelleher, owner of *The Star of the Sea*, built 1964, pitch pine on oak, Gardner 6LXB diesel engine, was planning to convert her to a live-aboard and sell her in England as a classic. That was the way the industry was going, with falling quotas. The drift-netting was completely gone now, all those boats lying idle, families that were taking salmon for generations. Whitefish quotas were fucked, mackerel and herring were fucked. Now they were offering money for the big pelagics to come ashore. Eddie was thinking maybe he could get in on the decommissioning. Time was the owner burned the boat and that was that. But now it was all approved environmental standards. Still, the conversion was a good job to come in so late in the year when the yachts were all launching.

Mattie Lantry was thinking that it was a fine dry day but the ground was still slightly damp so there was no dust. He was thinking about what Richard Bitmead wrote about French polish and the correct application of varnish to a newly prepared surface. The surface is rubbed down with fine glass-paper, after which a coating of varnish is applied with a sponge or a broad camel-hair brush, giving long sweeping strokes. The tool should be plied with some degree of speed, according to Bitmead, as spirit varnishes have not the slow setting properties which distinguish those of oil, and care should be taken not to go over the same part twice. This he felt was good advice. He had marked it the night before. Pencil sharpened by light bulb-shaped sharpener. All the advice in *French Polishing* was good. He went over the section he was about to start on. He wiped it once more with a cloth charged with white spirit. He had persuaded Eddie to let him French-polish the wheel. In French polishing the wood, by some magical process, is made to resemble marble, and has all the beauty of that article with much of its solidity. He said so to Eddie and Eddie said they'd give it a garry as the man said and he could always strip it back if it didn't work out, but varnish would be good enough for the brightwork. But when he asked Eddie Ross for a camel-hair brush Eddie said, I'll give you camel hair by Christ, am I paying you by the hour or what?

He was grateful to Eddie Ross for the work but the man had no sense of what could be achieved with French polish and a camel-hair brush.

And his grandad was not happy about him spending every Saturday in Eddie Ross' yard. What you want work for Mattie lad, you best keep your head in your books, how long now before the Leaving? It's just Saturdays, Grandad. Still and all. It's my first job, Grandad. My first job was as a telegram boy with the ruddy Posts and Telegraphs. They gave me a bicycle and I thought I was farting on a velvet cushion and I'd be right in no time. And then what did I do? I cycled down to Queenstown and signed on for the ruddy Andrew. Join the navy and see the world? All I saw was the insides of a ruddy ship is what I saw.

Mattie worried about his grandad. It seemed to Mattie that he wasn't moving so much. And his ticker was always flying. What's wrong, Grandad? Anno domini, Mattie boy, none of us are getting younger. His grandad was almost eighty. Maybe he was eighty. Sometimes Jack Lantry was confused. The old noggin was not what it used to be. When he was confused he would call things the whatsit. I was down the whatsit. Or pass me the whatsit. Sometimes he called it the feckamecallit. I got the feckamecallit for you, Mattie.

Here Mattie, his grandfather said, we had the guards at the door about school. How you going to get to college if you're AWOL half the time?

I got suspended, Grandad.

Mattie had the pleasure of breaking Longy Long's nose. He was the bane of Mattie's life and on a previous occasion, before his grandfather had taken his education in hand, Longy had given him a bad hiding. As a consequence his grandad had told Mattie all about the Sugar Ray Robinson–Randy Turpin fight out Harringay, fifteen bloody rounds, there was more in that boy Turpin than anyone expected, what a night that was, old Jack Solomons lived out Hackney way, he was the promoter, he always had a big cigar, Robinson comes over cock of the walk, expecting an easy title like see. But Turpin put manners on him.

This was the necessary gen to showing Mattie how to hold his fists and how to balance. Balance is everything Mattie boy, he says, you got to be light on your feet like old Randy Turpin.

As for that matter with the boy Long, your chum had it coming to him, but you were supposed to report back to school last Monday. I got the chit somewhere. Monday it said.

Considering Jack Lantry himself ran away to sea when he was younger than Mattie, Mattie believed he was perpetrating an injustice by getting mad at him for not being at school. His grandad did not see it the same way.

You go to school on Monday next or mark my words I won't be responsible for my actions.

Jack Lantry tapped his skull where there used to be hair. I got a pain in the noggin thinking about you. You go to school, chum. Learning is no load.

It was a mine that did Jack Lantry's noggin. Up in the Kara Sea somewhere near Novaya Zemlya circa 1942. It was trapped in the Oropesa Sweep and there was nothing to be done only turn to and shoot it. You

51

had to hit the casing to detonate it, shooting from a pitching deck. Jack Lantry was the best shot on board. Of course some of the officers were good shots too, but you never saw an officer potting a mine. Class, see. Officers shot grouse. Poor bloody Jack Tar had the pleasure of shooting mines that might or might not be too close for comfort. It took four rounds and when it blew the force of the explosion knocked him back against the superstructure aft. Cracked the noggin. Oh Jesus what a head. I drank with Yanks in Shanghai when we were up the Yangtze river and I drank with Scots in Scapa Flow, but laddie, what a head the day after I shot that ruddy mine. I never felt anything like that mine gave me. When them mines go off it's up the spout for you Sunny Jim. Best keep off if you can. That was in the old *Britomart*. Christ, she rolled like a pig in a heavy sea and we never had enough to eat. No storage on a minesweeper like see? We were hungry sods on board of the old *Britomart*.

Mattie charged his brush and began to cover the surface with broad sweeping strokes taking care never to go over the same part twice. The wood came alive under his hand. The low spring sun glowed in it. Outside the yard was the golden sea. He found that when he was varnishing the only thing in his head was music. At the first touch of the brush he heard in his head the words of a song about someone called Daniel travelling on a plane. The fellow singing said he really missed Daniel. He heard it on the radio. He didn't know all the words, but next time it played he'd get the rest of them. It was a sad song but it made Mattie Lantry happy. He swept sunlight into the wood and heard that voice and nothing else. The *Vierge Marie* was due back this evening with gearbox trouble he heard Eddie Ross say. The news came in on the VHF. Eddie Ross would haul her tomorrow. Mattie thought he might go down the pier and see if the *Vierge Marie* had fish. His grandad said the skipper was all right. He drank in the Harbour Bar.

Longy was on the road home. He could identify the characteristics of Longy from three miles, which was the distance from eye to horizon. That way of leaning slightly, of one shoulder higher. He saw they were smoking shit. They were passing it around.

There were a few others, including Harney and Jimmy Winter, Massey and Nailer O'Neill. Why was Jimmy Winter there? That was a turn-up for the books.

They weren't exactly partying no matter what they were smoking.

Mattie had the impression they were there especially for him. They were frankly thinking of jumping him. And he was afraid. He wondered if he could defend himself against more than one or two. Longy was strong on the Theme of Revenge. They did it in English. Nearly everyone has it in for Macbeth. Mattie was in favour of the king killing business and so was his grandad. Only one thing for royalty, Mattie boy, up against the wall. He thought about turning back but you can't. If you run away you're finished. Next time he might bring something, a spanner maybe, a chisel. If he had a chisel now he'd do Longy for once and for all.

Harney and Longy were the Terrible Twins. That's what Mrs Ward, the French teacher, called them.

They were smoking their made-up cigarettes. When Mattie reached them he said, Hiya Longy.

Longy said, Come here boy.

Mattie said, The small pig Sus andamanensis is to be found in the Andaman Islands, hence Andamanensis.

They laughed.

Mattie was angry with himself. These things just came out of his head at the wrong time.

A fucking pig, Massey said.

A small pig, Nailer said.

Longy said, You're in trouble now, boy. They're going to throw you out of the school. You're on the agenda for the next staff meeting. You assaulted me and caused grievous bodily harm. Know what that means? The high road for you.

You assaulted the son of a government minister, Charlie Harney said. You can't do that.

They don't want people like you, Massey said.

Natural like.

Your type, Longy said. You look like a scanger, Mattie boy. A knacker like.

Everybody laughed except Mattie.

You broke my fucking nose, Lantry. You got to pay, boy.

He noticed that Longy and Harney, Massey and Nailer were moving into position on different sides of him. He could see immediately that this would give them tactical freedom as well as possibly the element of surprise. Jimmy Winter was looking for something in the ditch, maybe he was looking for a stone or maybe he didn't want to get involved.

55

Mattie thought he could do with an extra hand here, if Jimmy knew which side he was on.

Longy was doing his dog poem now, which meant things were going from bad to worse. He did the poem when he got excited. He was saying, This dog is dog a dog good dog way dog two dog keep dog a dog stupid dog bastard dog busy dog four dog twenty dog seconds dog. In two ticks they'd jump him. So he kicked Longy in the knee very fast and Longy fell down shouting. Mattie was proud of the move. He had shifted his balance smoothly and quickly and leaned out far so the blow wasn't hard enough to break anything, but it had an excellent effect. Wearing Docs helped. Now he only had to deal with Harney and Nailer, and Nailer wasn't really up for it. Next time he'd bring the chisel. Longy's pain sounded like a curlew but very loud and close up. He thought about kicking Longy again but it wasn't necessary.

He was about to walk away when someone jumped him from behind. It turned out to be Charlie Harney. The weight brought him down. Now Longy was up, limping towards him.

Fucking spa, Longy said.

He kicked Mattie in the stomach. For a while Mattie couldn't breathe. While he was trying to get his breath Massey stamped on his hand. Longy kicked him again, aiming for his face, but this time Mattie rolled a little and the kick landed partly on Harney's shoulder. Harney rolled off and Mattie was up.

Fuck, Harney said, Longy, you fucking kicked me.

Leave him alone, Jimmy Winter said. Come on lads, it's not a fair fight.

It looked like Nailer O'Neill agreed. He was standing back.

Winter was standing well back. He didn't have a stone. It didn't look like he was at action stations.

Fuck off, Winter! Longy shouted. Mind your own business.

They were backing away now but Mattie landed a punch on Harney's chest. It wasn't a good punch. Harney laughed nervously.

Fuck off, spa! Longy said. You got what's coming. Fuck off home.

Mattie rounded on him but Longy took two steps back. Lay a finger on me and I'll report you to the guards. Who do you think they'll believe?

The minister's son, Charlie Harney said.

Mattie walked away. Longy shouted, Go home to Mammy, spa!

Mattie's stomach and hand hurt. Luckily Massey didn't stamp very hard. He might have broken a finger. Mattie imagined a cloak of invisibility that he could draw around him like darkness.

I haven't been called Jimmy since I left Rally. At college I was Jim and I have been Jim since.

Harney, Massey, Jimmy Winter and Nailer O'Neill. My father would have been happy to think of me in the company of respectable boys like Harney and Nailer, but that was because he didn't know them. He tended to view families through the perspective of their bank accounts. I don't remember this fight. But then it may not have happened. I feel sure my name is an afterthought. Does she know who I am? Is she trying to flush me out? Who the actual fuck does this woman think she is?

Or is it my paranoia speaking?

According to Catherine, I do manifest symptoms of paranoia from time to time. The measured judgement of a loving wife is not to be set aside lightly.

I will not allow myself to react.

Her Mattie Lantry character is exactly as I remember him, even turns of phrase that I had forgotten. How does she do it? I recall one of his teachers saying that he always had his head in a cloud or a book. His mother was dead, father unknown and he was cared for by his grandfather. Old Jack Lantry was an ex-sailor, by all accounts something of a bruiser in his time and inclined to spend his pension on the horses. They lived on Connolly Road, which someone had nicknamed Korea at the time of the Korean War. And I remember when Mattie started working at Eddie Ross' yard because we were all jealous of him. He was making good money when I was picking potatoes for my uncle Peter Winter and paid by the bucket. Only someone who actually knew Mattie would know these details.

And she has the language of the fishermen too. Perhaps some of the references are anachronistic. Were they selling the big boats already in the late seventies? I don't know, and fact-checking is not my business. She knows the material and understands the time. But the book isn't going anywhere, despite the characterisation and the period detail. It's relatively static, moving from one isolated episode to the next. There's no forward motion, no suspense, no sign of a plot, no character development. No one will publish this.

I toy with the idea of asking her straight out who she is, but I realise that this could only have two possible outcomes. The first and best is that she would tell me, possibly slowly and partially, but I should be able to put the pieces together. The second, catastrophic outcome would be her disappearing. This would be especially likely if she had real information, which would make it all the harder for me. After all I know nothing about her except her *nom de plume* and an email address which was specifically set up for the workshop in the same way that mine was. The risk of the second outcome is too great. If she disappears I'll never know. My second thought is that I should wait and see how her novel unfolds. Depending on how well she can manage the revelations, it could be a fascinating six months. A piece of my youth that has been missing would fall into place. And it's not possible that she knows everything because whoever she is, she wasn't there when it happened. The cast of that particular scene is strictly limited and I know all of them.

Of all the girls I knew at the time, and who might have known Mattie well enough to be able to write about him, the only names that stand out for me are Aisling Reck because in truth Ash became a wreck afterwards, or so I heard, and Miriam Healy, my first love. Did one of them ever live in England? Because Deirdre has something English in her accent. Who is she?

After work Ash Reck was waiting. Mattie and Ash walked on the strand on the edge of the afternoon, sunset getting its act together over beyond the harbour. It was an unseasonably warm day and they had their sweaters tied around their necks. Mattie's was frayed at the edges. Ash's was perfect. Mattie wanted to feel it. The wool was so fine he'd never seen anything like it. But he was too nervous to touch it.

Ash said, You heard about Nicky Wherley.

I was the one who found him, Mattie said. The car in the water. At the top of the pier. I saw it.

It's sad.

Mattie nodded. I don't know how you could do it. Just sort of decide.

I do.

Mattie looked at her and she shrugged. Was she talking about suicide?

Sometimes, she said. But she said nothing more.

He didn't like to ask. Frankly he wasn't good with asking people things. He was fine with telling, but asking was different. Apart from his grandad, who liked to be asked.

You know what they did, she asked. Longy and the others?

Mattie didn't, frankly.

I'll show you, she said.

She led the way back over the rocks and into the woods. He knew where she was going. Nicky's caravan was in among the trees here. He'd worked for Eddie Ross too, a first-class rigger Eddie called him, and one time he invited Mattie in for a cup of tea. Mattie liked the caravan. It was snug and clean and Nicky had Fig Rolls. Nicky had learned his trade in Portsmouth where they had a lot of rigging, why he got on well with Mattie's grandad. They both knew all about Portsmouth.

Someone had spray-painted Queer and Homo on the side of Nicky's caravan in big red letters. Mattie knew what queer meant because they often said that's what he was. Sometimes when he passed them in the corridor in school they made tutting noises and whispered *queer queer queer*.

Want to go in? Ash said. It's not locked.

I been in there, Mattie said, for tea and biscuits.

She looked at him. There was excitement in her eyes suddenly. Did he try anything?

Mattie blushed. I'm not a homo.

But did he try it?

No, he just made tea and told me about working on racing boats in England.

Are you sure?

Course I'm sure.

She looked disappointed. We might as well go back so if you don't want to go in.

I don't think it would be right, he said, Nicky being dead, see?

She nodded. The others would have gone in for a laugh, she knew. Longy would have wrecked the place. Or they'd have used it for drinking. But Mattie wasn't like them. It was one of the things that attracted her to him. Another thing she liked was how he loved his grandfather. Everyone else she knew hated their family but Mattie always spoke affectionately about the old man. She remembered the first time she was in his house. It was after the fight, the time Longy gave him a black eye and she walked him home. Old Mr Lantry stood up when she came in, lifted his hat and said, How do you do miss. And when she said, Nice to meet you, he said, My pleasure I'm sure. Like something out of an old English film, the ones on telly on a Sunday after dinner. And she thought it was funny that he wore his hat in the house but Mattie said he kept it on because the old noggin had a crack in it. Because this was Connolly Road she was expecting it to be shabby, but the place was scrubbed raw and smelled of carbolic soap and Vim and the walls were freshly painted in what looked like whitewash. There was a shaving brush and a razor on the sink and clothes soaking in the bath when she went to 'powder her nose' as old Mr Lantry called it. She was surprised that a man would do the washing. Never mind the dobeying, he told her when she said she would go to the loo, Monday is make and mend. She didn't know what make and mend was but she assumed the dobeying was the clothes. Old Mr Lantry thanked her for taking care of Mattie and he was so gentle cleaning the cut and putting an Elastoplast on it. His big rough hands were just tender. She knew immediately that he was kind to Mattie.

So they went back to the strand.

Do you think that's what made him do it? Having that stuff on his caravan?

Mattie shook his head. Nah, he said, Eddie Ross said his father fell off the back of a P&O line ferry but everybody says he jumped. Suicide. Runs in the family like wooden legs.

Ash laughed. Mattie, sometimes you're like an old man.

It's one of my grandad's.

He could smell a fire. Someone was burning somewhere upwind.

I'm worried about him, Mattie said. My grandad.

God I'm sorry, she said. I never asked.

It's OK, Mattie said, but I don't want him to die.

Like I wish my parents were old enough to die.

Mattie said nothing. He didn't look at her.

I hate them, she said.

It's just anno domini, Mattie said, at least that's what he tells me.

A trawler was letting go at the pier. Mattie would like to be in her. He couldn't wait to grow up. He would like Ash to be waiting at the pier when he got back but he didn't see much hope of that frankly. Her parents were psychologists.

A ragged line of weed and sticks stretched out along the strand, inhabited by a million creatures so strong they could survive any storm in two worlds. The sand was their desert. Mattie heard what sounded like an ocean in the distance, but it was only the sound of the wind moving the sand. The sand was always changing. Billions, uncountable billions, of grains all touching and grating and wearing each other down, that must make a sound. We're crossing a desert, Mattie said suddenly. And Ash stared at him. It's true, he said, if you were a sandhopper this would be the Sahara.

It's getting dark. I'm getting cold, she said.

When he stood still he could feel the sandhoppers abandoning ship. Under a magnifying glass they looked invincible and dangerous in coats of mail but in the light their armour was frosted glass. You could see their black hearts. If they had hearts.

That last paragraph. And the ending: *You could see their black hearts. If they had hearts.* It's beautiful. Who the absolute fuck is this woman? Could she be an already published author? I try to imagine who of my contemporaries could be playing this game. Maybe only Banville could better that and he wouldn't be trying his hand at an anonymous writers' group. The idea is ridiculous.

I wish I could have written that line.

I discuss it with Catherine after dinner one June evening. We're sitting out late, enjoying the lingering warmth, finishing a bottle of wine. Rather than going to the supermarket and risking infection we're getting Dunnes Stores to deliver, and when they don't have our favourite red from France they stick in whatever is to hand. Tonight it's something from South Africa that tastes as if it's been boiled in the remains of a wood fire.

I explain the situation, which necessitates telling her an abbreviated form of the actual story of the murder of Mattie Lantry, and give her my question, and her immediate reply is that it has to be this Reck girl. Deirdre is using the third-person narrative to distance herself, but the only way she could know what Ash Reck thought or what was said between Mattie and Ash is if she herself were Ash. I object that by this standard she also knows Mattie's thoughts and she could hardly be Mattie because he is definitely dead. There follows a tongue-in-cheek lecture on the perils of seeing fiction as autobiography, which almost finishes with me getting half a glass of red wine poured on my head.

But who else could it be? she asks. Are you sure Deirdre is a woman?

Yes, I've heard her speak. A touch of an English accent, south of England, much the same as Nicky Wherley's, but also something else in it. I'll listen more carefully next time but it's possible she's Irish. The problem is rhoticity. They pronounce their 'r's down there in the south of England – just as we do. If it was a Home Counties accent we could be surer. No rhoticity there.

And are you sure Deirdre is the writer? Not just someone doing the public side of it? For example, supposing someone whom you knew is writing it and asking his or her partner or daughter to stand in.

Someone I knew?

Someone who knows who you are.

That's impossible.

Nothing is impossible on the internet.

I explain again how far I've gone to disguise my identity. But as I'm saying it I'm asking myself if she could be right.

Deirdre is too involved in the Zoom meetings. She's completely committed to them and to the feedback I give her. If she were a stand-in, I don't think she'd be so determined. There's no sense of there being anyone else there behind her. But I hadn't really thought of someone recognising me. I just think it's very unlikely that anybody would have discovered who I am or that they would be writing an entire novel to get at me. I mean, how far do people go in these things?

Very far, is the answer. People travel round the world for revenge.

Nonsense. That's like a Tarantino film. Not in real life.

You're a bit fascinated by this, she says.

I am. You can imagine why. I mean I recognise most of the events she describes, or at least the setting of the events. I can remember someone telling me that Longy couldn't understand what Ash Reck saw in the 'spa' as he always called him.

You have a clear memory of some things.

Mattie was really handsome and Longy was a thick brute with a permanent sulk. Class was involved too, of course. Longy's family was well-to-do, a minister's salary, land and an auctioneering business. Ash's parents were professionals. It rankled that she split with the rich kid and dated an orphan from Connolly Road.

Does it occur to you that she's writing it for you?

I laugh and shake my head.

You think she knows who I am? She couldn't possibly. I haven't given her any leads.

Wittgenstein remarks that whether a proposition can turn out to be false or not only depends on what we count as determinants for that proposition. Your problem is to know what counts as a determinant. You should draw up a list of things that only someone who knew you at the time could know, because if I'm right, Jim, sooner or later you're going to make an appearance in this narrative.

I don't want to tell her that I have already been named.

And, by the way, how have I lived with you all these years and you never mentioned that your best friend was murdered?

Reading about plagues gives me something else to think about besides arguing about memory and repression with Catherine; a different time, a different culture, other people's lives. I have been dipping into *The Diary of Samuel Pepys* again after many years. Pepys lived through the plague years and survived. Today is the tenth of June and his entry for that date notes the arrival of the pestilence in London in what I think is a very moving note. That morning he 'lies long in bed' and then, in a phrasing that sounds completely modern, is 'all morning at the office', lunches at home and then 'to the office busy all the afternoon'. It's easy to forget that Pepys was a civil servant and such work must continue, plague or no. Nowadays people would be talking about him as a 'frontline worker'. There would be signs on the roadsides thanking him for his service. But coming home in the evening he hears the dreadful news that 'the plague is come into the City' and, worst of all, that it's in the house of his 'good friend and neighbour' Dr Burnett of Fenchurch Street. His immediate instinct is to put his own affairs in order and I am reminded that at the beginning of the outbreak Catherine and I had a similar conversation. In fact, we went to our solicitor and, for the first time ever, made a will. There was nothing very special about it, but it gave us – and our solicitor – some satisfaction. I joked that Petrarch had left fifty florins in his will to Boccaccio to buy a warm winter overcoat. I wonder who among our friends needs a coat? We'd need to scale that up for inflation, our solicitor said. He told us that we weren't the first. There had been a steady stream of clients making or adjusting wills since the virus was reported in Ireland. We came out of his office a little shaken.

So this is really serious, Catherine said. It's the plague, isn't it?

I'm afraid it is. We must be careful.

She squeezed my hand. We won't take any chances.

From: writers.anonymous2020@outlook.com
To: der-driu101@hotmail.com
Subject: Lantry Novel

Dear Deirdre,

You're really on fire here but the narrative, as it presently stands, is too episodic and fragmentary. You need to create linking sequences and a narrative thread that the reader can follow. I can see that you're drawn to the intensity of these moments, but so much is missing – the world of the text we could call it. You need to tell your readers about the place, the time, the people. We need to learn more about how they relate to the other people in the story. What was the weather like? What was happening in the town?

You're handling the developing friendship between Mattie and Ash really well. But I suggest you need to deepen that relationship. It would be a way of humanising Mattie who at present seems a little too extreme to be sympathetic to the reader.

WA

From: der-driu101@hotmail.com
To: writers.anonymous2020@outlook.com
Subject: Lantry Novel

Dear WA,

I attach a new piece – I hope you like it – I'm trying to do what you suggest here – I need to maintain Mattie's eccentricity while, as you say, 'humanising' him – I'm not finding it easy, as you can imagine – Thanks for your help and advice.

This is what Mattie understands by the word love. Once Jack Lantry wanted Mattie to excel at athletics. He was a good runner until the teacher who was training the athletes left and there was no more training. And then there was a time when his grandfather wanted him to defend himself; at that time he was inclined to teach Mattie certain esoteric defence techniques, including the famous rabbit punch. But after the nose-breaking episode and the goings-on that followed he gave up on self-defence. But not before he taught Mattie the orthodox stance for a modern boxer that enabled Mattie to get in four blows to Longy's one. Stand like Turpin. Keep your head boy and you'll be all right. To be honest his grandfather just wanted him to grow up normal.

And he tried to teach him about the sea and fishing. Mackerel skies and mare's tails make lofty ships carry low sails. Harbour rots ships and ruins men. Old Chinese saying, man who fish never go hungry. Even though they passed many a day catching passing oarweed until the mackerel came in. You could get very hungry in a boat.

Mattie was trying to explain this to Ash because she asked him if he was ever in love. They were sitting in the shelter of the rocks in a cold sun. A howling gale blew away over their heads and the dry sand hissed and stirred. They had their hands in their jacket pockets, sitting side by side, looking towards the harbour.

That's not what I mean though, Ash said. That's how your grandfather loves you. I'm talking about *in* love.

Of course it's not easy, Mattie said.

Ash was used to his strange thought processes at this stage. She smiled.

What's not easy, Mattie?

Mattie blushed and looked away.

Ash got up on her haunches and squatted in front of him. The sand whispered against her jacket. The small grey waves blew away eastward.

What I mean is.

He looked at her and she looked at him. She was smiling and leaning close to him. He knew what she wanted and he wanted it too but he was paralysed. His ticker was flying. In his pockets he could feel his hands trembling.

They looked at each other for what seemed a long time and then she said: It is easy. It's this easy. She reached out and put her hands on the rock on either side of his head and leaned in and kissed him softly on the lips. Mattie stayed completely still, hardly able to believe what was happening. When she pulled away he said, Thanks.

Thanks?

Of course, that was lovely.

She kissed him again, laughing. Mattie Lantry, she said, you're a pain in the hole.

But this time he leaned forward and kissed her and she put her hands around him and they kissed properly the way Mattie had seen it on the telly. While it was happening he was trying to calculate how many other people in the world were kissing at exactly that time. It would be thousands, he thought. The world resonating to a thousand thundering hearts. If ten million people had elevated heart rate would it affect the spin of the earth or was that covered by the law of conservation of energy? Later, after he had walked her to the foot of Union Street, he went over the whole sequence in his head. They met at the pier and decided to go for a walk. Ash was quieter than usual. The gale blew into their faces. They had to keep their eyes half closed against the sand.

She told him that her parents were definitely sending her away to boarding school if she failed her Leaving. They wouldn't talk to her about it. She was thinking of running away but she didn't know where to go. She was desperate, she said. I won't fail though, she said. I just won't.

Obviously he couldn't remember how they got from there to the stuff about love. But he remembered the kiss in quite good detail. The taste of Silvermints. He wondered if she was his girlfriend now. And should he tell his grandad?

I'm conscious of a strange binary mode of reading this material. On the one hand I know what I'm reading is intended to be a piece of fiction, but at the same time I have come to believe in its reality. It's not that I think of it as memoir or biography – they have their own rules of engagement – but that the people and the world of the book are completely real to me. I would call it hyperreality except that an actual real lies behind it. Still, hyperreal is a good word for how I feel about it. I *believe* that Ash Reck was already kissing Mattie Lantry even before the summer. The reference to the 'nose-breaking episode' places it after the second fight. He kept his kissing a secret whereas Longy boasted crudely about it. I'm shifting Ash Reck lads – she's a bit needy lads, know what I mean? (Winks, nudges, knowing laughter.) Like she needs it *all* the time. Not that anyone really believed him, except maybe the Priest Curran who was as thick as a ditch. In the pathetic fictions of teenage boys we all know what we're talking about, every hint is understood and we're all men of the world. In reality, none of us knew anything much. And we all knew that too, it was the unspoken tragedy of our lives. Herself has the curse, I remember him telling a group of us, and you know what they're like around the curse time. He made a groaning noise. Fucking insatiable lads, fucking insatiable. I remember it because, having no sisters – or a brother for that matter – I had no idea what the curse was about. Girls got it once a month, that was all. It was one of the sorrowful mysteries and seemed, inexplicably, to involve blood like some bizarre ancient ritual. Between women and men it was treason to even mention it. I wasn't at all certain, at that point in my life, that I would ever unravel the facts. Sex seemed like an impossibly remote eventuality. No girl I knew was having it *ergo* no boys were either.

So all of these actual memories are linked in my mind with Deirdre's narrative, blending into a single solid conglomerate 'faction'. It is not so much a willing suspension of disbelief as an inability to think of it as anything other than the story of my youth told through someone else's eyes. It is unsettling.

She continues to send episodes and makes no effort to provide a linking narrative. Each piece reads more like flash fiction than an element in a novel, snapshots and cameos and brief moments of conflict. I haven't run a word count on everything but my guess is she has hardly sent me twenty thousand words. A quarter of a novel, a third of a very short one. But she has told me that she's concentrating on writing what she calls the most intense parts and plans to write the linking story later with a more conventional narrative. It irritates and disturbs me, partly because I need to know how she is linking these events – because I need some understanding of what she knows and how she knows it. I literally need the detail because I believe the detail will reveal all.

Mattie was talking about Jimmy Winter. He didn't understand, he said, why Jimmy was hanging around with Longy so much. Jimmy didn't like Longy even.

He told her about something that he had seen. Longy and Harney were down by the back of the chipper where the cars park at night and Harney was arguing with Jimmy Winter about something. Mattie wasn't close enough to hear and at first he didn't think they saw him. Then Longy stepped in and told Winter to apologise. On your knees Winter, he told him. And the strange thing was that Winter got down on his knees. Longy and Harney laughed at him.

That's so weird, Ash said. Why did he do it?

Search me, Mattie said, a rum do whatever way you look at it.

A rum do, Ash said. What's a rum do, Mattie Lantry?

He looked at her as if she had asked him the third secret of Fatima.

What's up, she asked.

Nothing, he said.

And Ash was thinking that he was the strangest boy she had ever liked. Her mother was always talking about what she called Ash's Weirdoes. But there was only one Goth girlfriend when they lived in Dublin and a boy whose estranged father lived rough in the Wicklow Mountains. Her parents wanted her to go into counselling. Psychologists think counselling fixes everything. But Mattie was truly strange – in a good, or at least interesting, way.

The thing about Mattie was his mind. She wondered if he was just a genius.

He was always first in Maths and Physics and second in History and he was good in other things too. French, for example. He liked French because there used to be a café that he liked and the waitress was French. Ash suspected he had a crush on her. But the girl was gone now and he never went there.

He said the only thing that was keeping his grandfather alive was the coffin-nails. He's a forty-a-day man. The lungs are buggered and he has a dickey ticker.

Ash said, What about coffin-nails?

Frankly, all the evidence suggests that it's the coffin nails that are killing him.

What coffin-nails?

The ruddy fags, Mattie said. Woodbines. Or John Player.

Ash said nothing. He wondered if she was laughing. She was angled away from him. He walked around to the front but her face was normal by the time he got there.

What? she said.

I was wondering if you were laughing.

No, I wasn't laughing.

Did I say something?

Just you said ruddy.

Did I?

Ruddy is a funny word.

The *Susan Deane* was making the entrance in a hurry. The pelagic fleet. She was making waves. The buckled sand would remember for a while.

Mattie, she said, looking very serious. Longy really hates you.

It's because of the how's your father, the time I broke his nose.

Are you worse today?

Worse?

Sometimes you sound like a British comedy. An old one like *Carry On Talking Funny* or something. Today you're worse than usual.

It's my grandad. He says things.

Ash smelled of disinfectant. It was a surprise. Mattie had expected girls to smell of perfume always. She said her mother had signed her up for supervised study. She didn't think her mother wanted to see too much of her, anything to keep her out of the house. The sun went down somewhere behind pewter clouds. Mattie thought that he hadn't kissed Ash yet today, when were you meant to do these things, but somehow she was his girlfriend. It seemed to be a reversal of the usual arrangements. It was unorthodox. The only thing that might be relevant was *Social Life or The Manners and Customs of Polite Society* by Maud C. Cooke. Express affectionate fondness in your visits and letters; the more the better, so that you keep it a sentiment, not debase it by animal passion. The book ended at page sixty, but the Contents page gave a further six chapters. He didn't express himself, he knew that because Paddy Clancy, their

English teacher, told him twenty times a day. And he had never written her a letter. Probably her parents would intercept it anyway. They were like the ruddy CIA. And he wasn't sure about the animal passion stuff. And then there was all the stuff about how to dress. A woman's dress should be so much the expression of herself that, seeing it, we think not of the gown, but of the woman who is its soul. Ash turned her school skirt over several times on her waist to turn it into a miniskirt. She said her school uniform was disgusting. Like basically she was wearing a purple sack. Her mother thought it was very becoming. Becoming what? Becoming a shopping bag?

You would be charming even in a shopping bag, Mattie said.

He was quite pleased that he said it. He didn't usually say things like that. He didn't even think of them. And it made Ash smile. He liked making her smile.

She took his hand and he liked the softness and smallness of it. Whereas his own hand had callouses from sanding the *Kittiwake*, built 1927, gaff-rigged, carvel hull, pitch pine on oak. He had it back to the bare wood but it had taken him weeks. Eddie Ross showed him how to use broken picture glass to get the worst of it off and that saved time but you had to be careful not to gouge. He was going to varnish her the way he did the brightwork for the *Star*. And she would be a beauty.

It's true that in those days I was torn between my friendship and admiration for Mattie and my longing to fit in. I have since met other children of peripatetic parents – sons and daughters of bank managers like my father, police officers, diplomats, soldiers – and I have found that we all share that same need to belong to a group. We're needy, or needier than others, while at the same time assertive of our own independence. We revel in being outsiders while longing to be inside. I'm not proud of the fact that I was a hanger-on in Longy's crowd, but at the time I felt differently. Thinking back now I realise that I somehow idolised Longy in the way that people sometimes set their worst enemy on a pedestal. His violence was somehow noble to me, heroic, crazy, powerful. I wanted it. At the same time I wanted Mattie's gentleness, his brains, his big heart. I suppose, when I couldn't have his heart, I settled for Longy. Who never had a heart.

I can't help admiring how she achieves the character of Mattie. His oddities of language, his obtuseness, his difficulties relating to Ash paint a very clear picture of a naive outsider wrapped up in his own world.

The *Kittiwake* was the doctor's boat, the oldest in the harbour. I crewed in her quite a lot and I remember the time she was varnished. It was my last season racing in Rally. I haven't sailed since.

The doctor was a hard driver on a boat and he could curse his crew like the first mate of a clipper ship, but the minute he stepped ashore he was gentleness personified. He was a calm and comforting presence at the bedside or in the dispensary, soft-voiced and kind. He had been a commandant in the War of Independence and when he had a few drinks after a race could usually be prevailed upon to sing 'The Boys Of Kilmichael'. He was retired by the time Deirdre's story is set, but had been a family doctor for years. Strangely for an old IRA man he always drove an English car, a Morris of some sort, and when he drove he wore leather driving gloves. It was known that he had killed at least one man in cold blood, a British intelligence officer shot coming out of a hotel with a prostitute on his arm.

No one died today, at least not of coronavirus, and there are only twenty-four new cases. The plague is abating, it seems. Though all the scientists predict a second wave in the autumn, today there is some slight cause for celebration. We take a bottle of prosecco (Dunnes Stores age-restricted item, alcohol 10.5) and a few slices of cheese onto the patio in the evening sunshine and begin to think about the future. The newspapers say lockdown will definitely be lifted in a few days and our plan is to go to our holiday house at Gortnacarriga, which, as it happens, is about twenty kilometres further west than Rally. Catherine has remarked in the past that having been eager to flee the area as a young man, I was equally eager to renew my acquaintance when the chance of buying the holiday home came up. The exile's return to exile. Internal exile, perhaps. Although I had, in fact, driven through Rally once or twice, I had visited the town only once to meet the solicitor who organised the house purchase. I drove in, went to his office and drove out as fast as I could.

It was my uncle Peter's house and it came up for sale when he moved into a retirement home. Though we offered the ridiculously low asking price, the old man insisted on giving us a family discount. The result was that we were in a position to renovate it fully. We have owned it now for a little over five years. There is no telephone and no internet connection, no television. On the other hand, mobile phone reception is good although it's 3G only. In the rambling old bungalow with the sea in our eyes and the huge sky we have done our best work.

Looking out from my window I can see occasional passing container ships, trawlers, naval vessels, the occasional sailing boat and the whole sweep of the valley. Our neighbours are all farmers and there is a constant movement of cows to milking or to grass, sheep on the hills, tractors and machinery and an occasional quad bike used for getting around the rougher areas. You hear birds, sheep, donkeys, cows and the near-constant rumble of sea against stone. Water comes down the hill in winter or bad weather and flows around us so that on wet days it can feel like living on an island and we are but a stone to trouble the living stream, as Yeats would have it. The house was built in the 1960s to replace the old farmhouse further along the road, now a shed falling into ruin. It has big picture windows and no insulation because when it was built it looked like oil would last forever. We were lucky to have the money (thanks to Uncle Peter's insistence) to fit double-glazing.

Now we are sitting in the sunshine making lists of things to pack in random order. Toothbrushes, chargers, blood pressure tablets, hedge-clippers, coffee …

You're excited, Catherine says.

I can't wait to get out of the house. Remember that line in *The Plague* about the crazy need for life in the midst of every catastrophe? That's how I feel.

She grins. There's more to it than that. There's this Deirdre story. You're going to be back in the same place. I think I can recognise when you have an idea by now.

I wave my hand dismissively.

She's the one writing the story. I'm just the reader.

But you always say that the reader recreates the book.

Quoting my interviews at me when you know we only make stuff up for them.

You know, Jim, sometimes you come across as a pseudo-intellectual shit.

Anyway, I'm not recreating her book. I'm just wondering where it's going.

You know where it's going. The murder of Mattie Lantry.

I don't know that. I suspect it, maybe.

Aren't you curious to see if she can solve the mystery? The guards couldn't do it, after all. Has new information come to light, as they say?

Let's not talk about it. It's a beautiful evening and we're going to be free soon. Let's not spoil it.

She is silent for a while. I watch a blackbird searching for worms in what passes for a lawn after two months of drought and above-average temperatures – that brutal stabbing beak and then the triumphant lifting of the head, the worm coming out of the ground like a piece of string. I always think of blackbirds as fascists, blackshirts, strutting about and terrorising smaller birds. Robin, with his faded red breast, on the other hand, is a communist, a comrade or at least a fellow traveller.

Catherine (staring into the southern sky where blue is resolving itself into pink as the sun drops lower): Is there something you're not telling me?

Me: No, not at all, why?

Catherine: Because now I don't think it's excitement. I think you're on edge. You're nervous about something.

On the twenty-ninth of June the government lifts the quarantine requirement to stay within two kilometres of home. We plan to leave for Gortnacarriga the following day, so I have called in the latest work from my workshop. There's no internet down there so there will be no further Zoom meetings. This is a relief to me.

Tom's is the first to arrive. He has been struggling with an idea for a historical novel set on the Irish coast in the early nineteenth century, or possibly late eighteenth. We have discussed the problem of finding a voice to tell the story in, something he has never thought about, he says. He always thought of books as just words put down in the right order. So far none of the four attempts has proved fruitful, but today's email has a hint of excitement. *I think I've found it.* I know that excitement too. The realisation that a character or a narrator is finally speaking through you. You feel like a conduit, a medium, an amplifier, rather than a writer in control of his material. At its best it is a kind of possession; at its worst it's the voice of failure that will not leave your head. I open the file and am immediately struck by the change in his style.

Tom Clinch pissed into a stand of nettles. He was thinking of the pull of women, their long scope and certainty, as a durable cable that is drawn surely through its block.

It's like nothing he has sent me before. The tone is right, the crudity. The simile of the cable and the block. I read on.

Then, looking over his shoulder as he watered, he thought that between the scrawny pigs and their masters there was little to choose, not in the November gloom, the day's low cloud threatening rain or at least drizzle. Yet the buying and selling went on apace, new animals being driven in willy nilly from every direction, the haggling and the bargain-making, the pigs squealing and cattle bawling, the tanglers, their hand-battering and spitting, buying here, selling there, hens squawking, a baying hound, the clop of horses and the calls of the peddler and the balladeer. He saw one or two that he knew, the rest were all mere Irish. There stood French of Ballintray, a rack-renter, one who had been shot at twice but had a charmed life. French was a hard horse too, aye, and had laid information against his own tenants in ninety-eight. The thin man in black cloth was Lord Inchiquin's man of affairs, treading delicately between the horse shits and the cattle shits on his way to the lawyer's office ...

I find myself reading on compulsively. Tom Clinch is a Protestant widower with three sons, a small landowner who keeps boats and does a brisk trade in smuggling brandy, port and playing cards among other things. His sympathies lie with people of his class rather than with his fellow Protestants, though he is not a markedly sympathetic man. He has come to the fair to buy a wife. A man called Patrick Lynch has brought a woman for him and they go to a woodland clearing so he can examine her. I am struck by the fact that he examines her as he would a horse, even lifting her petticoats to look at her arse and legs. The woman is a beauty, Lynch insisting the only reason he's selling her is that she's barren and he needs children. Clinch, by comparison, is a widower and has enough children. He needs a woman. And Clinch is smitten, but hard man that he is, he bargains, walking away more than once. Eventually they come down to dealing.

'I'll give you two guineas for a bad bargain. Will you stead me?'
'Two is it? Look at her eyes. Only that she's barren I would not part with her.'

I remember my uncle Peter bargaining like that. He would arrive at our house in his ancient Opel Kadett estate. Will you come for a garry, Jimmy? I'm buying cattle. He always knew where cattle were ready for finishing. He smoked a pipe, but for the purpose of tangling, as he called it, he would take his time about cleaning it out, filling it, lighting it, letting it go out and starting again. As a natural psychological strategy it was brilliant. Say me fair now, I'll give you ten pound and the luck money. Twelve Peter and she's yours. Ah now Andy, say me fair, say ten pounds and ten bob. Afterwards there would be a call to the Elm Tree Bar and Ballad Lounge or Sullivan's for a whiskey and a chat and I would get a glass of Murphy's, something my parents didn't allow.

Tom Clinch and Patrick Lynch eventually settle on six guineas, ten shillings and a crown for the luck money. Clinch sets off for home; he does not own a horse, and tells the woman to 'walk on'. But he says it gently because he knows it's hard on her. This is a telling moment in the narrative because it's the first sign of a softer side to Tom Clinch. It's clear from the opening chapter that Clinch will fall in love with the woman. There is a hint of *Poldark* about it, including the hybrid language, the sense of a clash between the common farmer/smuggler and the lord of the manor. Then there's the specifically local conflict between Protestant and papist. I like it and I write immediately to Tom and tell him he is onto something, that the writing is true and appropriate. I list the things he has achieved – the voice, the characterisation of Tom Clinch, the atmosphere, the setting, the first step in the plot. Well done, I finish. I look forward to reading more.

What I don't say is that reading this at a Zoom meeting is likely to lead to unholy fireworks – Deirdre demanding that he cut the sexism and Emily objecting to wokeism and political correctness. There would almost certainly be blood. But there won't be another Zoom meeting for the foreseeable future. I'll be out of reach.

I feel a sense of satisfaction though – a writer was floundering and I have set him on solid ground. A justifiable sense of satisfaction. Tom, it turns out, has 'always been into old books' and he's drawing on his wide reading for the story and the language. He's grateful for my comments and delighted that I think there's something in it.

I print all the other files without looking at them and put them in a cardboard box in the boot of the car. I pack around the box – the car fridge to bring perishable food with us because we don't know which local shops will be open, our gardening clothes, the hedge trimmer, the petrol can, an overnight bag, wetsuits, books, Catherine's papers because she'll be reading a PhD thesis while we're down there, a half dozen bottles of wine from at least three continents. Finally, we're ready. We lock the doors and flip the catch on the windows, check that everything that should be disconnected from the electricity is disconnected, pick up a random selection of CDs and set off west.

I'm pleased to see that Catherine is relaxed and looking forward to the break.

The first CD we play is *Kate and Anna McGarrigle* and Catherine skips straight to the 'Swimming Song', our favourite holiday music. Her next choice is the beautiful 'Mendocino' and we are driving into a westering sun with California in our heads.

There is a point in the road when the rock begins to emerge from the fields and, gradually, you slip from lush pastures into a landscape that is dominated by sandstone and bracken and stunted thorns. We are always exhilarated by that moment, that sense of entering a different world. The roads are almost empty and so we drift lazily into the evening as the world turns to stone around us.

Our little house is there, with its back to the rock and the valley stretching down from our front door to the Bawn of Cannavee and the dunes. These dunes still archive the tsunami that created them from the great Lisbon earthquake of 1775. Sand has been found in the fields at thirty metres above sea level. The seabirds soar away over Mallavogue Head and beyond that can be seen the great whale's hump of Castle Island. At night you can see the loom of the Fastnet Rock light. A single house slightly further along the boreen, a holiday home used for only two or three weeks of the summer, and then an old abandoned farmhouse, its rooms still full of moulding furniture, settles and a food safe, a deal table and chairs, before the bracken takes over, stretching away to the cliffs of Dunlough and the sombre sea. Every few days Johnny Whelan, a local farmer and our nearest neighbour, drives past our door. He waves and we wave back. He told me once that the house was built on the ruins of an old school and the slate on the pump-house roof came from there. The minister built it, he said, during the Famine and the scholars that went were given the soup. There were a few soupers around here at the time and who could blame them if they were starving, you'd do it yourself. From time to time he brings us a bag of turf or a few stone of potatoes. The well is the sweetest water around, he said, and it never runs dry even in the worst drought. They must have had a mighty douser in those times or else the minister had the power himself. He laughed when he said it about the minister but I had the feeling he wasn't entirely sure it mightn't be the case.

Gortnacarriga in Irish (*Gort na Carraige*) means the Field of the Stone, and, in fact, a hill of Old Devonian sandstone rises directly behind the house, buried in the first instance in furze and bracken, but turning into farmland beyond our boundary. If you dig you strike bedrock at slightly less than a spade's depth. And so the house sits on the edge of a ghost desert of petrified sand laid down three hundred million years ago, on the side of the mountain they call Cnoc an tSionnaigh, The Fox's Hill, looking down on the brilliant white strand of Cannavee.

The first days are always busy. There are bushes to be trimmed, briars to be dug out, bracken to be controlled. The wilderness takes a step closer every year and every year we push it back. Because the house has been idle during the pandemic, birds and animals have grown bold. A hare crosses insouciantly in front of me on a morning walk. A family of rabbits takes the early sun on the concrete in front of the house. A robin perches on the handle of my shovel when I rest. Catherine is in her element, deep in the bracken swinging a slash-hook to left and right. If we were to come under attack from the ancient dead pirates of the bay she would be a fearsome defender. And pirates there were. This area was lawless and impenetrable for hundreds of years. Passing ships paid taxes to the chieftains who kept the castles and towers along the coast.

One time, digging out the root of a particularly tenacious briar that had grown against a convenient flat stone, we unearth something white and too regular in shape to be a stone. We prise the clay off it and dust it down and find it is the bowl of a clay pipe that had been cast with a set of oak leaves at the side. Someone, a man or a woman, had sat smoking contentedly on that stone and perhaps, in knocking the dottle out, had broken the bowl from the stem. Clay pipes were cheap and he or she would simply have discarded it and replaced it with another. Later, sitting on the stone together, we speculate about the life of the person whose pipe it was.

Sometimes, as we strip back the bracken and the blue-grey sandstone appears beneath, I think of how Deirdre has made Mattie Lantry see the landscape. I am looking down on the ocean and at night I can see the loom of the light. There is a passage that I have marked in one of her chapters in which Mattie imagines the Gulf Stream vanishing.

> He was hoping for a switch in the Gulf Stream because it would make a change of scenery and there would be icebergs. This old harbour was on the same latitude as Cape Bauld, Newfoundland. *Britannica* said the lighthouse at Cape Bauld marks the eastern entrance to the Strait of Belle Isle, which was ice-bound for half the year. He imagined it white as death, only the ghosts of white bears moving. Today the sea looks cold and the rock looks lonely enough and it is already too late to see the flash of the light.

I am surprised to find myself living in a strange layered topography – the past and prehistory of the coastline, my own present, my childhood and the parallel world of Deirdre's text, which seems to partake of all of the other times because she is a living person writing now as I read, and because the events she describes are part of my own past and the history of the place. I've had these experiences before but never so intensely – walking out of a film about a part of Italy I know well, for example, or with certain books – Saramago's *Blindness* was one because I began reading it at a festival in Lisbon. And on another occasion I was reading one of Ian Rankin's Rebus novels, I forget which one, and as the plane settled into the descent to Edinburgh airport I lifted my eyes and looked out at the city and had the distinct impression I was descending into a crime scene. It took me some hours to shake off the feeling. I have met readers who experience these states of intense duality and we have talked about passages, books that evoke the feeling, but my own writing never takes me that way. It's always the work of others.

Deirdre's email says that she has worked out some details of the plot and one morning recently she woke up with a passage in her head that describes how Mattie's grandfather Jack Lantry reacts to hearing the news of Mattie's murder. She encloses it, because although it's from what will be the end of the book, she feels she had to put it on paper. She hopes I don't mind it coming in out of sequence. She thinks of it as just a *possible* ending for the book and she may change her mind. She reminds me of something I said about endings in one of my emails: that there are numerous possible endings at the start of a book but by the end most of them have vanished into the air, yet there are still several ways to close it and the skill is in finding which one fits best.

I have a vague memory of having written it. One way or the other it's true. The process of writing a book closes off numerous histories, so that by the last third the ways it can end are quite limited. Characters can perform certain tasks but there are a billion others that they cannot be imagined doing. That is the structure of a character. The end, in a way, is contained in the beginning.

But I'm worried and irritated that she has skipped forward to after the death. I want her to spell it out, how she sees all that, who she suspects. I don't want her glossing over things, teasing me with half-answered questions, I want to know what she knows.

The passage tells how the guards find out who is Mattie Lantry's next of kin. Their crude comments contrast with the solemnity of their duty. Little fucker from Connolly Road. Next of kin is the grandfather, a right piece of work, permanent resident in the Harbour Bar. The narrative follows the streets from the graveyard to Connolly Street. They knock on the door and eventually Jack Lantry answers. They sit down with him and tell him the news and they can see that he's having trouble taking it in. They offer to stay but he shakes his head. They leave. Then a break in the paragraphing to indicate the passage of time and we are plunged without warning into old Jack's fractured consciousness. The shift in style is startling.

Jack Lantry felt something go in his head. It was like a strained cable parting. He saw one go a long time ago. He saw how just before it broke steam came out. That was the strands losing their power to hold moisture. And then the cable snapped and he saw a man's arm taken off as neat as a surgeon and a hole punched in a lorry. The man bled to death. A long time ago on the Yangtze. He was watching the news now but he wasn't taking it in. For days he had been listening to the sound of a distant engine, running smooth and clean, steady and true, and the occasional ding of the engine-room telegraph. It was the sound of a ship running over a flat sea and it was inside his head. He was listening to his heart. Anno domini for the time-expired man. What he wouldn't give for a coffin nail.

He felt a prickly heat all over like in the tropics. He didn't like it. They used to swim every morning until someone reported a shark. It was just someone larking but the old man, old Bone Dome, took it seriously. That was the last time they heard the pipe of Hands to Bathe Over the Side. The darkies didn't care about sharks. They jumped in off the mole. They could swim like fish. That time they had a stoker whose name was Jimmy. Jim and Jack Lantry were thick as thieves, because they were both in the Party.

The ruddy Internationale. I tell you one thing, Jim, when the revolution comes there's one or two people I know that I'd like to put against the wall. You put 'em against the wall, Chiefy, and I'll pull the trigger. That always made them laugh. Chief Petty Officer Jack Lantry RN. Had to keep membership hush hush of course in case officers got wind. Jim knew his stuff too. One time the yanks were in, Jim issued a challenge but the Yankee boxer wouldn't fight him. Old Gentleman Jim was in the Kandahar when she went down. You can't box your way out of that, not when you're just a stoker down below. There's no way out for those boyos. It's down to Davy.

They say Mattie is dead. So they say. Young Ash said so. She was here five minutes past. Come to think of it, she might still be here. Upstairs in Mattie's room. A young lassie like that, who would have thought? So polite. How do you do, Mr Lantry. Very well I'm sure. And tears in her eyes. The whatsit came first. A young un' barely able to fit his uniform, and an older chap. What rating was he? A sergeant maybe. We regret to inform you. Like the telegrams. His Majesty regrets. His Majesty regrets that another good man is gone to Davy Jones. His Majesty doesn't give a damn point of fact. His Majesty is farting on a velvet cushion and poor Jack Tar is on half rations. Poor old Mattie. Did I want someone to stay with me, the bobby asked. And they were hardly out the door than young Ash Reck popped in. Oh Mr Lantry. Tears and lamentations. Go on up young Ash, take whatever you want, I'm for the high road, it'll all go in the bin in the heel of the hunt.

Mattie dead.

He couldn't take it in. They said he was already in the graveyard. That made no sense. If there was a funeral, Jack Lantry would have known. Studied the Births and Deaths every day. Something missing. The how and why. Why would a boy be dead? There's not a ruddy war on, is there? Time was you didn't have heart to grieve. You stepped in to see Sparkie on your way off watch, Anything in the signals, Sparkie? They got the *Neptune* Jack, my cousin Dan was on her. Then down to the non-com's mess. They got the *Neptune* boys. What's for tea?

He felt a wash of cold run down the back of his head. He didn't try to touch it. When the cable parted he'd heard the sound of water in his head. Nothing was happening now except the blood noise and a little scratching like an insect. He judged from the way he was seeing that he had lost the sight of one eye. The water sluicing along the deck in a seaway. You could slip away then easy enough. Once on the China Station in a typhoon he had seen the ship bury her bow. That was the heavy cruiser *Kent*, can you believe it? He was on watch. He saw the wall of water and the old *Kent* climbed up it, and then she went down so far on the other side he thought she would never come up again. But she did, didn't she? He had a feeling his bow was going down for good and he'd never see the other side of the next wave. One thing I will say, this time I hope the whole ruddy lot goes down together. Lost with all hands. Gone to Davy. He didn't want to finish up with tubes out of every bastarding orifice. They used to say when your number is up your number is up. Well, the bastarding medics stuffed that one right and proper. They just can't leave well enough alone. All the things he knew. The procedure for testing the automatic sight on a Mk V mounting. He had it all in there as clear as a light. Where did it come from after all these years? Balance the gun as if loaded, see that the correct sight-bar is fixed, find the index error of the clinometer, place the tide lever at MTL and the error of the day drum at zero. He could do it now. Stand him on a gun deck and he could load and train the old Mk V and ruddy fire it too. All the things he learned in his life and lost. The error of the day. If he had to go himself well and good. He'd faced it many's the time. So be it. Clear away for action stations. So comrades come rally, the last fight let us face. He tried to sing it now but his mouth was stopped up with something. Nothing came out. He felt the ship going to slow ahead but he never heard the telegraph. It was five bells in the first watch. A long way to up spirits.

It's odd that both Tom and Deirdre use the image of a cable. (Tom: Tom Clinch pissed into a stand of nettles. He was thinking of the pull of women, their long scope and certainty, as a durable cable that is drawn surely through its block. Deirdre: Jack Lantry felt something go in his head. It was like a strained cable parting.) In fact, now that I think about it, I realise there are definite similarities in style between the two of them. I am uneasy about it though I know that strange concurrences are thrown up by the zeitgeist. I recall a time when Irish poetry was full of references to pig-killing, as if it were something that poets did as a by-trade. I can imagine the conversation between Heaney and Montague: I'm doing pig-killing nixers, Seamus, there's good money in it. Me too, John. Maybe I could go down to Billy Regan's bar where there's public Wi-Fi and Google images of cables. Or maybe they're somehow the same person, the Zoom call a set-up, some sort of sinister collaboration specifically against yours truly. A vendetta. I know what Catherine would say – I'm becoming paranoid. On the other hand, she is the one who suggested that Deirdre was specifically writing the book for me. In any case, it seems obvious to me that Deirdre's style is a woman's whereas Tom's is clearly masculine. I check back and find the passage about how he examines the woman he is going to buy.

Tom Clinch walked slowly all around, admiring the set of her shoulders, her broad hips. He stood behind her and lifted her petticoat to examine the stretch of her legs. She drew away of a sudden but stood still afterwards, at a word from Lynch. Tom Clinch lifted the petticoat again and held it high. Her legs were shapely, well-rounded and not thin. Where they rose to her undergarment there was a suggestion even of heaviness, a pleasure rare and a sign of good feeding. She trembled slightly as she stood, like a frightened mare. He dropped the petticoat and walked around in front of her, studying her a moment more.

'She won't do,' he said, knowing he would not be believed.

I am reassured. The thought had occurred to me that it could be someone who decided to apply twice using two different kinds of work in order to maximise her/his chances of getting into the workshop and was now carrying on with the charade, even using a collaborator, a boyfriend or partner maybe, to take the place of the second person on voice calls. An elaborate piss-take, a sour joke on me. Often when writers are at the earliest stage of their development they try out different styles, sometimes influenced by the last good book they read. I myself could find a few attempts at historical fiction somewhere in my drawers, typed and discarded before ever I owned a computer. Such experiments are part of finding your own voice. In fact writing courses sometimes encourage people to imitate the masters. Or at least the successful.

But Tom's is a masculine sensibility. And I was certain that the description of Ash Reck kissing Mattie Lantry was written by a woman. In fact the difference in the two styles is obvious now. *The Bought Woman* (his working title) is an objective narrative; *Lonely Rock Light* is full of subjectivity. And no man would have written that a girl smells of disinfectant.

Still, the coincidence of imagery is striking.

Exactly as I expected, Catherine tells me I am paranoid. I try to explain that a writer may be more sensitive to these techniques, but she's having none of it. She even calls me a wanker for saying it. We're sitting in the evening sunshine with our backs to the gable wall because the easterly wind means we can't sit on the terrace at the front. The mountain stretches ahead of us, its side a patchwork of mown fields and pasture rising to the line where the land is no longer productive, a great mass of bracken and heather and scrub sally trees and thorn. The light on a mountain is always uncertain. Clouds cast certain rocks or fields or streams in shade and then the sun follows and picks them out in silver, silk or bronze. The exchange of colour and tone.

I have a copy of Defoe's *Journal of the Plague Year* beside me. Earlier I was looking at the page where he first mentions the increasing numbers of deaths recorded in the quaintly termed Bills of Mortality for each of the London parishes. He and Pepys record exactly the same terrible dread as the pestilence creeps across the Channel and up from the south coast. But to my mind Defoe, whose book is based on research and is essentially a work of historical fiction, does it better. I'm arguing for literature over documentary evidence and Catherine is winding herself up for a serious argument. But suddenly she changes her mind.

It's a beautiful evening, she says, who cares about truth just at the moment?

I'll drink to that.

She smiles at me and raises her glass.

Here's to good news, she says.

And today, there is something good. The business news is reporting that shares in AstraZeneca rose almost six per cent following reports that it was about to publish positive results on a Covid vaccine. Social media is full of dire predictions about the Deep State microchip plan. Here it comes, they say. AstraZeneca is the chosen mode of delivery. The New World Order or the Illuminati or the Elders of Zion – whichever fits the conspiracy theory of the moment – are moving in on us. Defoe has this stupidity nailed down: 'They were as mad upon their running after quacks and mountebanks, and every practising old woman, for medicines and remedies; storing themselves with such multitudes of pills, potions, and preservatives, as they were called, that they not only spent their money but even poisoned themselves beforehand for fear of the poison of the infection.'

There's a gentle easterly breeze blowing over our heads and seabirds are dreaming on the updrafts from the valley. The furze is an electric yellow and a faint smell of dung drifts up from the farm below us. If I look over my shoulder I can see the back of Castle Island and the ruined tower like a broken tooth.

Mattie pushed the trolley down the slip until the water took up the weight. It was a magic moment that always made him giddy, when the wood suddenly became paper on an ashen sea. He pulled the boat alongside the slip and helped Ash in. Ash was as light as a bird, barely disturbing the sureness of the boat, the constancy of the water. Jimmy and Miriam followed, Miriam already in her swimming togs with a big jumper over them.

He pushed off lightly and the boat drifted out and he unshipped the oars and sat on the thwart and began to pull steadily around the pier. The day was a glass, calm and clear from blue sea to blue sky. Mossie Sweetnam, the Art teacher, told him once how they used to make sheets of glass by melting a vat of lead and then pouring the molten glass onto it and the lead cooled first, so the glass set into a perfectly smooth surface. Mattie tried to imagine what it would be like if someone blew on the glass as it was setting, a tiny transparent wave rippling away from his breath. When people looked through it they would think they were looking out from inside the sea. Mossie Sweetnam was OK. He told Mattie he had a gift for recall and that he should study to be an architect or an art historian. That was a nice thing to say.

When he was clear of the pier he slipped back to the transom to sit by Ash. She stuck her elbow in his ribs. When he looked at her to see what it meant she winked and nodded at Jimmy and Miriam. They were sitting on the thwart holding hands. He lowered the *Seagull* and primed it and flipped the starter cable and the engine started uncertainly at first, a stuttering machine gun on the still morning, then settled down. He directed the bow towards the island and Ash began to sing. It was a radio song. 'Rivers of Babylon' by Boney M. They sang the words together and after a time Jimmy and Miriam joined in. They sang it four times. Ash taught Mattie the words. Then Miriam sang 'Brown Girl in the Ring' and they all sang the chorus. Frankly even Mattie knew the words of that.

He stopped the engine in the Castle Grounds, which was a good fishing area. Willy Morrish had told him so. The *Susan Deane* was out today but Willy wasn't on her because he had injured his arm.

He handed a line to Jimmy and Miriam and another to Ash. He showed them how to lower it and troll it up and down so the fish thought the feathers were high tea.

They could see Lonely Rock. A yacht was going round it very slowly. Mattie remembered his grandfather saying, That old rock, I been looking at it off and on for nearly ninety years. I used to see the light in my dreams. There's no sun in the winter up there in the north, Mattie boy, and in the summer there's no night. There used to be a light on North Cape, a white flash every thirty seconds, but Jerry knocked her out. Aid and comfort to the enemy see. But whenever I seen a light at sea I thought about that old rock. Nobody knows about Hell till they sailed the winter between North Cape and Spitzbergen. Cold? Hell is a cold place, Mattie boy, if there is another one.

The boat drifted on the tide. They heard the distant moaning of seals on Carthy's Islands. No fish came to their lure, though they felt the bottom tugging at the lead. So after half an hour they hauled their lines and moved on. Mattie brought them into the old slip on Castle Island. He pointed out the ruined tower and told them the legend of the child who fell from it in the sixties and the hippy family who used to live here. The child's name was M, he said. In those days hippies gave children names that were just letters. They didn't want Christian names.

They decided to see if the house was still there.

Mattie dropped the anchor in four feet where the tide swirled around the pierhead and rowed the chain away until it was shallow enough to get out. Then he brought a rope ashore with him and tied it off so that when they came back he could haul her back to him.

The pier was covered in lichen, an intense cadmium yellow pocked with blue-grey from another dimension. An ancient grass roadway ran along the back of the island between two high ridges. Now the banks had fallen in places; sheep had broken them down or worn them out. There were places where the road had gone into the sea. They walked on the springy island grass that the sheep had eaten down, then up through a field of bracken. There were some ruins near the tower, old houses empty since the Famine. They moved Ash to tears. Think of the babies, she said, the mothers and the fathers saying goodbye. Mattie didn't think of babies much. He very rarely saw babies. But now he tried to think why mother and father would be saying goodbye to their babies. He asked Ash and Ash said not to be stupid, she was talking about people emigrating, about mothers and fathers knowing when their babies were born they would have to leave the island.

Then they came to the hippies' house. They had to step over the broken lintel stone. The same psychedelic lichen in the curves of the limestone, but overall a kind of verdigris. The inner lining of the chimney had fallen down through the chimney breast and the flue was exposed. They could feel the earthen floor under their feet, even through the nettles and scutch grass.

Mattie said, The Famine killed a million people but it killed poor devils only.

Is that a song, Jimmy Winter asked.

Old Karl Marx, he said. And he said the emigration after the hunger should have ruined us but instead it became industry number one. And worst of all, wages were as low after as before. It was all round a bad show, the Great Famine. *Capital*, volume one. It's like undertakers, isn't it? Making a profit out of other people's sorrow.

Karl Marx? Ash said to Mattie.

Volume one, he said, it's in Grandad's room. It's on the stack under *Cyclopaedia of Literary and Scientific Anecdote*. That was a bargain. But we only got volume one. Of *Capital*.

Look, Ash said, two doors. One for the sunrise, one for the sunset.

They looked through the door at the distant mainland. The hills were the colour of smoke. Sheep or stones littered them. In the east the sky was breaking into a glittering evening. A seal was passing on the tide a hundred feet below them. He was unhurried, curious, sensual. Mattie didn't know where Jimmy and Miriam were. They looked in and then they went somewhere else.

Mattie and Ash sat down in the sun in a nest of bracken by a drystone wall under the lighthouse. They whispered even though the island was empty. When they lay back the bracken fronds were like a delicate embroidery above their heads. They heard the creaking of the stems and the sound the swell made among the pebbles of the shore. They heard the drumming of a trawler engine, the calling of gulls, something like a sigh that could have been a whale or a wave or a ghost. And six weeks later Ash Reck would know for certain that she was carrying a baby. She would know that only Mattie Lantry could be the father. She would have been to his funeral by then. She would have seen him put in the grave and know for certain that her Mattie was gone forever. That day of the funeral she wanted to die herself. In fact the pain was so bad she thought she would. She thought once darkness fell she would lie down and close her eyes and there would be no waking.

But wake she did, to her sorrow that day and many afterwards.

Now, going home in the sunset over a still sea, she leaned her head on Mattie's shoulder and held his free hand and happiness was her lot. Ahead of them Miriam and Jimmy were kissing. Her skin felt taut and hot and she tingled all over. She whispered to Mattie, This is the best day of my life. But Mattie couldn't hear over the noise of the engine.

And what was Mattie Lantry thinking?

He was thinking of the rivers of Babylon and wondering where Babylon was. They had B so he could look it up.

And he was wondering how Boney M got their name.

And he was thinking that *The Irish Coast Pilot 1968* said there are no dangers inside Lonely Rock and the harbour affords sheltered anchorages to vessels of moderate draught. There were beautiful drawings in the Views section, showing the shore from the seaward side. As they motored home Mattie tried to imagine that there was a town ahead of them that was completely free of danger. He thought of Ash Reck lying in the nest of bracken. He used to think of Ash as a sparrow, shy and cheeky at the same time, but now he saw she was a seabird, one that needed the freedom of green water and grey air under its wings. He could imagine her floating high over the Castle Grounds. She would be the lonely cry that seamen heard as they neared the shore. The sound they took for sirens.

I'm driving to Rally, down the valley and then right at the main road and over the next hill. I'm uneasy, anxious, unsettled by Deirdre's book, by the story of Mattie and Ash in particular, and the day seems to have adjusted itself to my mood. The light is a strange brown tint, sandy looking. It reminds me of a scirocco I saw once in Italy. The sea appears and disappears on my right until the road winds inland temporarily, then I'm dropping down the mountain road, the wayside aflame with the bloody skirts of the fuchsia and the bright orange flags of montbretia gone native. A scattering of sails like seagulls speckled between the islands. There are so few boats this year. Someone told me owners are not putting them in the water. There was no maintenance during the lockdown, and now races and regattas have been cancelled. Everyone is afraid of a second wave, another set of quarantine rules, closures and travel limits. Nobody wants a boat in the water if they can't travel to it.

The town looks quiet, but then everywhere is quiet now. Though people have permission to mix, some residual dread prevents it happening a lot of the time. I have seen articles by psychologists musing about whether we'll ever get back to casual mixing, hugging, kissing cheeks, even handshakes. Many say no, that after the Black Death society changed and this pandemic will change us too. I say no, the instinct to hold someone in your arms, to hug, to shake hands, is too deep, at least in our part of the world. In a few years we will all be hugging like there's no tomorrow.

The place looks a bit more down at heel than it did last time I drove through. A few of the older shops have closed and it has all the signs of being permanent. One of the pubs is gone, its windows covered in plywood. There's a derelict house on the main street and shops and cafés with For Sale signs.

I park the car near the pier, take my face mask out of my pocket and lock the doors. The reproduction number of the virus rose above one yesterday, which means it's spreading again. Treat everyone you meet as though they were infected is the advice. I'm reminded of the warning given to Dante in the *Inferno* – '*guarda com' entri e di cui tu ti fide*', watch how you enter and in whom you trust. I note a personal reluctance to meet new people. As I walk down to the pier I am glad to be anonymous. The mask helps. There are no friends here in Rally to greet me.

I sit on a bollard and watch a man in a small boat casting off under sail. He has his main up, his jib flapping. He heaves hard on the mooring before dropping it, giving the boat a little forward impetus, and then bears away, filling the main neatly. Now he is hauling the jib and the little boat is skimming away between the moorings. This is a man who knows what he's doing. Just before the rocks he tacks and suddenly he's heading down harbour under a light easterly. It's a perfect day.

I'm thinking about the song that Deirdre mentioned – 'Rivers of Babylon'. I remember the crossing, the sound of the engine and the sound of Ash singing above it. She had a hoarse, throaty singing voice. I remember Mattie taking his shirt off and the ripple of his muscles, the straight breadth of his shoulders, the powerful chest. I couldn't take my eyes off it. I was conscious of a fierce jealousy. I wondered if Miriam was attracted to it too, but she was looking at me. The heat of the day despite the movement of the boat. Who else could have known? Only Mattie and Miriam – and Mattie is dead.

That Ash Reck was pregnant is a shock. It had simply never occurred to me, any more than it occurred to me that they had sex. But now her disappearance makes sense. She went to Trinity at the end of that terrible summer but with Mattie dead, no doubt, she was in despair. An abortion probably looked like the best solution but in the Ireland of those days it was a criminal act and an unspeakable shame. Like many girls of the time she would have taken the boat to England. Very likely she never came back, like many before her. The National Health System would have taken care of her without passing judgement. In 1980s Ireland she might have finished up in a Magdalene Laundry or one of the notorious Mother and Baby Homes, her child taken from her and sold to rich, barren Irish-Americans. She had a lucky escape.

The otter boards and nets are gone now and no trawlers ride the high tide. Off to one side beyond the slip there is a stack of lobster pots and buoys with black flags on fibre-glass masts. A pair of potters lie against the wall, another moored off, a scattering of yachts and motor boats. Unused mooring buoys bob in the distance. There is a sense of recent collapse, of something that preceded the pandemic. The fishery is dying, someone said to me once, it's all the big boats now, they fish off the coast of Iceland or West Africa and land their catch in Spain or South America. A large warning notice on a metal background says: *Vessels may be made fast in a harbour only to the bollards, mooring rings or mooring buoys provided for that purpose. A rope, chain or similar impediment shall not, except temporarily in case of emergency, be laid or run from a vessel in a harbour across any steps or stairs* … I am attracted to the precision of public and legal notices. I take a photo on my phone and remind myself to transfer it to my laptop when I get home.

I walk up into the town. Young people lounging in the open air on benches, many wearing masks. The virus is their atom bomb. The anxiety that they will hardly feel until long afterwards, circumscribing their lives, their liberty. We lived with it in our day, the sense that we could all be wiped out in the blink of an American or Russian eye.

I stop at Dr Charles Harney's rooms. I don't have an appointment, I'm hoping to get in early. His secretary is pretty and smiling, in her early twenties at most. She gestures to the electronic hand-sanitiser on the wall beside the door. I hold my hand underneath the machine and it ejaculates exactly the right quantity of soap. I rub it round and round. Out damned spot. Then I stand the requisite two metres back where she has placed lines of yellow tape for patients to queue. Her mask is on the desk beside her and she puts it on in response to my masked face. When I tell her I'm an old friend she says the doctor hasn't come in yet as his surgery hours don't begin until ten, but he's usually in with twenty minutes to spare. We make small talk. I ask her name and wonder if I knew her father and she tells me that her father died of Covid in the spring. Her eyes fill with tears and she has to turn away. All I can do is apologise for asking the question, but she waves my apology away.

There's hardly any here now, she says, but back then we didn't know what was happening. My dad fitted central heating boilers. He got it from a customer. He had asthma bad.

Then the door opens and Charlie Harney comes in, a man of about my height now, carrying considerably more weight, florid of complexion, a receding hairline, pinstripe suit and sailing-club tie. He carries the obligatory leather bag. A classic country doctor, anxious to advertise his status. He does not recognise me, so I introduce myself.

Jimmy! What a pleasure to see you again. Carrie, this is Jim Winter, our most famous Rally boy. Jimmy is a writer. I didn't recognise you with the mask.

Carrie makes sounds of amazement but clearly my name means nothing to her.

He leads me into his office.

A desk, a computer, a couch with a screen that can be pulled around it, two large metal filing cabinets, framed certificates.

Sit, sit. Excuse me if I go through this mail while we talk.

He slits an envelope open with what looks like an ornamental dagger, frowns at the contents, puts it to one side and opens another.

You went to Italy after uni, didn't you?

I did, I was two years in Rome.

Lucky you. What did you study?

I did my thesis on neorealist film.

I grimace at the words, a reaction that has become instinctive over the years. Don't take me seriously, I'm saying, but also take me seriously. I catch myself doing it sometimes and wonder where I became so cynical.

Altro Che La Cultura was the title. Other than *culture*. It was a nod to an article by the novelist Elio Vittorini. A pretty good film critic himself.

Dr Charles Harney has hardly heard my display of erudition. He is studying a report. He frowns again and again puts it to one side.

That's not good, he says. He picks up his phone and tells his secretary to phone Mrs Margaret Murphy to make an appointment to come in. Make it for tomorrow morning, he says.

Then he goes to a sink in the corner of the room and washes his hands thoroughly.

So what brings you back to Rally after all these years?

I have an answer prepared for this.

I'm planning to write a memoir of growing up here. You know the sort of thing, happy childhood by the seaside, school, sailing, characters I knew on the boats, friends and so on. Nothing special.

He returns to his chair, tilts back and folds his fingers together.

A memoir? I'd say there'll be a few people around here who won't be happy to hear that.

He's still wearing his reading glasses but he's looking over the top of them at me. He reminds me of one of our teachers but I can't remember which one. Butty Sullivan maybe. Or Paddy Clancy, the English teacher who first encouraged me to write. You can put it together Jim Winter, you have the gift, you should write stories or poems and send them off to the American Midwest, there's thousands of magazines there. I had the feeling it was a strategy he had tried himself in his day. Did Paddy Clancy once want to be a writer? He certainly loved his Shakespeare. I can still see him reciting from memory Macbeth's 'Out out brief candle' speech. There was a point where I thought he was about to burst into tears for the dear departed Lady Macbeth, regicide and potential child-murderer (I have given suck etc.). Paddy Clancy lamented her passing as though he had been married to her himself.

I won't be settling old scores.

We gave you a hard time though, Jason, myself and the lads.

I shrug. I want to convey the impression that it's water under the bridge, we're all grown-ups now, bygones are bygones and other ridiculous clichés. In reality I still hate his guts but there's information I want from him.

Sure it was all good fun, Charlie, just boys being boys. Our kids are the same. Have you kids? I have two. I'd say the same is true in every school in the world. And look how things worked out. I'm a writer, you're a doctor, Longy is in the Dáil. I'd say whatever was in the water at that school had success built in.

I can see him relaxing. The hands drop to the desk and he spreads them flat.

You know what, I'd say you're right. And you forgot Marty Curran.

The Priest?

Dr Charles Harney laughs. The very man. He's principal of the community college now. You mightn't remember Peter O'Leary? He was two years behind us. He's CEO of one of the big pharmaceuticals in California, I forget which one. He sends the family home every summer. The kids are lovely. You'd never know their father was a high-roller. He comes over himself whenever he can. Still sails with the club the same as if he never left.

Quite a scattering.

My father used to say that wherever you went in the world you'd find someone from Rally.

The fishing is gone?

All the big boats are gone since the quotas. But there's a fair amount of inshore stuff still going on. You'd be surprised. And the sailing club is going from strength to strength. The last race in September we had over fifty boats out. Pre Covid of course. That's a change from your time. We're not so reliant on the boys coming down from the city anymore. Plenty of people live out here and commute and they keep their boats here. Though, not this year, as you'll see if you go down the harbour.

I nod. I saw that. A lot of empty moorings.

Most people haven't the heart for it. Although I will say this, there's nothing safer than being in a boat. Fresh air is the best preventive.

I could hear him telling that to all his patients.

You remember Longy's girlfriend Aisling? Aisling Reck?

Longy is a married man with four kids now. He wouldn't care to have Ash brought up.

Names have been changed to protect the innocent, I say, grinning behind my mask and hoping it shows in my eyes. I won't be naming anybody. It'll be fully anonymised. The legal people will insist on it anyway. You know publishers. They want their ass covered. I just want to get my facts right.

What about her anyway?

Did you ever hear of her after she went to Trinity?

The phone rings and he answers. Yes, hello. Yes, they came in this morning. Your ESR is a bit high again. I'd suggest we send you up to the boss. I'd imagine she'll want you back on the Ritux. How do you feel about that?

121

He nodded a few times. I'd say you might count on writing off the day after the treatment, but otherwise it has a positive effect by all accounts. She wrote to me after your last round. She thought there was a benefit. You respond well seemingly.

Nodding again.

Right. Go ahead so and make the appointment and I'll write her a letter. Call in for it tomorrow. Carrie will have it for you. Take care now.

Bad news? I ask when he puts the phone down.

Chronic rheumatoid arthritis. She knows the score. It comes and goes a bit.

So I was wondering about Ash Reck?

No, I didn't keep track of her after Trinity. But I know where your ex is. Miriam Healy?

That was my next question.

She runs La Galerie. The restaurant. You'd have passed it if you left your car down at the pier car park. On your right as you came up the hill.

I remember it. Looks nice.

They do coffees in the morning and a bloody good lunch if you feel like renewing your acquaintance. I might add the dinner is excellent too. She's divorced. The husband was French. They do a great steak and the seafood of course. Straight off the boats. Your man was a bit of a chancer. Temperamental French type. And he left one or two *leanbh mishtakes* around here, if you get my drift.

Leanbh mishtake is a sarcastic local term for a child born outside wedlock – a mistake baby. A mixture of Irish (*leanbh*) and English (mistake).

He gives me a broad wink and stands up. My first patient will be waiting, he says. I won't shake your hand, if you don't mind, and I can't be doing this ridiculous elbow-bumping thing they do in England. Did you see your man Johnson at it? A chancer. I never thought England would elect such a clown. I trained over there you know. General practice training. We didn't have it here at the time. Be careful, the virus is still around. We'll have a second wave once the cold weather comes back, mark my words. Wear your mask and wash your hands.

I'll be careful, don't worry. Can I leave you my number. Just in case you think of anything that might be useful to me. About Ash and those days.

He writes it down on a Post-it note with the name of a drug at the top. I have a feeling it will go into the bin once I'm out the door.

Thanks for your time. Nice to see you again.

You have a house over in Cannavee, he says, I seem to remember reading about it.

I do. That's where we are at the moment. Gortnacarriga actually.

The stony field. Safe as a house on fire over there. I don't think they've had a single case of it. It's good to catch up, Jimmy. And I'm glad to see … things went well for you. Wife and family and all. Sure we all make mistakes at that age. And it would be an age where people experiment. You know what I mean.

I stare at him. I'm thinking, For fuck's sake shut up, Charlie.

Well, anyway, all's well that ends well. Carrie will let you out.

An elegant elderly woman sits in the waiting room. I notice that she's wearing a pair of brogues polished to a mirror. I have a vague feeling I should know her face. We nod and Carrie comes from behind her desk to open the door for me. Her mask makes her eyes glow brighter.

We keep it locked, Mr Winter, she says, usually we only let people in by appointment because of the Covid.

Professional. She registered the name in one take. The perfect doctor's receptionist.

I pass La Galerie on my way back to the car – Steaks and Seafood, Wine Licence, Coffee Mornings, Large Groups Catered For. Someone is sitting inside the big picture window with a calculator and some sheets of paper on the table in front of her. She does not look up. Is it Miriam? It's been forty years and I don't want to stare. Sunlight is glancing off the glass. I have the impression of a capable, slim, elegant woman. And then I have a sudden, almost physical memory of her mouth. By the time I drive past on my way home there are gleaming steel chairs and tables on the footpath and a handful of people sitting in the sunshine drinking coffee. The table inside the window is empty.

Mattie Lantry was walking Ash home after a concert. He was explaining to her how nuclear power involved so many hazards, from uranium mining to fuel enrichment to reactor operation, and then there was the problem of what to do with nuclear waste. There is no known method of disposing of nuclear waste, he said. He had a leaflet he could give her called *Nuclear Power No Thanks*. Ash was smiling in the dark. This was a side of Mattie that she loved. He just hoovered up facts. He could talk forever. When she met him first he knew nothing about nuclear power and neither did she. Now they knew all about it but he explained it all again anyway. He explained how fission works, the vast displacement of energy from cracking an atom. He told her that when they dropped the first bomb, the pilot who flew the plane, Colonel Paul Tibbets, said the explosion was brighter than a thousand suns. Think of the energy behind that. The plane was called the *Enola Gay* after the pilot's mother. It was a bit of a turn-up for the books that they were the first generation of human existence that had the power to completely wipe itself out. He'd bring her the leaflet next time. It was frankly excellent. And he was holding her hand and the music was still in her head. It was a band called The End. They were good.

They turned off Union Street and onto her road and straight away she saw someone in the shadows under the chestnut tree and she knew something was wrong.

Longy came out of the shadows, zipping up as he came. Mattie could see he was drunk. He wasn't at the concert.

He stood in front of Mattie with his fist to his mouth, tilting a little on bent knees and waving his left hand. Mattie didn't understand. What was it supposed to mean?

Ash's house was just ahead. Ash was thinking if she could get Mattie as far as the house Longy would be afraid to do anything. But then Jimmy Winter appeared suddenly from behind the same tree. Mattie was surprised to see Winter there. He heard Ash say, Jimmy? Why are you with them? But he didn't hear Winter's reply because Charlie Harney came out of the shadows doing his hyena thing. Mattie had seen a wildlife documentary on the telly that did hyenas. They had a bad name, apparently. The laugh travelled far in the stillness. Mattie thought you could hear it down the town. People would turn over in their sleep and think, that's all we need now, the ruddy hyenas. People with moggies would worry about the consumption of moggies by hyenas. Did hyenas eat moggies? Very likely if they were presented with the opportunity. Though he didn't think hyenas could climb trees, in the documentary they were just terrestrial.

Heeehahaha heeeeeeehahahaaaaa, Harney wailed.

Look at the fucking spa shitting himself now, Longy said.

Mattie was not shitting himself. He wondered how Longy had formed that impression.

A light came on upstairs in Ash's house. Ash knew it was her parents' bedroom. She felt sick.

Come on you fucking langer spa, Longy said. Hit me. Try it.

Just get out of our way, Mattie said. Or I'll do you again.

He said it calmly but he was frankly very worried for Ash.

Ash said, Oh no, Mattie. No more fighting.

Longy looked up at the window.

Look there, boys and girls, Mr Reck is awake.

Shut up, Longy, Ash said. For fuck's sake.

Hey Mr and Mrs Reck, Longy called. Hey Mr and Mrs Reck. Hey Anne, hey Tom.

Stop Longy, don't, Ash said.

Hey Reck!

Charlie Harney was pissing against the gate now. He was looking back over his shoulder at Longy and Winter. Far out, he said. He was smiling like a child. Mattie guessed they were stoned or worse. Two more came out of the trees to see the fun. One was The Priest. The other looked like a visitor from town. There were no street lights up here so it was hard to be sure, but he had a T-shirt that said *No Nuclear*.

A window opened and a man's head came out. Ash's father. He looked older and balder in this light.

What's going on down there? People are sleeping.

Charlie Harney finished peeing and climbed onto the gate pillar. Ash noticed that he hadn't buttoned up. He put his hands in the air like a soldier surrendering.

Come out now, he shouted, come out now.

What's going on down there? Mr Reck shouted. Clear off or I'll call the guards.

Ash was moving back towards the shadow of the chestnut tree.

Where's your daughter, Mr Reck? Longy called. She's not in her room.

Shagging Mattie Lantry the scanger, Charlie Harney shouted.

Everybody laughed again, except Mattie and Ash. Ash was sobbing and holding her face in her hands. Even Jimmy Winter was laughing and Mattie couldn't understand that. Not after being out on Castle Island with them in the boat. He thought Jimmy Winter was a friend. But Mattie knew he wasn't good at understanding people.

Charlie Harney suddenly started howling like a wolf, howooo howooooo, and Longy started reciting that crazy poem that he always said when he was excited, This dog is dog a dog good dog way dog two dog keep dog a dog stupid dog bastard dog busy dog. Nobody knew what it meant. A light came on in the next house.

Your Aisling Reck is a bit of a bicycle, Mr Reck, Longy Long shouted, we regret to inform you. She's riding that fucking waster. That's your Ash under the tree. She wasn't happy with the decent people of this town. She likes the bit of rough from Connolly Road Mr Reck, I regret to inform you.

Mr Reck at the front door in his tweed dressing gown. His face red with fury. Harney and Longy scattering back towards the shadow of the chestnut tree.

What's going on here? You! He pointed his finger at Mattie. Jesus Christ! You stay away from my daughter. We don't want you here. Clear off the whole lot of you!

Mr Reck looked around and saw Jimmy Winter standing in the light of the streetlamp.

Clear off, he said again. I'll tell your father.

Ash walked towards Mattie but her father came out and caught her. He pushed her back. Get in there, he said, get in, get in.

Mattie said, I love her.

Mr Reck was standing three feet from Mattie.

By Christ you do not, he said. If you think my daughter is going to be seen with you, you waster, you can forget it. Now clear off before I call the guards. I'll get you charged for assault.

When the door closed Mattie could hear shouting inside.

She is setting Longy's gang up for the murder. It's a reasonable assumption. The guards made the same connection at the time, perhaps responding to other people's accounts of the bullying, although they kept it quiet. As far as the newspapers were concerned all of Mattie's 'friends' were interviewed, but in reality they concentrated on Longy, Harney and Nailer. I was never really part of the gang, just someone hanging around on the periphery. There was, according to the only accurate article that actually made it into print, a 'history of violent confrontation' between Longy and Mattie (*The Southern Star* – you could always trust the locals to find the grit). Longy's father pulled all the strings he could find to keep it out of the papers and not another word was printed with the name Long in it, but he couldn't stop Longy himself talking. He was proud of the attention the guards paid him. Why would I kill the fucking spa? Just because he got Ash Reck? I wouldn't touch her with a barge pole. Ash Reck is a bicycle. A 'bicycle' was slang for a girl who slept around. If Mattie had been alive he'd have beaten the shit out of Longy for saying that. No file was ever sent to the Director of Public Prosecutions – ostensibly for lack of evidence, but everyone said it was because Longy was the son of the Minister for Industry and Commerce and Mattie Lantry was an orphan from Connolly Road.

Mattie knew Ash was in trouble. He was worried too that Longy and his friends would be waiting for him again somewhere along the road. Mr Reck was very angry. Mr Reck imagined Ash having poor babies. His grandchildren would be poor, maybe the children of a man who painted boats. Mattie had already considered the possibility of spending the rest of his life on the lump in Eddie Ross's yard and rejected it. Instead he imagined that he, Mattie Lantry, would go to university and get some sort of a job and then Ash would have their baby and he would be the acknowledged father and would take care of them. It seemed to Mattie that this was a reasonable expectation. He saw a lot of it. But he had also thought about the poverty business. People were against poverty. They said things like, people like you. If you had to give your address for something people noticed it. The time he applied for the position of temporary postman he was fine until they came to address please. Someone else got the job. There was good money in temporary postmen but he thought boat-painting was almost as good. Mattie understood that people didn't want poor babies. They didn't want their daughters being seen with a poor boy. They did it in school. In Civics and Religion they discussed it. Even though Mattie was an atheist he wasn't able to get out of Religion. In his school Religion was compulsory. One time when his teacher mentioned capitalism Mattie told him he thought very highly of Karl Marx after reading volume one of his book and so did his grandfather. He said Karl Marx said nice things about religion but was against it in the heel of the hunt. The teacher was furious. Religion was against Karl Marx, he said. He said that Karl Marx was an atheist, which was fine by Mattie because he was one too. He didn't see the point of imaginary beings quite honestly, there were enough real ones to keep you interested for a long time. And frankly the religion teacher went and told the Principal that Mattie was an atheist and the Principal was incandescent. Mattie liked incandescent. He had seen it in a book about safety at sea. Incandescent flares were an essential safety item for any boat. The Principal called Mattie into the office and told him that he shouldn't be telling people he was an atheist. He told the Principal that mostly they watched videos in Religion class so religion or atheism didn't come up very often anyway. The worst video they watched was called *The Tin Mountain*. In business class they had not discussed Karl Marx either, even though it was obvious because Karl Marx's book was all about business.

Ash would be punished for being out with him. Would she say that Mattie was her boyfriend? Would she say they were kissing and that something happened on Castle Island? He didn't think so. Mr Reck would be incandescent about it if he knew. And it wouldn't help that Mattie loved Ash as much as he loved his grandad.

He tried to imagine what her punishment would be. She had been grounded before and when she was grounded she told him she got very lonely. Mattie Lantry knew all about lonely since his mother died when he was seven.

He saw someone on the road ahead of him, but when he got closer he saw that it was only a shadow coming and going in the moonlight. There was a light breeze now. The fish and chip was closed. A new billboard sign on its gable said *Sudocrem a great friend of the family*. He didn't know what Sudocrem was. Lonely Rock blinked and darkened and the sea was its usual dark invisible.

From: writers.anonymous2020@outlook.com
To: der-driu101@hotmail.com
Subject: Lantry Novel

Dear Deirdre,

Firstly, well done on sustaining that voice for so long. The character of Mattie Lantry is taking shape very nicely and you're building a certain level of suspense, which is good. I have the feeling that all of this is based on real events, am I right? That's a good thing, it means you've convinced me that the world of the novel is the same world as that which I inhabit. If it works for me it should work for general readers.

That said, the absence of an overarching narrative line will make it very difficult for the general reader to engage with those characters. You're already challenging the reader with your style (which I love) and I'm not sure he or she will respond well to being fed isolated episodes in an impressionistic structure. In short, you need to start writing the in-between bits that you keep telling me you're putting off until the end. Otherwise you may exhaust the potential of the story in the episodes.

I also think this chapter could do with more context. For example, perhaps you could describe the concert in some detail, or even begin as they leave it with a description of the crowds. I get the feeling that you're excited by this material and you're rushing towards the conclusion. You should slow it down more.

The Karl Marx stuff is too much. I'd suggest reducing it to a passing reference or deleting it altogether. We already know he read *Capital* and that his grandad is an old commie. By the way, that's a backstory that might be worth exploring in further revisions.

So, apart from the narrative problem, these are all minor changes. What I want to emphasise is that this work is excellent and feels like it could well shape up to a full novel. And of course, the artistic choices are yours; what I've said here should, as always, be taken as a suggestion, no more.

Kind regards,
WA

I'm hoping the question about whether the events described are real will bring some sort of an explanation. I see two possibilities: 1. She simply comes out and tells me that it's based on a true story and that she was there at the time or she knows someone who was there or she has been researching it or 2. She doesn't answer, in which case she knows who I am and the story is directed at me, as Catherine suggested. I suppose a third possibility would be that she lies, but if she does that it means the same thing as 2.

Catherine is conducting a job interview on her 3G phone hotspot connection, which drops out occasionally. I can hear the frustration level rising from the other room. I pity the unfortunate candidate, not to mention the other members of the interview board. We're both on edge, having received a text message to say that a friend of ours, Mike Cosgrove, has been intubated and put in an induced coma. We had not known he had Covid until two days ago. At that time the news was he had been showing symptoms for over a week but was struggling through and even managing to work a little. In the space of a few days it has come to this. We fear the worst.

It's a beautiful morning. I take my laptop and drive down to Ballynaule, to Billy Regan's bar perched on the old stone pier over the bay. I order a pint for an outside table and log onto his Wi-Fi. Billy comes out to chat.

Ye're down again?

We are.

Great weather for it.

Very few boats in the water, Billy?

He shakes his head. His mournful face is habitual now. Everything is going to hell for Billy Regan and has been for all the years we've been coming here, but every year it's a fresh hell. Nevertheless he is kindness itself. Once when our daughter Aoife fell off the pier and had to be hauled out, he took us into his care, fed Aoife copious bowls of hot chowder and lemonade (hot whiskey for us) and regaled us with tales of lobstermen and gill-netters that had us in stitches for an hour.

The Covid has everything fucked, he says. They're all talk about staycations now. That's a new word on me anyway, *staycation*. They didn't teach us that in Cannavee National School in the old days.

We used to call them holidays.

He gives me another mournful look.

Will they be drinkers, that's all I want to know. This country has no use for teetotallers. If it was up to the teetotallers GDP would be in the ha'penny place.

I laugh and he shakes his head sadly. I know his humour by now. Billy Regan is a character, they all say.

Have you had a visit from the guards? They were saying on the radio this morning that a lot of publicans are to be prosecuted for serving drink without food. A breach of Covid regulations and all that.

I glance in the direction of a solitary old man at a bench by the closed door, nursing a pint, his back to the wall and his face turned up to the sun, eyes closed. No sign of a plate in front of him. Billy purses his lips but does not reply, his eyes fixed on the bay in front of us.

I'd say we'll have crab before long, he says, nodding at a potter festooned with pink and orange buoys making its way between the moorings on the still harbour water. I'll put you down for the usual sangwitch.

John Brien?

The very man. He done up the boat during the lockdown. He had Ross' yard put a new motor in. A Yamaha, he tells me. Yamaha make a great engine. You'd hardly hear it at all at all.

The noise of the engine travels clearly over the still water and I wonder if Billy Regan is going deaf.

How's Eddie? I heard he got a bit of a fright.

Quadruple bypass. They told him when they opened him up they thought about throwing the whole shooting match in the bin. Seemingly the valves were set like concrete. Surgeon Power has a boat as you know. Would you treat a seacock the way you treat your heart, he said to him.

Chuckles. Billy likes a good turn of phrase. He saves them up.

Anyway, Billy says, as he begins to move away, the guards around here is decent skins.

That man forgets nothing, I think. As he begins to serve another customer I press send on the email to Deirdre.

Billy Regan's famous crab sandwiches. Crab is on the menu but anyone ordering it is likely to be told the boat never went out or hasn't come back yet or the Japanese are buying all the crab, or the French. John Brien is a big customer of Billy Regan's. He plays the bodhrán like a man possessed and when there's a session the night before he's likely to rise late. On those days the crab is off. And the sessions are famous. A pair of mad fiddlers from the mountains, Mick Healy's button accordion – 'the box' – some young fellow on tin whistle and John Brien's bodhrán. Songs too. People come from as far away as Tiraneering, Goleen, Rally. There's some Irish still. For any stranger who chances by it will be a night to remember, though nobody knows when it will happen except the musicians themselves. Some kind of secret code passes along the valleys or through the veins of the hills. Billy Regan's tonight. Another night it will be Rumley's or the Lobster Pot or the Harbour Bar in Rally, but there's no session like the one in Billy Regan's. There's magic in it.

I scroll through the newspapers. Doctors are warning about the dangers of breaching the regulations, the importance of hand hygiene, the oxymoron of *social* distance, avoiding large crowds. They worry about rising infection rates. They have access to figures that suggest people are mixing more frequently. It hasn't gone away. At the same time, something deep down in my psyche is telling me that everything is fine and that it will all be normal in a week or two. It's an insistent little voice that I find hard to ignore and which does nothing to help my general anxiety. It's as if a friend is reassuring me that all will be well while he shoves my head underwater.

I haven't been sleeping well. My dreams are full of contagion, strangers with infected handshakes, people breathing on me, the horror of infected surfaces. Sometimes I see them as if they were crime scenes covered in bloodstains.

Then the ping of an email. It's from Deirdre.

From: der-driu101@hotmail.com
To: writers.anonymous2020@outlook.com
Subject: Lantry Novel

Dear WA,

Your words make me feel I'm doing something right – I'll make the changes you suggest – You're right, it's partially based on real happenings.

I hope your own work goes well,
Deirdre

So neither 1. nor 2. then. She admits it's true but does not elaborate. I'm annoyed that I didn't set a more comprehensive trap. I am not a very intelligent detective. I decide to take it a step further. I'm on my second pint now and I'm eating a simple ham sandwich. The crab is late.

From: writers.anonymous2020@outlook.com
To: der-driu101@hotmail.com
Subject: Lantry Novel

Dear Deirdre,

I'm just very slightly worried that you'll run foul of the law or end up being sued for defamation.

And to be honest, I'm also worried for myself as your mentor, in that if the book should be published I might be joined in any case, criminal or civil. Which parts are true and which are fiction? Can you point me in the direction of some articles that I can research?

Another alternative would be to fictionalise it more.

WA

I press send again and close the laptop. I don't expect an immediate answer. She'll have to think about it.

There's a radio on in a car parked behind me and I can hear the voice of an American saying that Biden was a disastrous choice for the Democrats, he's too old and too traditional and too much of a compromiser. Not that Sanders would have been any better. It just looks as if Trump is a steamroller. She concluded, Get ready for four more years of weeping and gnashing of teeth, folks. Like most of the world I dread a continuation of that whining, passive-aggressive spoilt child. But then, I tell myself, there are more pressing problems than what happens in an American election.

Billy Regan has carried a tray of pints to a table closer to the water's edge. John Brien's potter has come to rest gently against the pier. Soon crates of crab are coming up to the young Lithuanian man who has worked here for years. The crates are labelled *Union Hall Fishing Coop*.

Billy stands beside me watching the unloading. They're saying we'll have more of this after the summer? A second wave they say.

It sounds like it.

Do you say so. By Jesus we'll all be ruined.

They're saying the summer season will be good though. Everyone is staying at home.

He lifts and drops his head in a dismissive nod. Look at that. He points to four empty tables, a seagull standing on one. His brilliant yellow eye. I should be full on a day like today. There was a time when we took bookings. Would you believe that now? Things were hard enough around here before the fucking Covid. You know what they say, you can't ate the scenery. Never was a truer word said.

But if it wasn't for the scenery no one would come down here at all, Billy.

I can see him processing that thought. It will come up in conversation at the bar one of these nights. It doesn't seem to have occurred to him until now.

The road home winds along the coast, climbs to a height over the bay called Lackenakea where there is a viewing point wide enough for a car to park. The land here is half-rock half-heather, and the sands of the Bawn of Cannavee stretch out below like a silver ribbon in the afternoon sun. I get out and take my swimming togs and towel from the boot and follow the path on my left that drops over the cliff and down a valley between the rocks, thick with softly scented meadowsweet and high grass. Locals use it. At the bottom is a tiny sheltered bay. There's no one else here. Further out I can see the half-tide rock they call *An Diabhal* – which means The Devil – breaking the water like a surfacing submarine. Nearly at the horizon a naval vessel goes by at speed, a low shape almost indistinguishable from the colour of the sea. I know from experience that someone on a trawler or potter will be whistling into a VHF radio on Channel 16 at this very moment and passing the word 'Grey fella gone west', meaning a fishery patrol vessel is on its way. The faint throb of the engines is comforting. I change quickly and plunge in fast. The water is icy but it empties my head and sets my skin pulsing. The sandy bottom is as clear as through a pane of rippled glass. The slightly exaggerated undersea. I swim hard for five minutes and then return to shore on an easy breaststroke. I lie down on the warm sand and try to think, to remember the night Deirdre wrote about. I've always done my best to avoid thinking about it – if psychology has discovered anything it is that we have all betrayed someone, we all have our burden of guilt – but her images fill my head, they have a reality that I cannot gainsay. I feel disorientated, unmoored, adrift. I am being told a version of my past that I feel I have only half-lived. As though someone else has inhabited my childhood. An incubus.

I am filled with uncertainty and dread, possessed by the feeling that I must talk to Catherine about all of this, I must somehow tell her all. Deirdre's book is a small controlled explosion in my life. But it has the potential to blow everything up. I need to find the right time.

She is moving back in time, she says, filling in some of the background as I requested. She has studiously avoided my comment about defamation and my request for articles for research. I wonder why. This next chapter takes place in April, before the Leaving Cert and a couple of months before the events described in her most recent piece. She is conscious of a change of tone and looks forward to hearing from me on it.

The Principal slipped today's positive thinking card out from today's page in his desk diary, read it, then slipped it back again. *Live in the sound of the bell.* He hadn't a clue what it meant, though it sounded fairly positive all right. He supposed whoever thought it up wanted him to think about it. Just at the minute, though, he would have preferred something more useful. Ideally something about staff meetings. They were his nightmare.

Afternoon light streamed through the library windows, warming his back. Golf called, but it would not be today. A discipline item on the agenda was a guarantee of a long day. Mrs Cleary was talking about Mattie Lantry as if she knew something that nobody else did. He had long ago decided that this was a game of Guidance Counsellor's bluff, covered by some kind of code of omertà or the silence of the confessional. Nobody was going to ask her for chapter and verse. To be fair to her, she was usually on the boy's side. Lantry was, she told them, far from intellectually challenged as everyone knew by now, but he was socially awkward and he did have a number of conditions and, of course, there were the family issues. Butty Sullivan wanted to know what kind of conditions. Of course they were confidential. Butty wondered how they were supposed to teach little fuckers like Lantry if they didn't know what was wrong with them. Mrs Cleary said it wasn't a matter of wrong. Well, Butty said, resorting to his usual position, I told you this was going to happen the very first day I laid eyes on him when he came into first year, I could see it in him. All we ever hear about these days is conditions, someone said. There were nods of agreement. A pity we didn't impose a few conditions on him, Peter Doyle the Mathematics teacher said.

Laughter.

The Principal could see his well-ordered agenda slipping away. He looked at Paddy Clancy. Usually you could rely on the old hands to talk sense, but Paddy was red in the face and doodling on the printed agenda in front of him.

Mrs Cleary said Lantry had a home situation and Butty Sullivan said everyone knew his grandfather let him run riot but what could they do. He himself had considered making a report but the way things were … More nods. Nobody made formal complaints to social services because you could be held legally liable for the consequences. There were mythical teachers who had been sued for reporting child-abusers to the guards or the social services. Nobody, of course, had ever actually met one of these unfortunate, honest teachers.

Nevertheless, the law was there. The Principal was sympathetic. On the very rare occasions when he had been forced to act he had made damn sure to have the school's solicitor on side first, even on one occasion getting an opinion from a barrister.

Mrs Cleary, the Principal said, could you sum up the situation for us?

Mrs Cleary nodded and began counting the issues on her fingers: a difficult student, only works in the subjects that interest him, does not conform to the rules, socially awkward, high-functioning especially in Maths, Physics and History but generally doing well, tends to speak out of turn, no friends until recently when the new girl Aisling Reck started to be nice to him and possibly Jimmy Winter the bank manager's son, bullied incessantly by Jason Long until recent fracas, lacks organisation except in the subjects mentioned, difficult home situation, in particular lost mother at young age in tragic circumstances.

Butty Sullivan said the grandfather was an alcoholic who spent half his time in the bookie's and half his time in the pub.

One of the PE teachers said, How bad.

Laughter.

He must be nearly a hundred, Butty Sullivan said, and one of these days he'll snuff it and the boy will be taken into care anyway, and the thing is if he was taken into care now …

Mrs Cleary interrupted. He won't be taken into care, he's almost eighteen.

Butty Sullivan looked around him for support.

146

He's a caffler, he said, nothing but a caffler.

Mossie Sweetnam the Art teacher said he'd seen Long and Lantry in the yard and he was prepared to say that Long provoked it.

Ah but, someone said, there's Mrs Long on the board …

A fine half, someone else said.

One of the PE teachers, the Principal couldn't see which one, groaned suggestively.

Laughter.

Helen Ward pointedly took some copybooks from her bag and opened one of them, pen poised.

Sweet Jesus, the Principal thought, it's going to become a fucking feminist issue when all it was about was the juvenile mentality of male PE teachers.

He rapped on the table. Ladies and gentlemen, he said, come on now, this is a serious matter. The question is, what are we going to do about this boy? We can't just let him carry on, for his own sake as well as for everybody else's. We're all agreed he's on the wrong road.

A caffler, Butty Sullivan repeated. There's a proposal that we should resign our charge. Are we going to vote on it or not?

You know me, the Principal said. I'm a consensus man, votes are divisive.

Somebody muttered that they were only divisive when they were going against him.

Mossie Sweetnam said he was against expelling Lantry. He was a gifted artist. If they dumped him they'd be cutting him loose, you needn't think any other school would take him at that age and with that record. What would happen to him then?

We're obliged to find another school for him, the Principal said. It won't be easy.

See? Nobody's talking about just dumping him, Butty Sullivan said.

You are, the Art teacher said.

The Physics teacher said, He's quite good at Physics. Himself and Jimmy Winter are top of the class. Now that I mention it, Winter is another outsider. No wonder they're friends.

As much as Lantry has any kind of a friend at all, Butty Sullivan said.

Exactly, the Physics teacher said, they're two of the brightest lads in the school and you're talking about dumping one of them.

Peter Doyle, Mathematics and Applied Mathematics, was also a member of the Urban Council with aspirations to run in the next general election. He said, Every kid is entitled to an education and nobody has a right to deny them that same education. But that's what young Lantry is doing to the others in his class. He's literally denying them an education. He's always asking stupid questions, he's out as often as he's in, he attacks people in the yard, Butty is right, one of these days he'll go for a teacher. He's violent and he can't control himself. I mean to say, we have to do something. We can't just stand idly by.

He slapped one hand into the other in an overly dramatic gesture. We have to act and act now.

Everybody looked at him and wondered what the future of the country would be like in his hands if he won the election. It was a bleak prospect, even for people who agreed with him.

Or we could not act like a little Hitler, Paddy Clancy said, half under his breath. The people around him sniggered. Nobody liked Peter Doyle.

Sure his grandfather has no control of him, one of the younger Business teachers said. What can you do when the home isn't behind you?

The Principal reflected that there were too many business teachers in the world. He himself had been Latin and Greek, and while there was still Latin, just about, Greek was long gone. There were times when he wanted to retreat back into a bit of Pindar. Reading in Greek took him away from himself.

Let's get real here, Butty Sullivan said, he's a troublemaker, he's a dangerous little fucker and handy with his fists. You all saw the way he flattened Jason Long. We're very lucky the school isn't in the courts over it, only that Mrs Long is on the board.

Thanks, Butty. We knew all that already. That was Paddy. He could get sarcastic give him his due.

The Principal looked appealingly in his direction. Paddy, what do you say yourself?

It's all going against him, Paddy Clancy thought. Otherwise he'd never have brought me in. And he really doesn't want to expel the boy. He can be as hard as nails, but he has the best interests of the kids at heart.

Butty Sullivan said, His coat is covered in badges, political stuff, nuclear power, bands. A parka no less. Army surplus. By Jesus, I won't have badges in my class. I told him take them off. What did he do? Only added another one. In German this time.

Atomkraft Nein Danke, the German teacher said approvingly.

Helen Ward, who had been correcting French homework and may not have been listening until now, closed the last copybook and looked up. She had a high-pitched, piercing voice that could penetrate the walls of three classrooms in a row.

He's never in uniform, she said, his hair is too long, his shirt is always out, he wears runners, does he ever wash himself, he never has his homework done. He's like a tramp or a hippy.

She began to sort through the copybooks.

Look at this, she said, picking out the rattiest one. It's like a dog slept on it.

She flicked the copy open and blew on it.

All smudges. His grammar is good, now that's true, he has the grammar. But I ask you, do we have to put up with people like him? Only he's filthy.

You mean he's poor, Paddy Clancy said.

Oh no, Mrs Cleary said. That's not true, Helen. His clothes are in tatters, yes. But he's always clean himself. That's one thing I'll say for him. And that house of theirs is spotless. You could eat your dinner off the floor. You often find that with old sailors. They're used to cleaning things. The old man calls it dobeying. I remember an old uncle of mine calling it the same. The boy is always clean, you can't say that.

You should see his Physics drawings, the Physics teacher said. Like something out of Leonardo di Vinci.

Da, Paddy Clancy said.

The Physics teacher looked at him strangely. Russian now, Paddy?

Well whatever, Helen Ward said. I think he's a disgrace. He's letting the school down.

Dear God, Paddy Clancy said. The school is being let down, that's final then. Let's dump a child just before his Leaving because the school is being let down.

Imagine what parents are saying, him running wild all over the town, beating people up and that haircut, I mean really. He's like a Teddy boy.

There's a proposal to resign our charge, Butty Sullivan said, rapping swiftly on the table as if he were the one in charge of the meeting. I put it on the agenda. I'm sick of the little fucker. Will we or won't we vote on it and for God's sake let's get back to the fecking agenda.

Vote, Helen Ward said. I'm for the motion.

I'm against it, Mossie Sweetnam said. He'll get an A in Art. If we throw him out he's finished. He hasn't a hope. He'll get a scholarship to uni too, mark my words.

Helen Ward raised her right hand, glaring defiantly at him. Well he'll get an F in French, she said.

Someone said, I'd like an F in French.

Mossie Sweetnam said, You said he's good at the grammar. What did he get in the pre?

Helen Ward blushed and looked down. She didn't answer because everyone knew he got a B. She had made a song and dance about it at the time. This nasty little tinker never does a stroke in class and he gets a B? She was implying that he copied someone else's work.

In one last bid for the boy, Paddy Clancy said, He's the only one in my class that understands a word of what I'm talking about.

Butty Sullivan said, The only one in the school, Paddy.

And there was laughter.

But people were putting their hands up.

Wearily the Principal counted and to his surprise (what was it the card said, live in the sound of the bell?) the staff was evenly divided. Outside the bright sunlight was filling with wind. He sighed. Even if he got out to the club there'd be no point in playing in a gale of wind with his handicap.

He asked them to raise their hands higher. He asked Butty Sullivan to count with him. They conferred.

It's eighteen eighteen, he said. That means I have the casting vote.

Somebody groaned. The sound came from one of the two PE teachers who always sat together. During meetings they whispered jokes to each other. One of them had long black hair. Yoko, the boys called him.

Look folks, the Principal said, you know I was against it from the start, but I'm a consensus man, so instead of just casting my vote what I'm going to do is suggest a compromise.

He didn't tell them, but they all knew anyway, that from the moment Butty Sullivan put the expulsion on the agenda he had been planning to introduce this alternative solution. For a moment there he'd thought he'd lost his chance.

How about putting him on a last warning? One more incident like the one with Long and he's out. I'll call in the two of them – himself and the grandfather – and lay it on the line. How about that?

Vote, Butty Sullivan said.

And make him stop cutting his hair like a bloody gangster, Helen Ward said, and tuck his shirt in.

The thing is, the Principal said, there's right and wrong on both sides. Lantry really is handy with his fists. And the family situation is terrible, the grandfather is useless, and anyway he must be ninety if he's a day, what do you expect? But on the other side, as Mrs Cleary has said, there's the fact that he lost his mother. And the grandfather is genuinely fond of him. I think we could do a lot for the boy.

It's not our job to save him, Helen Ward said. And as we're on the subject, I think your man Winter is on drugs. You should see his eyes on a Monday morning.

Father a bank manager, Peter Doyle said. I believe we bank with him.

Himself and Miriam Healy are doing a line.

Is she over the anorexia, one of the PE teachers asked. I'd say she's a potential danger to herself if she's going out with Winter.

It wasn't anorexia, Mrs Cleary said. And none of your business, Barry. She's doing well now. She's over the worst.

We could give him a second chance, the Principal said. Lantry I mean.

Oh for heaven's sake, Helen Ward said.

Vote, Butty Sullivan said. Vote, for God's sake, or we'll never get home. This is like a bad play.

The vote was carried. They would give him a second chance. They moved on to the remaining item on the agenda: what to do about parking, which was, according to Butty Sullivan, absolutely fucking chronic.

I don't know what the reference to Miriam is about. She certainly didn't have anorexia. She was beautiful, almost as tall as me, well-built, a fine figure. To me, a complete innocent, she seemed very self-assured. She it was who first kissed me, much as happened with Mattie in the scene on the beach during the gale. Except ours happened against the side wall of the Bayview Cinema after seeing *Kramer vs. Kramer*. She was a big fan of Irish and was always trying to get me to speak it to her. Before she kissed me she said, *Tá póg ag teastáil uaim* (I want a kiss). Then she kissed me. It was a shock but also liberating. After three dates I was still desperately trying to work out how the kissing might start.

From: writers.anonymous2020@outlook.com
To: der-driu101@hotmail.com
Subject: Lantry Novel

Dear Deirdre,

I'm not sure where this chapter will slot in with your present scheme. It's very well done, of course, which I have come to expect from you, and as a former teacher I may tell you that you capture the dynamic and atmosphere of a staff meeting to perfection – that mixture of weary cynicism, moral outrage and kindness that is so hard to describe to outsiders. Can I take it that you are or were once a teacher?

I suppose we'll have to wait and see how the book as a whole takes shape. I'll know better when you've pieced together the first draft. I may be advising cutting this chapter or I may not. We'll see. By the way, I'd delete the line 'This is like a bad play.' Whatever about the reading public, Irish and English critics hate anything that smacks of self-referencing or meta fiction. Much too continental don't you know.

On another note, I've been doing a little research myself. It wasn't hard to track down a murder in the town of Rally. I must say I think you're running the risk of litigation. Lantry, Long, Harney, Healy, Curran and Winter are all the real names of people who were interviewed or referred to by journalists at the time. You can find them with a cursory search of the Irish papers. Any one of them might sue. The suggestion that there were drugs involved is enough to cost you a fortune unless you happen to know that they have actual criminal records.

I suggest that you rename the characters. A simple search & replace will do it. But choose names that do not sound like the originals, no rhymes for example.

Oh, you also need to change the name of the town. Otherwise, fictionalising the names will just seem like a cheap trick.

Aside from that, keep up the good work.

WA

From: der-driu101@hotmail.com
To: writers.anonymous2020@outlook.com
Subject: Lantry Novel

Dear WA,

Healy and Winter were never interviewed by journalists and don't appear in any newspaper articles – though you're right, their names are real.

I will give thought to your suggestion.

It seems to me you're unusually worried about the legal side of things – why is that? After all you don't even know me, I'm an adult and can look after myself and think for myself.

Thank you for your comments about the piece generally. I agree we need to wait and see how the book as a whole takes shape.

Kind regards,
Deirdre

So who is this Miriam Healy, Catherine says. The radio news is announcing that Trump has formally notified Congress that the USA will be leaving the World Health Organisation effective yesterday.

You read the chapter?

The print-out was sitting on your desk. Why? Was I not supposed to?

She was my girlfriend at the time.

So I gathered. Why did you never mention her before?

Do you want a coffee?

Sure, decaf for me. Why didn't you tell me about her?

I fill the battered old Bialetti stove-top coffee pot with decaf and wait for the rumbling volcano that tells me when it's ready. All this time my back is turned to her. From the corner of my eye I can see that she is sitting at the kitchen table watching me closely. I can see there is anger in her, I can read her like a book.

It wasn't a secret, I say, I just never thought it was important.

Your first girlfriend? I told you about mine.

Yes, but that was because you wanted to explain to me about girls' relationships at that age. If you remember it was in the context of a book I was working on. You wanted to explain crushes and all that. Convent schools.

Don't change the subject.

I'm not.

Tell me about her now.

I sit down opposite her and pour our coffees. Over her shoulder I can see the gleam of water on Cannavee Strand. There are people swimming. There are splashes, and someone on a paddle-board headed towards The Devil.

First love, you know. She was my first kiss. We dated from about March of my Leaving Cert year until maybe August or September.

She is silent. She finishes her coffee in one gulp but does not look at me. The silence grows and seems to fill the room. I sense danger.

What are you working on? The Trump essay?

She is writing an article for an edited collection. The article is provisionally entitled 'Trump: The Meaning of Meaninglessness'.

It's going well, she says.

I look forward to reading it.

And this murder. The Lantry boy. Tell me something, Jim. You've mined everything that's happened to both of us for your books. Everything turns up in some form or other. You remind me of that David Lodge crack about writers using up experience at a dangerous rate. But it seems you have a reserve that I didn't know about. We haven't reached peak experience yet. The murder of a school companion sounds like a good thing to keep in store for your old age. I would have thought you'd have been eager to write about it before now. But you're not. Now why would that be?

I take my time about replying and she lets the silence sit. In the end I say, He was my only friend. I don't think I've ever processed his death properly.

Bullshit. That's exactly the kind of conflict you'd have for breakfast. You love that kind of unresolved tension. You're hiding something.

Why would I hide anything? He was in school with me. For a time we were best friends, until I met Miriam. Then we drifted apart. By the time of the murder I hardly saw him. And he had his own girlfriend by then. I was devastated by his death. I blamed myself for having abandoned him. He was one of nature's innocents.

And why do I get the feeling you had sex with this Miriam and that's why you didn't want to tell me about her? Some sort of vestigial guilt. You've told me about all your other partners and conquests. Or have you?

I didn't have sex with her. This was 1980. You didn't have sex then if you remember.

Have you had affairs since we got married?

Catherine, what's got into you today?

What's got into *you* is a better question. Ever since this Deirdre started writing to you you've been away in your own world. I can see you're nervous about something. Why don't you just tell me?

The news is over and we are now listening to Rihanna singing 'Desperado'. Catherine switches it off and in the silence we can hear the sea falling on Cannavee.

I haven't had affairs. We're honest with each other. If either of us had an affair the other would know.

What makes you think that?

I stare at her. Well, it's true. Isn't it?

She turns to look at me. Her face is pale and pinched. I've been having an affair off and on for nearly ten years.

What?

It's true. And I assume you've had yours too.

Who?

A man I met when I was on the fellowship at Fordham. We spent that six months together and we've met at conferences since then. When you were doing your Italian tour three years ago he came here with me.

Here? In our bed?

Spare me the melodrama. Where do you think we'd sleep? In the spare room?

Fuck you.

I don't love him, in case that's your next question. I love you. I like him a lot and he's fun. But he's not you.

That's a consolation.

She shakes her head. You're not very good at sarcasm.

Why are you telling me now?

Because it's time you knew. And also because I know there's something behind this fucking story this woman is telling you. You know who she is now, don't you? Did you sleep with her? Did you see her since then? Since 1980? Did you jilt her? Is this her revenge? What's going on about this murder? I'm tired of you disappearing with your head full of the past. You're obsessed by this woman.

That's bullshit. Now you're just changing the subject. You had an affair. You're still having one. Stay on that.

It's over. I wrote to him two months ago. I can forward you the email if you like.

Fuck off.

So what happened in 1980, Jim? What happened with Miriam? What happened with Lantry?

I never had an affair.

Bullshit. When you were in London you did.

I didn't. She was just a friend and she was a publicity agent. And you toured with her.

That was the following year. We did two festivals. It wasn't exactly a tour. And we didn't sleep together.

I don't believe you.

160

Is that why you went with this guy?

I was in New York, you were wandering around England with this beautiful young woman in tow. I was lonely. I'm not making excuses. I deliberately decided to let it happen.

Jesus fucking Christ! I did not sleep with her. Get it? I just fucking didn't. These people meet a hundred writers a year. They can't afford to sleep with them.

Absolute crap. Despite all your supposed political and literary daring you're just an old bourgeois, as conventional as they come, and you'll have had all the conventional indiscretions, Jim. I know you. But you'll never be able to admit your dirty secret. You'd never be able to bring yourself to say it like I just did. The words would poison you. You don't have the courage to admit to your infidelities.

I stand up.

I can't believe you had an affair.

And I don't believe you didn't.

We stare at each other.

I know you're lying, she says. I always know when you're lying. Your face becomes a mask.

Clearly I don't know when you're lying.

I never lied. You never asked me. If you had asked me I would have told you.

That's good of you.

You're a cold bastard.

I pick up the car keys.

Where are you going?

I don't know.

Don't go out. You're angry. Stay.

Fuck you.

No sooner have I slammed the door behind me than I realise what a ridiculous figure I make by comparison with her. She is sitting there calmly telling me about a ten-year affair and I am behaving like a child. I drive out through the gate without even thinking there might be something else on the road and immediately have to brake hard. Johnny Whelan's ancient Massey Ferguson is trundling towards me, his two dogs loping along beside him. Johnny owns the fields around the house which were once owned by my uncle. Ignominiously, I have to reverse back into the gate to let him pass. He gives me his usual papal blessing as he goes by and then I see him look up to the house and wave again. I know Catherine has seen the whole thing.

She is behind the counter, her background a wall of red wine. From where I sit most of what I can see is French. I watch as the last customer pays by card and, simultaneously, she takes a booking over the phone, the handset cradled against her ear. Above her olive-green mask, her hazel eyes glow. I remember those eyes. The restaurant decor is from the nineties or earlier – all pine tables and pine wainscoting, old photos of the harbour in the days of sail, exposed beams overhead, though to be fair, the beams are solid oak and ancient and worth exposing – my guess is the house itself is two hundred years old. The menu fits the decor well – prawn cocktail, pâté de campagne, duck à l'orange, crab salad, fillet steak, lobster Thermidor (in season), fresh strawberry pavlova, tarte aux fraises.

On the way here I heard the weather forecast on the car radio. There's a code red storm warning – the highest level. The core of the storm has an exceptionally low barometric pressure, so they expect a storm surge and coastal flooding. High levels of rainfall may cause rivers to overtop their banks. The wind will be strong enough to do structural damage. I am conscious that I will need to get home early or find some place to stay. It is not a night I can be out.

The customer goes out and I watch him at his outside table gathering baby things and a shopping bag while his wife settles the baby in the buggy. Finally he takes a small plastic bottle of alcohol soap from the shopping bag and sanitises his hands. So much hand-washing all over the world, a universal parting ablution. We have the cleanest hands since Pontius Pilate. Then they go off down towards the pier. I hear Miriam say, See you Thursday night then, John. She hangs up and comes round the counter to stand at the next table to mine looking straight out the window. Following her gaze I see the pierhead and a scattering of sailing dinghies from the sailing school, Optimists and Lasers mostly, milling about waiting for an instructor to arrive, trying to get their day's sail training in before the wind gets too strong.

So Jimmy Winter is back in Rally after all these years, she says.

She is speaking directly at the window.

Or should I say Jim? The famous writer returns to his home town.

She is slim and dressed in a simple cotton dress, no jewellery, flat leather sandals. There's something slightly unconventional about her. She fits well with the faded-hippiedom of Rally. In the sixties and seventies this area was a focus for disaffected lefties and alternative living enthusiasts from France and Germany, the post-'68 generation finally giving up on changing the world and opting out of it instead. Their children now drive the local food industry – air-dried hams and speciality cheeses, beautiful complex breads, fresh organic vegetables. You can still buy the best weed here, they say, polytunnels dual-purposed for spinach and cannabis. It's the perfect soil and climate for it.

Hiya Miriam.

How did you find me?

I was passing the other day and I saw you in the window.

She nods slowly. Something tells me that the nod means she doesn't believe me. That seems to be my certain fate these days.

And you recognised me after all this time?

I did. You recognised me too. Even with the mask on. We haven't changed that much, it seems.

You're in the papers sometimes. We get to recognise you whether we want to or not. But you didn't come in that time you passed. You walked by and saw me but you didn't come in. Why was that, Jimmy?

She still hasn't looked at me.

Any chance of a glass of wine?

She shrugs. Lunch is finished.

Italian if you have it.

You don't take no for an answer?

You didn't say no.

A young man comes out of the kitchen, followed by a middle-aged woman.

I'm off now, Miriam, the young man says. His accent is eastern European.

See you tomorrow, Stepan.

See you around ten, the woman says. This time it is a French intonation.

Thanks, Yvette. See you then. By the way, lobster will be on tomorrow. He's bringing it in shortly. There'll be no fishing for a few days after this gale.

On verra. What he promise last week too.

When the door closes behind them I say: It looks like things are going well for you. I hear great things about the food.

I'm not supposed to sit near you, but I assume you don't have the 'rona?

I've been out in Gortnacarriga for the past week. The only thing I'm likely to catch up there is nostalgia.

That'll be a turn-up for the books.

She sits across the table from me, not in the seat opposite, but the one on the diagonal. She carefully removes her mask and places it face up on her side of the table. I take mine off and fold it into my pocket. I've noticed that, as with Arabic women who wear the niqab, the eyes of people who wear masks seem to shine all the brighter. But Miriam's are just as bright without the mask.

I wouldn't shake hands even if I wanted to, she says. It's against the rules. Why are you here?

In the narrow street outside, a huge SUV is refusing to give way to a small Toyota. The driver's window of the SUV comes down and a heavy-set man with a florid complexion puts his head out. Back up, he shouts, back up! He waves his hand to indicate direction. The woman in the Toyota gets out of her car, closes the door and locks it. Then she steps onto the footpath.

Back up you, she says, or I'll leave it where it is and do my shopping from here.

Miriam and I burst out laughing.

Fair dues, Miriam says.

After some gesticulation and what sounds like muttered obscenities, the SUV begins to reverse up the hill, slowly and noisily. When it is back at a wider patch the young woman returns to her Toyota and drives past him, waving a big thank you and grinning all over her face. Then the SUV proceeds down the hill, the window rolled up fully, red-face looking neither to right nor left.

You went to college on the eighteenth of September 1980, Miriam says, and I never heard from you again. You never came back, not even for summer holidays. You never wrote. Not a postcard to say goodbye. You just left.

My dad was transferred. You know, bank managers. They always have a limited time wherever they are. He was lucky, he was left in place longer than most. By Christmas we were living in the city.

But I was still living here. And I had a postal address.

I'm sorry, Miriam.

I was crazy about you.

So was I about you.

She looks at me. There is hardly a mark on her face, hardly a line. She's the same age as Catherine but she looks twenty years younger.

You were crazy about me too? But you just fucked off, Jimmy. You dumped me without a word. One day we were talking about getting married, counting future children, planning a house, all the silly things teenagers in love do, and the next day you were gone. You even left a week early so you wouldn't have to say goodbye.

Feebly I wave my hand. You did all right.

In November of that year I tried to kill myself.

Oh God, no.

Oh God, yes. I took two boxes of Panadol. I only stopped because I was passing out and they were sticking in my throat. My brother came in to ask me something and saw what was happening. He ran next door to Wallace's Lounge where they had a phone and called 999 but the ambulance took so long to arrive my dad put me in the car and drove all the way to the city. He was stopped by the guards going down Patrick Street at sixty miles an hour and when they saw me in the back they gave him an escort to A&E.

Jesus, Miriam, I'm sorry. I'm just so sorry.

Not your fault. I was already screwed up when we met. But you really seemed to care for me.

I did.

Then why did you just fuck off?

I look out the window. The dinghies are more organised now and everyone in sight has a lifejacket. There's a RIB with an instructor. *Rally Sailing Club* is printed in bright red on the sponsons. There's money in the old club now. In my day it was perpetually broke. As I watch, the Optimists all swing onto a starboard tack and begin to move forward together. The Lasers are further off, racing round buoys. A large classic sailing yacht, something like an Amel Maramu, is making its way between them under motor. Forty years ago I would have been that instructor, though in those days the club had a twenty-foot wooden yawl with a dodgy Yamaha outboard, and health and safety was not all that important. Probably none of us would have worn or owned a lifejacket and there were certainly no wetsuits.

She's waiting impatiently. The fingers of her left hand tapping gently on her right forearm. I remember that she was left-handed.

I was frightened, Miriam.

Of me? For fuck's sake.

You know how it was then. People got married at twenty. They started doing a line in their teens and as soon as they got a job they got married. Five years later they had three or four kids and a mortgage. Or not.

In 1980? Don't be ridiculous. And anyway, you wanted to be a famous writer. You wanted to be fancy-free.

The famous part never came into it. I just wanted to write.

A look from her that I can't read. Ironic or just quizzical? A moment's silence. She moves a wooden block with the number four on it. I see her purse her lips and notice a fleck of some sort of red sauce where the block stood. She takes a tissue from her sleeve and polishes it clean.

You're married? she asks. Two children, I seem to remember.

Marcus and Aoife. Marcus is in London teaching and Aoife is in the Irish embassy in Rome.

Didier, my son, is in London too. He's at the Dorchester now on a *stage*. He did his training in Switzerland. Hotel Management. He's a natural. He picked it up working here.

I heard about your divorce.

Who told you? Jesus, nothing is secret in this town.

Well, a divorced restaurateur is a public figure.

Yoann was his name, I just called him Yo. Yoann Trébaol, Breton to his core. He came here on a boat on his way to sail around the world and decided to stay. It was good while it lasted. But he couldn't keep it in his trousers. Eventually one of his women turned up here in a temper and broke glasses. That was the last straw. Luckily, the restaurant came from my money, from my parents' house, and luckily he was decent enough about it. He just left one night with the takings of the till and our car. When I woke up in the morning there was a note in French to tell me how much he took and that it was the price of his ticket back to Roscoff on the ferry and if I liked I could have the car back. I couldn't care less about the car. You know what I was most angry about?

Tell me.

He left in August at the height of the season and I had no cook. I had to close down for a week before I found someone else.

169

She looks up at me, cool and intense at the same time. Her poise is remarkable. Nothing in my memories of Miriam Healy could have prepared me for this tough woman.

Yo cooked, I was front of house. It only took me a week to replace him and the woman I found was a better cook than him too and a lot less trouble. And none of her ex-lovers turned up, if she had any. We got along brilliantly. I was well happy with my lot.

I know how you feel about the lovers, I say. My wife Catherine has been having an affair for the past ten years.

She stares at me. I shrug.

Her phone rings. She looks at the number and cancels it. A single, furious swipe.

Why did you come looking for me?

I told you, I saw you that day. I'll be honest, I didn't have the courage to just walk in and say hello.

That disbelieving look again.

You seem to have a problem with lacking courage. Look Jimmy, whatever you want I don't have it and if I did I wouldn't give it to you.

I swallow hard. If I leave now I'll never know if she's Deirdre. I'm trying to imagine what Deirdre's voice would be like without the distortion of the microphone and speakers, the filtration through audio systems and the internet. I don't think it's a perfect match for Miriam's but I could be wrong. The pitch and tone are right.

I need to do something. Something that will set her off balance.

I'm writing a memoir. About Rally and our time here. Summer days by the sea, sailing, swimming, schooldays. Our relationship. All that. It will end with the death of Mattie Lantry.

It doesn't have the effect I want. She leans back and folds her arms.

And you want my help in some way? Do you want me to jog your memory? I can tell you the gossip. We could all see how obsessed you were with Mattie. That day on the boat, remember? Going out to the island? You couldn't take your eyes off him. And then tailing along with him wherever he went, sitting beside him in school. And then one day you were with Longy, a hanger-on in the gang. It was pathetic. Everyone said you were a liar except me. Everyone said you let Mattie down. All the girls were for Mattie. I defended you, if you can believe it. And I can tell you all about the day I discovered you had gone early to uni. The way your mother pitied me. Though maybe there was just a tiny bit of triumph in her look, a tiny bit of I told you so. What would a simple girl from Rally have to offer her son when he could have college girls?

That's crap, Miriam. My mam was very fond of you.

A snort of derision.

Right. That's why she didn't give me the address of your digs.

I was just in a temporary place. I was staying with an elderly aunt. You know the type – no visitors, no smoking or drinking. I was looking for proper digs.

Your mother said she would tell you I called.

I shrug. I hadn't expected so much anger after all these years. She seems to me to be a spring wound up too tight. I have the feeling that she's going to explode into action at any moment.

Miriam, I'm sorry you're still so hurt about this. We were kids. We all make mistakes at that age.

I was a mistake?

Have you ever tried writing about it? I find it helps.

The way you've done about us? I've read one of your books. You made us sound like peasants.

I've never written about anyone here. You're just reading yourself into it. People do that all the time. I'm not responsible for it.

She does not respond. Silence grows between us. I see that I've wasted my chance. Outside rain is falling intermittently. Huge clouds are forming over the islands and the wind is rising. I can see it on the water, bullets, as the sailors call them, falling down from the high ground behind Gun Point, toppling dinghies. The club boat trying to herd them home. They may have stayed an hour too long.

I try a different approach.

I'm a mess, Miriam. Catherine told me this morning at breakfast. I've been driving around since. I have no idea where I've been. I'm lost.

I hope you're not expecting me to sympathise. I got that from Yoann. After every affair he was always the injured party.

Again I try the downcast look. I'm not expecting anything.

Just as well. I suppose it'll be material for your next book anyway.

I doubt it.

A consolation prize, Jimmy? You wouldn't say no.

But have you ever tried writing? The story of you and Yoann would make a great book.

A pursing of the lips and a narrowing of the eyes. She's wondering if I'm taking the piss.

I think about writing a cookery book sometimes. There's money in it I hear.

There's a market for divorce stories. The romantic Breton and the Irish woman, setting up the restaurant, the divorce. You'd probably have a chapter on the early days. You could have your revenge on me.

She laughs. Have you ever seen my writing? I can hardly read it myself. Anyway, you're the one who's writing about that. Why are you encouraging the competition?

I wonder whether this is an attempt to throw me off the scent or perhaps she really doesn't know that writers use computers nowadays. But I can't think of another way back into the question. I am a singular failure as a detective.

I watch her carefully. Did you keep up with Ash Reck afterwards?

After what?

After she went to Trinity. I heard she had a nervous breakdown and dropped out of college. Someone said she hit the bottle.

I had no idea. Ash was someone else who disappeared that autumn.

So you don't have an address for her?

No. And if I had, do you think I'd give it to a stranger who just wanders in from the street? Why are you asking about Ash anyway?

I'm not a stranger.

What makes you think that?

Another dead end. I decide to show my hand.

She's writing a book about the murder of Mattie Lantry. Or someone is. I suspect it's Ash.

Someone is? So that's why you came? In case it might be me. You were checking me out. That's why all the questions about writing. You were always pretty obvious, Jimmy. You never could keep your motives quiet.

You're in it too. Though she gets stuff wrong about you.
I'm in it too?
We're all named.
Our actual names or are you guessing?
Our real names.
Jesus, there's a few people around here that'll be rightly fucking pissed off about that. Junior Minister Jason Long, for starters. Good for her. I hope she puts everything into it. What did she get wrong about me, by the way?

I take a deep breath. She said you had anorexia.
She looks away. What makes you think she was wrong?
Did you?
More or less. Before I met you.
I shake my head. I knew so little about you, Miriam.
And about your wife by the sound of things. You should go back to her. Kiss and make up. Believe me, being alone is no fun.

I feel an anger surging through my veins that I didn't know I had. You should have seen the way she told me. It was like she was deliberately trying to hurt me.

Have you had affairs?
Suddenly the lights go. The dishwasher in the kitchen behind stops churning, the radio which had been tuned to Lyric FM drops out. I hear a click as the wine fridge switches off, and then we're sitting in complete silence.

Shit, she says. We're always the first to go. Why can't they bury the power lines and this would never happen. You'd better go home, Jim Winter. It's going to be a rough night.

Yes, I say, I've had affairs.
Silence for a full minute or more. Then she says: Christ, Jimmy, you really are a bastard. You haven't changed.

When I get back to my car someone has broken the passenger side window. They've stolen my camera from the back seat. It was hidden under a jacket. Fuck the bastards. In the wind I struggle to get the door open. I know these ferocious storms and how they work down here on the edge of the world. I had better be careful. Trees will come down, banks will burst, the coast road to Ballynaule will be impassible. I drive back over the mountain with the wind screaming through the open window. Every once in a while, just for fun, the car is blown wide into the other lane. I'm going to have to cover the window with something. There's a piece of plywood in the pump-house that I think I can cut to size.

I am climbing up into the crack of doom. As I crest the saddle I enter the cloud. Rain comes down hard but at least now the wind is blowing from the other side and nothing much comes in the broken window. The only other vehicle I meet is a coastguard jeep, comically out of place so far above sea level but also somehow appropriate in the deluge. He waves as he passes, almost losing control of the vehicle in a gust of wind as he does so. Everybody waves around here.

When I turn up the road to home I have to present the window to the rain. I won't be carrying any back-seat passengers for the foreseeable future. But public health advice is against hitchhikers, so the dampness is irrelevant.

And then Gortnacarriga is locked. Early darkness is setting in under the gloom of the sky and the wind is higher, driving the rain almost horizontally. I pull a jacket over my head and dash around the windows. Our bed is made but there's no sign of Catherine. I go round the side where a substantial slab of slate hides a hollow in the concrete path. I can't remember if the keys are still there. When did we last check it?

But there they are, rusting quietly under the slab. The hollow has filled with rainwater. I make a mental note to give them some WD40.

I let myself in. I am relieved to see that my laptop is still on my desk. When I touch the keyboard the screen comes to life. She was going through my emails. She must have used her phone as a hotspot. The Mail programme is open and the email is from five years ago. It's from Emma Thorne, the publicist, and is completely innocuous, simply giving me a list of places where she hoped the book of that year would be reviewed but cautioning me that it was becoming increasingly difficult to get reviewed as newspapers cut back their literary pages. The battery is at nine per cent. I plug it in but there is no power. I flick one of the wall switches. Then I check the fuse board. The electricity is down. It happens. Gortnacarriga is so far out on the peninsula that it's almost like being at sea. Fortunately, Johnny Whelan has a milking parlour and if anything is an acknowledged priority in Ireland it is the milking of cows. The fact that we get our water from a well via an electric pump and, without power, there will be no pump and therefore no water for drinking, flushing the toilet or washing lies far down the priority list.

There's an unopened email from Aoife.

Things are hard in Lombardy and the north, she tells me. Outside the windows the cloud has settled. Every once in a while the grey mantle is illuminated from the inside like some sort of bioluminescence – lightning happening somewhere I guess. At this height on the hillside of Cnoc a' tSionnaigh it is like being underwater. There are no lights to see in Cannavee, all buried by this great aerial ocean, the rest of the world a supposition based on past experience, one I hope is justified. It would be nice to see it again tomorrow.

But Rome is not bad, Aoife tells me, and the south in general is doing fine so far. I am not to worry about her. They move between the embassy and home and never go out except to shop.

Rain explodes suddenly against the window in front of me. The noise is like plastic wrapping being squeezed.

Some people who don't own dogs are buying dog leads, Aoife tells me, and when they're stopped by the carabinieri they say the dog has escaped. Rome is a ghost city. She doesn't think she'll be home before Christmas, she says. She hopes we're both behaving ourselves and keeping away from crowds.

As suddenly as it came the rain is gone and I am left with the cloud looming in the light from the window. A wall of cotton wool that I could almost reach out and touch.

If I see Seán Whelan of Cannavee I am to pass on her greetings. Seán is Johnny Whelan's son and Aoife's first sweetheart, a holiday romance at fourteen years of age. They used to swim together at Cannavee Strand and she became a fixture at the farm, learning to milk cows and turn hay. Seán is now a county engineer with responsibility for bridges. I remember him as a serious young man. Our bridges and our passages over them are safer for his care.

I check the bedroom and find Catherine's clothes are gone. A catch in my throat.

There's a note on the kitchen table.

Mike in last days of Covid coma. Not expected to live. I'm getting a taxi to the bus. I'll be with Danielle, C.

Mike Cosgrove was a colleague of Catherine's, a mentor in a way, the one who saw her through her early days of teaching. A fine scholar specialising in French existentialism, his biography of Sartre his magnum opus, published when he was already retired, a distinguished professor emeritus. He is seventy-two years old, lean, fit and agile of mind and body. Hillwalking is his pastime. His wife, Danielle, is one of those powerful Frenchwomen, ferocious in friendship and in enmity, a professional translator and a stunning cook, a passion Mike shared. Before Covid we met at least once a month for a meal out. They were planning a book of recipes that would be, as Mike liked to say, properly grounded in philosophy. I remember the title of its first chapter: 'If all things were turned to smoke, the nose would smell them out.' The joke, as he explained it to me, was that it was a quotation from the early Greek philosopher Heraclitus, and it would be about disasters in the kitchen. I did not ask what kind of an audience they had in mind for this Frankenstein of *rillettes* and aphorisms. Mike was as much my friend as Catherine's.

In bed I toss and turn, unable to sleep. I drift off around one o'clock and wake again at two to hear the wind raging around the house and the sea beating the rocks. I try to turn the heating on but the power is still out. I spend an hour or two pacing the rooms and trying to think. The noise of the storm is the perfect accompaniment to my despair. Catherine, I think over and over again, Catherine. We have been foolish, we have hurt each other, but we love each other and I can't imagine life without her. I have a sudden memory of the first time the reality of the pandemic struck us. We had watched a news report about a hospital in Bergamo and that night in bed we held hands under the duvet and whispered that we must mind each other. Now I can almost feel those warm hands clasping mine. What have we done to each other, I ask myself. How could we be so stupid. Me above all.

I think about texting her more than once. Would she be asleep? Or sitting up with Danielle waiting for word from the hospital? And Mike. By now we all know what it means to be dying of the virus, the isolation tent, the tubes, the oxygen. No human contact. I have been in intensive-care units and can recall the bleeping of machines, the whispering, the lights, the crazy rush when an alarm goes off. And now we understand the process too well. The lungs gradually breaking down under the assault of the outside world. Someone described an X-ray of an infected lung as like looking at a bag of ground glass.

I find a bottle of Black Bush.

The sky is clearing by now, the cold front coming through, and the moon is full and as it rises over the hills it lights the bay of Cannavee and the white tops of the waves with a soft, broken, golden colour. And out on the deep I see the slow, heaving passage of a ship like a city of light. A bad night to be at sea. The house is surrounded by water now, mountain streams falling down on either side through ancient cuttings that form our boundaries. Loud is the vale, her voice is up. I am islanded halfway between the earth and the sky.

The feeling comes over me that Deirdre is really my alter ego, a different, innocent me, writing the story of my

179

life, a part of me that I have never managed to access, a much better writer that I always believed I could be, braver and more daring and more distinctive in style, a part of me not subject to my mind's censorship. I think I could put an end to the whole thing if only I could summon sufficient concentration. I could unwind the clock and Catherine would be asleep in our bed and no anonymous writers' group would exist. It is a feeling of immense power and it comes over me like a fever and passes in minutes. Afterwards I'm exhausted and helpless and go to bed slightly drunk and toss and turn for a time before falling asleep in the early dawn and dreaming that Gorbachev is shuffling through my books and commenting on the things I have written in the margins. Apparently I have a headache. A bad case of false consciousness, Gorbachev says, pointing two fingers to his temple in a gesture that means shooting.

Before we parted at the door of La Galerie, both of us masked again, Miriam relented a little and told me that Ash Reck has been living on Castle Island for almost ten years. Or rather I stood in the doorway and she stood the requisite distance of two metres away, leaning against the counter with the shelves of wine behind her, looking relaxed and entirely in command of the situation. It was hard to tell from just her eyes, but I think she told me out of spite.

And why had she held this information back? Why, in fact, did she deny knowing anything about Ash at first? And Charlie Harney, as the local doctor, must certainly know about her and yet he too had kept his silence.

Why tell me now, Miriam?

A shrug of the shoulders and, She's old enough to look after herself.

She didn't know anything about her, she told me, other than that she had been seen in Rally shopping a few times. According to reports she had an English accent and dressed very mannishly (sic), with wellington boots and the kind of waterproof coat fishermen wear. Someone who knew her years ago had said hello and Ash had replied as if she didn't recognise him. These, she told me, are the kinds of things noted in a small village.

As if a woman in oilskins and wellies would pass unnoticed in a city.

Life on the island is hard, Miriam said. She must be one tough lady. If you talk to her tell her to get in touch with me. I'd like to see her again.

She told me that I would have trouble finding a boat to take me out there.

There's no ferry. Castle Island is essentially uninhabited. Except for Ash Reck, that is. There's all sorts of superstitions about the place. They say there are ghosts. One of them is a little girl who died there in the sixties. As a matter of fact Ash lives in the same house where the little girl lived. And one more thing. The man who brings us fish here tells me that Ash is a pretty fearsome woman. I suspect one or two fishermen might find the prospect of a woman living alone on an island an irresistible attraction. By all accounts she's ready to repel boarders.

I laughed. That sounds like Ash all right.

Does it? she asked. Not the Ash I knew.

The morning after the storm. Gortnacarriga is cold and damp. The salt of the sea carries on the wind and penetrates everywhere. It greys the windows. As I'm wondering whether or not I should light the stove to warm the place, the power comes back. I hear the fridge click and whirr and the pump scream into action out in the pump-house. The radio lights up to show 00.00 as the hour. I turn the heating on immediately. I hear the faint but satisfying whump as the boiler fires. I plug my phone in and wait for the screen to light up, then I text Catherine: *Give Danielle my love. Keep me posted. I miss you.*

I think about deleting the last sentence but just press send instead.

My phone rings. A number that's not in my contacts. I am disappointed to see that it's not Catherine. I'm about to cancel it – I get regular calls telling me that Amazon is about to close my Prime account, which I don't have, and that if I don't log on immediately, I'll lose it – but then I notice the prefix is local. Someone who still uses a landline?

Jim, this is Jason Long of Rally here, how are you?

His voice has a needy quality. How did he ever make it in politics? Not the sharpest nail in the box either, but a certain brute cunning. His father was the same.

Jason! This is a surprise. I'm fine thanks, and you?

Charlie gave me your number. I hope you don't mind? Nowadays we're all very conscious of GDPR and all that, but I thought, old friends, what's the harm.

Not at all, that's why I left it with him.

Good, good, good. I was just wondering if you'd come in for a chat and a cup of coffee? I'm down for a couple of weeks. The Dáil is not sitting in person, as you know, so I would be spending a bit more time with the family. I'd love a good chat.

To be honest, Jason, I don't think we have anything to say to each other. A lot of water under the bridge and so on.

I'd say you need to talk to Jason Long, Jason Long said.

Why is it that so many politicians have a habit of referring to themselves in the third person?

You could talk to me or you could talk to my solicitor. I needn't tell you Jason Long has a very good solicitor. I'd prefer if you came in to my constituency office. Would that be all right? I have a decent coffee machine here. One of those Nespresso things. And we'd have privacy and all the time in the world. How does ten o'clock Saturday morning sound? I have a meeting at eleven.

I don't have anything to say to you.

But I have something to say to you. I'll be here at ten o'clock on Saturday. Monday morning I'll instruct my solicitor. Come in or not, it's up to you.

I am spending an increasing amount of time in the car park of the Tourist Information Centre. It seems that it is somehow an expression of grief or at least loss, that without Catherine the internet is my only companion. One morning I watch *The Seventh Seal* on YouTube, another day it's Hitchcock's *Shadow of a Doubt*. Secrets and who knows them. I read the news obsessively – the electoral campaign in the USA, the politics of Italy, our own attempts to form a government after the inconclusive elections, though the eventual coalition has been obvious from the start. The slow march of the pandemic around the world is on every page, the crazy dance of contact-tracing and rising infection rates, anti-lockdown protests, the mythology of the Deep State, of the New World Order inventing fears in order to exert control, all the bizarre conspiracy theories. And then the hard fact of people gasping for breath in hospital.

I tell myself that there is work to do and sometimes there is. Work as a distraction from reality, that must be something new to philosophy though maybe not psychology. Something Marx and Smith couldn't imagine. A request for an 'interview' for an online journal called *The Refuge* from someone called Harman Baraket. The spelling in his message is American (catalog, license, color) so I assume he is too. It follows an entirely predictable pattern: When did I begin to write and why? What are my sources of inspiration? What is my relationship to the landscapes and places of my work? My style has been described as 'lyrical realism', would I accept that as a description? Do I really feel, as I argued in one essay, that 'writers are parasitical on the suffering of others'? And if so, do I believe that being a writer gives me the license to prey on others that way? Some critics have speculated about the origin of the darkness in my work: do I have anything to say on the matter? Personal and societal guilt is a major motif of mine … and so on. The questions reveal a mind well-stocked with banality.

I am at first tempted to refer him (I assume it's a male) to other, similar interviews where the answers to the same questions can be found. But after a strong coffee I decide to be polite.

I linger for a time on the landscape question. Before our quarrel Catherine had pointed out, somewhat gleefully, on several occasions, that a substantial part of my problem with Deirdre was that she was writing about the place and landscape where I had set no fewer than three novels but which I had steadfastly refused to revisit (or even name) until we bought the house in Gortnacarriga, and even then only to sign the contract. The implication was that in Catherine's view, Deirdre was better at it. She was echoing my own anxiety and so I responded even more indignantly than normal.

What is hurting me, I know, is that Deirdre is driving my story and she holds the reins. She has control of a narrative that should have been mine but that I lacked the courage to confront. It's not so much that she has appropriated my story as that she has turned it on me. My own material used against me. She has weaponised it. She might as well be the alter ego that I imagined the other night, but a relentless superego determined to fuck me up, not anything over which I can exert control.

I have always avoided writing directly about Rally. I have never once named it – the descriptions in my books could fit any fishing town, any hint of autobiography is curated for universality. Of course the locals read themselves into it, but that's just the autobiographical fallacy. What I write is fiction, lies, falsehoods, inventions without location in space or time, except the page, about people who never existed. Or so I write to Harman Baraket.

Not true, of course, it never is – or only true in the superficial sense. I cannot honestly plead not guilty. I am, I realise, very much unmoored, swinging between moods, unsettled. In fact I'm frightened.

To distract myself I turn my attention to the latest instalment of *Salter's Art*. That, at least, is predictable. Something has happened to Salter's suit as a result of his participation in some sort of anti-war demonstration. I could go back and find the file where it is described but I can't be bothered. Very likely he got blood on it. Salter, in Emily's imagination, is a conventional retired gentleman lost in a world of radical politics and police brutality. Blood then. Hard to remove. And Salter is not someone who can dispense with a jacket and a clean pair of shoes.

He needs a change. On the Via Condotti he finds a small clothes-shop that is less threatening than the smart boutiques around the Spanish Steps. He has been memorising useful words – *comprare*, to buy; *voglio*, I wish; *informale*, informal; *giacca*, jacket; *camicia*, shirt. To his surprise he needs them because the small, pinstripe-suited man with the oiled hair does not speak English. Albert silently christens him Mafia man. He begins by showing a cashmere jacket that Albert cannot afford. A pretence is made of considering it. It is rejected. The price drops and with it the enthusiasm of Mafia man. Each time a new jacket is produced a little dumb show takes place in which Mafia man invites Albert to feel the quality and then flips open the right-hand side to display the brand name: much raising of eyebrows inviting a comparison between the brand and the price in order to suggest an outrageously good bargain. By the time Albert is admiring himself in a pure new wool sports coat Mafia man has retreated behind his desk and is making a show of shuffling receipts and letters.

Now he needs a pair of shoes (*scarpe*). The shop he has selected seems to him a little too brash.

It goes on in increasing detail, prominently placed Italian words, different kinds of fabric, shoes in various sizes and no action. Everything happens in the tiny historical centre of Rome, which every tourist has walked. Nothing, for example, in Trastevere, where most of the students actually hang out. The culmination of five pages of text is:

Albert buys a pair of brown shoes. Later when he wears them to walk around his apartment the narrow toes pinch and he finds himself limping for no reason. Nevertheless they look stylish and new and he is happy.

The text is accruing local colour like a boat growing barnacles. But it is going nowhere unless in ever-decreasing circles around the city centre, an area that I know very well, so much so that it feels like an indulgence to read this material, if a pointless one. I write to her (to be sent later from the inconvenience of the car park at the tourist office) that I can almost feel the Roman heat, the smell of the city that is a mix of fumes and food and exotic perfumes. I can hear the voices of the salespeople. The shift to a third-person narrative (which I had earlier advised as a good strategy) has worked really well. The character is more credible now. But, I caution her, the novel lacks action, there is no sense of a plot in the course of unwinding, no forward drive. How long will the holiday experiences of the lonely Albert Salter hold our attention? I suggest that she should think of the novel in three phases, each of the first two phases culminating in a happening that is crucial and that changes the direction of the plot. The third phase must lead to a catastrophe, or at least a resolution, that has been in the making throughout. Without this sense of purpose, I tell her, beautiful writing will seem merely self-indulgent to the reader. Readers expect things to happen, I conclude – although having read a number of the new plotless novels that have become fashionable, I am no longer certain that this is the case.

There has been no communication from Catherine since the note about Mike Cosgrave, no reply to my message. Sooner or later one of us will have to make contact again. I know Catherine – or perhaps I should say I *knew* her: she is unlikely to break the ice. I should call her. I remember her quoting Herodotus to me once: Nothing is less intelligible than the human heart. On that occasion we were talking about the break-up of a friend's marriage, an apparently perfect couple suddenly spinning out of each other's reach in a fury of recrimination and pain. Is that what's happening to us now? Our unintelligible hearts. Do I want that? Am I prepared to lose her? I don't think her colleague/lover would be there for her if our marriage collapsed. It's very much a friends-with-benefits arrangement. She said she's never loved him.

Would I be there for her?

Strangely, it gives me no comfort to think of Catherine finding herself alone and unloved.

I turn my attention to my printout of Tom's manuscript. My first reaction is that the work is much harder-going than Emily's Roman story. The language is more awkward and the narrative more opaque.

Tom Clinch heard the clop of horses on the stones of the yard at early morning and went out with his gun, for whoever came a-horseback at that hour had travelled by night. He saw three riders in the gloaming. He cocked his flintlock and levelled the barrel.

'Stand or die!'

'Friends *in ainm Dé*.'

Tom Clinch recognised the voice of his neighbour. He lowered the gun but did not release the lock.

'What ails you, McCarthy, to be afoot at this hour?'

McCarthy leaned down in his saddle.

'I bring you bad tidings, Tom Clinch. The worse because I am in debt to you for sending me word of the militia.'

He swung out of his saddle and his two fellows did the same. Tom Clinch eased the flintlock and led him inside.

'I'm on my keeping these last two days, my boats cannot come to land. But I was down in the village after news of them that seek me and it was there I heard that your John was taken when they raided my country.'

Tom Clinch groaned but said nothing.

'Ye did not know?'

'This is the first news.'

There is more in that vein. Not an easy story to follow but against my better judgement I find myself wondering what will happen next. The world Tom has created is an interesting one. The neighbours, Tom Clinch and McCarthy (I don't think he has been given a first name), freebooters, smugglers, rivals but also co-conspirators; the militia searching for contraband; Tom Clinch's uneasy possession of Kate, who has been shown in previous chapters to have a mind of her own; the language differences; the hostility between Catholic and Protestant, between the Gaelic Irish and the English settlers – all of it is intriguing me. Because the episodes come in with long gaps between emails it feels a bit like a serialisation. By contrast with Emily's Salter, things are constantly happening in this book. I am certain it can be made to work, but I am equally certain he will have trouble finding a publisher. The industry these days is focused on pretty young things and books with clever takes on issues. A straightforward piece of historical fiction, no matter how well-written, will be a hard sell. It needs a twist, a mystery or some other driver to keep the reader's attention. And Tom's version of a kind of archaic English is too much. It will seem artificial to an editor, and in fact it is artificial.

I write to let him know that I think he should tone down the archaism. I warn him that there will be rejections because this kind of work rarely finds a publisher at the first outing. I quote Saul Bellow to him that rejections are not necessarily bad because they teach a writer to not give a damn. Bellow is always useful and I have discovered in the past that people who attend writing classes like quotations from famous writers, especially Nobel Prize-winners. I encourage him to continue with the story. It is worth writing, I say, and it *will* find a publisher if we can get it right.

Then on second thoughts I add a PS. Maybe he could make a virtue out of the archaic language, make it his own invention, a sort of dialect of the world of the novel.

Walter and Judy have all but dropped out. The last thing Walter sent me was an account of his days as a teacher. I suggested he read Frank McCourt's *Teacher Man*. A sour reply came back to the effect that if someone else had already done the job properly there was no point in doing it again and coming in second best. I was about to reply, in irritation if not anger, that he was far below second-best when I stopped myself and deleted the email. These days I have to control my temper. Events have unmoored me. Normally I am patience itself.

Instead I wrote that everything worth saying had already been said at least once, and more probably an infinite number of times, and that the only justification for any kind of literature was that we each say our truths in our own way and that uniquely told truth somehow resonates with the reader. Perhaps readers in every generation need their stories retold for them. Knowing that someone had written something before was therefore no excuse for not writing it again from your own experience. People are hungry for stories, I said, because humans need to share experiences. No further justification for writing is needed other than to say 'I have lived and this is how I survived.'

There is no reply.

Emily, on the other hand, keeps sending me, along with chapters of her *Salter's Art*, articles copied from sources that I have no interest in. There are times when the afternoon visitors to the Tourist Information Centre must be able to hear my groans through the windows of the car.

The Washington Post recently published a series of books called *Social Justice for Toddlers* under the advertising slogan: 'Start the conversation early.'

A conversation with toddlers? You heard right.

The *Post* quotes a pair of psychology professors who said that children develop implicit bias as early as three months and by the age of four are already aware of racial and class stereotypes.

If you just blinked and had to read it again, don't be surprised.

I had to read it twice. Two eminent psychology professors are saying that our children are already racist by four years of age.

Sometimes the email only contains a link, or a chunk of text. Sometimes there's a message. *Don't be fooled by Deirdre. She is a woke social justice warrior. These feminazis hate men. She will try to destroy you.*

I have to put a stop to it.

From: writers.anonymous2020@outlook.com
To: emilysmemily@earthlink.com
Subject: Your messages

Dear Emily,

If you don't confine yourself to samples of your writing then I think our relationship is at an end. It was never my intention to engage in a discussion about feminism or racism. If you persist in sending me this provocative and, frankly, distasteful material I will block you.

WA

I have left Deirdre's work until last. Each time I see her name in my inbox I feel a sharp pain in my stomach. Since my night with the whiskey I can't shake the idea that *I* am Deirdre, that somehow *I* am writing the emails addressed to me, some deeply buried psychosis is asserting itself in the text, a long-denied guilt is communicating with me. In some fugue state in the interstices of my days there is a *me* sitting at my laptop writing the story that I never wrote and hallucinating the video calls. My younger self's smirking revenge, to paraphrase *Fight Club*. In my rational moments I know it's not possible. When could I have done it? I couldn't simply repress all memory of having written this text and having set up an anonymous email. If it were me it would leave some trace of its creator, some sign, because the subconscious is not playing games, it is deadly serious. I try to analyse the text to see if I can find telltale indicators, turns of phrase or syntax that point to me, and even though I realise the style of the text is nothing like mine, still I find points of contact. I think of Catherine telling me that the book is written for me and rationalise that if I were writing a book for me it would be different to any book I would write for someone else. Is this why I find the style so attractive? And why I know the material, the setting, the characters so well? Even the chapter on the teachers' meeting I could have written. I lie in bed in the small hours trying to think it through, trying to calm my racing heart, to ease the savage spasm in my gut, conscious that the whole idea is mad but unable to shake it off. I drift into and out of an uneasy doze full of nightmarish scenarios, which have me at the centre, a kind of colossal egoism in which I am the author of my own suffering.

And then in my waking moments I convince myself that Ash Reck is behind the name and that she has worked out who I am. Although it's almost as frightening, the idea calms me somewhat. I try to work out how I gave myself away. *Healy and Winter were never interviewed by journalists. It seems to me you're unusually worried about the legal side of things – why is that?* It seems such a trivial slip. She must have already suspected something. Now, writing from her island, her fastness, she feels she can play games with me. She blames me for what happened to Mattie. I should have been his friend. I should have stood by him. Instead I threw in my hand with his enemies. This is the meaning of what Catherine said. This book is being written for me. Or *at* me. I am its target audience. And like Catherine, she probably wonders why I have never written a word about the murder. Why the secrets, Catherine said at one point. Why avoid this life-changing event, of all the events you have mined for your work? What was so terrible about it? The death of a schoolfriend, even the betrayal of a friendship, is not enough. There's something else.

I have asked around about someone to take me out to Castle Island, but nobody wants to do it, partly because fishermen have better things to do with their time and partly, I suspect, because of Ash herself. The one hope, I've been told, is Willy Morrish, now in his seventies and, according to most people I've spoken to, a bit mad. What that means in a place like Rally is anybody's guess. It could mean that he talks to himself, that he fishes in bad weather, that he doesn't talk to his neighbours or talks too much to them, that he likes espresso coffee – almost anything that is not expected of a fisherman. The problem is that he's in the category of people most at risk from the virus who have been advised to stay at home. It's called cocooning but, as Miriam told me, Willy Morrish is never going to turn into a butterfly. It's too late for that, if there was ever a chance of it.

Mattie was making a cup of tea when the kettle just stopped boiling. There was a soft pop and the noise went out of it. It was the last of old Nicky Wherley's gas. He shook the bottle but it was definitely empty. Ash was sitting up in the bunk with just Nicky's manky old patchwork quilt for covering. He could see her in the moonlight. She was beautiful frankly.

Come back to bed, she said. Never mind the tea.

It's late, Mattie said. I have to take you home. Your dad …

She got out and walked towards him. She was wearing only her white knickers. She put her arms around his waist and rested her head on his chest. Mattie liked the feeling of her soft body against his. He liked her breasts pressed against him. He felt a sense of responsibility, which is what their Religion teacher was always saying boys his age didn't have. He wondered if his father, whoever he was, had ever felt this way about his mother. And then he wondered if his mother hadn't died would everything be different now. He didn't know what his mother died of. His grandad had just blushed and said something about waterworks and lady problems, which wasn't very helpful, frankly. He should walk Ash home, but still he didn't want to leave. Frankly, if Mattie had his way they would just move into Nicky's caravan forever.

But there was his grandad. And then there were her parents. Ash did not approve of her parents. Earlier she was in a bit of a tizzy. She was giving him the going on strips on what her mother said at teatime. My mother is a cow, she said. She said I'd have to tart myself up. She didn't say tart. She said I'd have to start looking respectable. I'm not respectable and I don't want to be. She said I was a disgrace. She said I dressed like a slut. Well, she didn't say slut. I forget what she said. I'm not talking to her ever, like your mother saying something like that to your face. And Dad was just reading his paper. Hey Dad, Mr Psychologist, there's something happening here? Did you hear what your wife just said to your daughter? Like I'm stressed enough just moving every time he gets transferred and I have to deal with my mother. She's like Princess Margaret and I'm supposed to be, I don't know, someone royal too. Do I have to look like Princess Margaret? Just because I'm going to Trinity. It's not fair. And I don't want to go to Trinity. I want to stay here. In our school if necessary.

Our school is fucked up, Mattie said. It's schizo, frankly.

But he agreed it wasn't fair having to look like Princess Whatsit.

But who is she? That princess you mentioned?

If you don't know who she is there's no use explaining it. It's the British royal family.

My grandad says the British royal family is a feudal institution and they should all be put up against a wall like the Bolsheviks did. He says the Bolsheviks had a point when you come to think of it.

Ash had a window with access to the flat roof of the back kitchen and thus she was able to make good her escape as necessary. Otherwise she was grounded. Just that her parents never bothered to check. Mattie loitered in the trees every night. Actually he loitered some nights and she didn't get out. On those nights the loitering was not good fun but it was worth it for the nights she did effect an exit. The order of the day was, once her parents' bedroom light was out, he was to wait only fifteen minutes. Sometimes he waited half an hour and sometimes longer. They'd arranged a signal. A flashing bedroom light meant no date. If the light flashed once and then stayed off she would be coming out. But it became too confusing.

She started to put her clothes on. Mattie loved watching her find her bits in the dark. All he had to do was pull on his pants, his shirt and his shoes. But girls had extra stuff. She had her knickers and her bra and a vest and then a T-shirt and a jacket over that and then her bell-bottoms and her sneakers. And sometimes she had a hat too. When they were dressed they kissed again.

Oh God, she said, I want to do it again.

We have to get home, Mattie said. If they find out you'll never get away again.

I don't want to go home. I want to stay here forever.

As they closed the door they both said, Thanks Nicky. It was a ritual. They said it every time. That way they didn't feel like they were doing something wrong, using the dead man's caravan to have sex. Mattie said Nicky would definitely be happy that they were doing it. He always liked company. One night they even tried to make contact with him using a tea cup and a sheet of paper with *Yes*, *No* and *Maybe* written on it. But nothing happened. Mattie said he thought ghosts were all me eye and Johnny Reilly anyway. Ash thought that was funny. Who is Johnny Reilly when he's at home? Mattie said he thought he might be somebody his grandad was at sea with in the navy. He mentioned him often. Some politician would say something on the radio and his grandad would say, that's all me eye and Johnny Reilly.

They were headed home across the strand when they saw the fire ahead of them like a wrecker's light. Smoke was drifting out over the rising tide.

Even from far off Mattie could hear Longy going through his dog poem. He had a dead feeling and his ticker was flying all of a sudden. He didn't want Longy to find out they were using the caravan.

Longy was pretending he didn't see them, but Mattie knew he was watching. Longy always saw Mattie. There were whole areas of town that Mattie never went near because Longy might be there. Mattie felt he was like the lighthouse out on an empty sea, anyone who looked for him could find him. Maybe frightened people always felt like that. Until recently the strand and the harbour belonged to Mattie, but now they had this bonfire thing going. When they got close unfortunately Ash moved towards the heat. She stood with her hands held out.

Longy said, Howya, Ash. Story?

Ash said, Howya, Shorty.

The others laughed.

Want a suck of beer? Longy said.

No thanks.

Harney threw a piece of plywood on the fire. It looked like a broken hatch. Sparks streamed out around it. There was more smoke. It probably wouldn't burn. It was hard to burn anything that had been in the sea for a while. He knew that because he tried it one time the coal ran out.

Jimmy Winter was lying on the sand. He looked drunk, frankly. He didn't even look at Mattie.

What you hopping up and down for Lantry? Longy said. Want a drag on a fag?

Harney laughed. Mattie shook his head.

Longy was laughing about something and Ash was laughing too. She took Longy's coffin-nail and inhaled but when she breathed out Mattie saw no smoke.

This dog is dog a dog good dog way dog two dog, Longy said.

I have to go, Mattie said.

Go so, Longy said. Ash looked at him. Her mouth was open. He didn't know what her face was saying. When she looked away Longy pointed his finger at his throat and wiped it sideways and nodded his head sharply at Mattie.

Go home to Mammy, he said again, who's keeping you?

That's a curlew, Mattie said, that noise. Probably out poking shellfish.

Everybody laughed and Longy moved towards him.

What fucking curlew? Longy said.

Mattie didn't know why Ash was standing by the fire. He wanted her to come away with him but he didn't know how to say it. He started to walk away.

Lantry lad, watch yourself lad, you won't always have a girl to fight your fights for you. Some night you're on your own I'll be waiting for you.

Mattie stopped. He turned around. He stared at Longy Long.

Then Longy started his dog poem again and Harney did his hyena laugh. Jimmy Winter stood up. Mattie was ready to fight but Ash was walking towards him. The fire behind her. Sparks going off like rockets.

You're dead Lantry, Longy said. You're fucking dead.

Fuck off, Lantry, Jimmy Winter said suddenly.

Longy turned to look at him.

All right, Ash said. I'll go home.

Go home, babies, Longy called after them.

Ash caught Mattie's hand. Don't take any notice, she whispered. Keep walking.

Why did you go to the fire?

No reason. I didn't know what to do.

By the time they were climbing onto the pier they could hear singing from where the bonfire was. Mattie felt something dangerous almost happened. He wasn't afraid for himself. But what if Ash stayed? He squeezed her hand tight and she squeezed back. And then there was Winter. What ails him, he wondered. He was like a different person at night, like a whatsit, a vampire.

I know what you're thinking, she said. Don't worry. I'm not going with Longy ever again. I hate him.

Can I sit beside you on the bus to Carnsore tomorrow?

She laughed and caught his arm. Of course you can, silly. You're my boyfriend.

Carnsore. Ireland's one and only attempt at establishing a nuclear power plant. The minister in charge was James Long.

Mattie and Ash Reck, with the help of a marine mechanic called Billyboy Brosnan, a member of Friends of the Earth, organised a bus to the protest. Four pounds return fare, bring your own food and tent. And off we went, Mattie, Ash, Miriam Healy and me, and Nailer O'Neill who also happened to be anti-nuke. Ash wouldn't even look at me but Mattie was happy. I don't think he could bear a grudge but I remember blushing every time he spoke to me. And on the long bus journey I remember closing my eyes and dozing and dreaming of the night before. I don't remember telling him to fuck off but even now I can feel the remorse of whatever happened.

And there we are when I google it – the anti-nuclear crowd in Aran polo-necks, Fair Isle sweaters and flared jeans, cowboy hats, denim jackets, long hair and rolled-up sleeping bags. In one archive video from RTÉ our group can just be made out in the background among the tents, Ash with her back turned, me holding one of the stays, Nailer taking his jacket off. Mattie is not in the picture. Someone is handing loaves of bread out of a bread van. Someone has a news-sheet with the headline *Nuclear Power Is State Power* and there's a white flag with *Nuclear Ireland Never* on it. Communist propaganda, the local parish priest cries – with some justification, it's only the lefties who ever wanted to mention state power, the rest took it for granted, at least until the rise of the new right, which is so obsessed with the idea of the small state while simultaneously calling for a large military and police. In the background a forest of tents, mostly in colours of rust and brown, and one wigwam.

The Carnsore crowd was cheering. They put Mattie up on the stage. Go on, Mattie, they were shouting, Doubt ya, boy! Tell us about no nukes? Mattie liked the hippies actually. They listened to him. The man at the microphone, who was singing a few minutes earlier, called him over. Here you go young fella, he said. What's your name there?

Mattie Lantry.

You have the floor, young Lantry. Talk into the microphone.

As if someone from a small town like Rally wouldn't know what a microphone was.

Mattie stood in front of the mic and looked out at the crowd. Ash was in the front row, smiling at him. He could see Jimmy Winter at the back. And behind them he could see Miriam Healy and Nailer O'Neill. Nailer was all right. He was the only one of them who never said a bad word to Mattie. Even Jimmy Winter called him a spa once. Nailer just called him Lantry. How's she cutting, Lantry? Not too bad, Nailer.

My grandfather, Mattie said. He's fairly old, you can imagine. He fought in the Second World War. He was in the Arctic Convoys, bringing guns to Uncle Joe. His health is bad. He had a bad war, you can imagine. But one thing is, he says no to nuclear. He was against Hiroshima and Nagasaki too. The people putting this nuclear power station here are out for the main chance, he says, they're kiss-me-arse capitalists (cheers). There's money behind it, no doubt about that. But who makes the money? That's what I want to know. The man who owns that field? Or the people who make the cement? The half-life of a radioactive isotope like caesium or strontium is about thirty years. Picture that. If we get a leak here the farms and the sea will be radioactive for at least thirty years. Think about Three Mile Island. The government wants us to think that we're all good pals and jolly good company, well, they won't be here when people are sick, will they? I ask you, who in the government is going to live here when there's a nuclear reactor on their doorstep?

Mattie looked around. The crowd was getting bigger. People were coming from the camping field. Maybe they were curious about a kid talking.

Of course, if they put a nuclear power station here we'll all have to live with it. We're a small island. They say it's safe but what if they make a mistake? What happened at Three Mile Island was just simple. A two-way valve got stuck open. Just that. And half the reactor core melted down. What would happen to us if a valve got stuck? The first casualties will be here.

Mattie may have said more but people were frankly cheering too much. Afterwards he couldn't remember what he said. But people put him on their shoulders and marched him around the camp. Somebody said he was their mascot. He didn't actually know what a mascot was and when he asked his grandad later he was told that they had a dog on the old Kent which was their official mascot. Which frankly didn't make any sense to Mattie.

But afterwards there was the how's-your-father with Jimmy Winter. Winter said, All that about your grandfather, for fuck's sake, Mattie.

And Ash said, I thought he was brilliant.

Winter: You would.

Ash: What's wrong with it anyway. His grandad fought in the war. He knows what war is about.

Winter: It's not a fucking war though, it's a nuclear power plant. Mattie can't say a fucking thing without mentioning the old man.

Miriam: What's bugging you, Jimmy? Everybody cheered.

Winter: It was all old shite, that's all. (Turning to Mattie) You shouldn't have got up on that stage. Leave it to people who know what they're talking about.

You're just jealous, Ash said.

Mattie was probably the most committed of all of us, as he was in everything. He had a box of anti-nuke leaflets and stickers and when we got home he went door to door handing them out to whoever replied to his knock. Not very many. By then the government was under serious pressure to reconsider and there were calls for Minister Long's resignation. In fact, historians have concluded that the failure of the nuclear reactor plan was the end of James Long's political career. Afterwards, he was embittered, sidestepped in various reshuffles and eventually shuffled onto the back benches. Most likely that was one of the many reasons Longy hated Mattie. He saw him as the incarnation of the people who were destroying his father.

But that argument between me and Mattie never happened and, anyway, Mattie never spoke to a crowd apart from Religion class, if that counts, and he certainly didn't speak on our trip to Carnsore. This, I realise, is the first fully fictionalised piece she has sent me and, on the one hand, I think it proves that I didn't write it and on the other hand I resent it.

Many, possibly most, readers expect that fiction is a disguised form of autobiography, that hidden beneath the encrusted detail are shining diamonds of truth about the author's life. I have spent my writing life asserting that this is a fallacy, or at least that any factual background is transformed by the act of writing or has no more than a symbolic relationship with experience, and here I am secretly demanding veracity from someone else. At the same time, if I am to discover how much Deirdre knows I need to see it in print and if she switches to fiction, even to properly fictionalising the facts, I may never know.

I drive down to the Tourist Office and log on to send my replies.

From: writers.anonymous2020@outlook.com
To: der-driu101@hotmail.com
Subject: Lantry Novel

Dear Deirdre,

I've read this chapter several times and I'm afraid it's just not credible. Firstly, Mattie never spoke to a crowd. He's far too shy and withdrawn. And you make him much too confident. It's unrealistic, false to his character. Mattie's speech is the first failure of your characterisation. It's just bad writing and completely out of character for him. And for you, I might add.

In fact, his shyness and his inarticulacy are important aspects of his character. They can't just evaporate. It's back to the drawing board, I'm afraid.

WA

Almost immediately, as though she has been awaiting my message, the reply comes back. No 'Dear WA' this time, just the bald statement:

From: der-driu101@hotmail.com
To: writers.anonymous2020@outlook.com
Subject: Lantry Novel

Mattie never spoke to a crowd? It sounds like you knew him.

I know I have slipped up again. I'm slightly disappointed that it's not my subconscious after all, that I haven't been waking in the night and writing and then repressing all memory of it. Or writing in some sort of psychotic trance. How did I even think it? Come back, Catherine, I need you, I'm in danger of going crazy.

Now I'm certain Deirdre knows who I am and this book is some kind of revenge plot. An elaborate one perhaps, but I can imagine someone – Ash Reck say – feeling frustrated for years that the guards had abandoned the case without charging anybody and eventually deciding to write a book about it herself. Fiction as the weapon of choice could have seemed like a clever move, something that would give her the classic cover – it's only fiction.

Did I give too much information away in the ad? Did she guess who I was at that point? Or was it later? She has been careful to associate me with Longy and to point to the fact that I played both sides, befriending Mattie and also his tormentor. But looking back over the earlier chapters it seems to me that I was included as an afterthought. I wasn't originally in the story and she wrote me into it sometime after I took her on for the workshop. In other words, she worked out who I was and started to bait me.

I have decided it's time to confront Ash Reck and I've come down to Rally pier to find Willy Morrish's *Star of the Sea* lying quietly alongside. He's supposed to be cocooning, but his cocoon seems to include the stretch of the Atlantic he normally fishes. I doubt the public health authorities would approve, though I can't see how he would catch Covid out there. There are other boats and I now see that, as Charlie Harney told me, the fishery is not entirely dead here – the *Guillemot*, a potter, straining at her mooring off the top of the pier, white water blowing past her; the *Breizh Arvor* further out, her skipper leaning over the rail talking to someone in an open boat resting against her in the lee. A yachtsman's gale is blowing outside. Force six gusting seven or stronger according to this morning's forecast. A whole gale blowing further north. A stack of lobster pots, five high and fifteen long. Which boat is big enough to hold seventy-five pots? None that I can see.

I go down the steps and introduce myself.

Christ, Jimmy, long time no see. I wouldn't recognise you hah? How many years now? We're not getting any younger hah? Not a bad one today? At least we didn't get the rain?

He has a habit of finishing every sentence on a question, I notice. I agree that it is not a bad one. At least we have a bit of sun after the past few days. Fair bit of wind though.

The forecast is shite again though? I might get a bit of fishing in before the wind gets up if I can fix this yoke.

The wind already looks up to me.

He is replacing a hand-operated bilge pump set into the starboard gunwale. It would be for emergency use only. I can hear the electric one pumping out over the port side as we speak. That stale smell of salt and diesel and dried fish scales and blood.

What brings you back, Jimmy?

That's what everyone wants to know.

Fair dues.

I've been asking around to see if anyone would take me out to Castle Island.

Willy Morrish shakes his head. They won't touch that place.

Why not, Willy?

He chuckles.

Scared of their shite, Jim boy. First of all there's the bogeyman and then the ghosts. You couldn't make it up. The stories they tell about that place. Your wan put the *ruaig* on them too. I may say she has a double-barrelled shotgun. Sean Hennessy says she nearly shot the arse off him one time. He came out of the island like shite out of a gannet's arse. He does a bit of shooting and the place is haunted with rabbit, hah? Pure haunted. They'd walk up to you and shake your hand. But herself is not having it, by Jaze. If anyone shoots a rabbit on her island it'll be herself. You know who I'm talking about?

I do.

Sure yourself and herself were great one time. I forgot that.

Not me, Willy. I was great with Miriam Healy.

Fair dues. Long time ago now, Jimmy, hah? Water under the bridge, hah? Is it herself you want to see? She's not inclined to visitors.

Someone told me you might take me out.

Willy Morrish raises his chin and nods abruptly. I'm the one that brings the supplies anyway. I gets on fine with herself. She never fired a shot at me yet. I'd be a waste of a cartridge, tough as old boots.

You remember her well from the old days.

A sorrowful face all of a sudden.

I do. I was fond of her and Mattie. You remember Mattie?

What's she like now?

She has a tidy business there, I'd say.

So what do you think? Could you take me out?

If you don't mind being peppered with shot?

I'll chance it.

Braver man than most, hah?

How about today?

He straightens his back and looks towards open water.

It's blowing shite outside. Are you up to it still? You were handy in a boat one time.

I sit in the shelter of the little cabin. Willy has the helm. I notice that he is slightly lame. A bad set, he tells me, the time he broke the leg, out off the Porcupine Bank. The skipper was following a mark, he said, along the deepwater edge, a big one, and the seas were bad. A slip on the fish deck and the leg caught and he swears he heard the crack. The mate and the engineer set it. There was no way the skipper was turning back or calling for a helicopter.

Hard times, hah? The same skipper, the boat sunk under him by Jaze, an exhaust fire, but didn't he get them all off alive. Fair dues. That was after my time. I had the *Susan Deane* by then. I bought her myself. How about that?

The inboard hammers us into each oncoming wave and cavitates when the stern lifts on the down slope. Ahead I can see the waves boiling over the Castle Grounds, sunshine gleaming on the white tops. I remember the doctor taking the shortcut across the Grounds one time for a race and, hanging over the windward side, I watched the rocks go by beneath the keel. We shaved it, the doctor said, when we found deeper water again.

Willy is staring out towards the horizon and musing about advertising. He has been watching an ad about Norwegian fishermen. They have a fierce care for their hands seemingly, he says, and they does be using this Neuter Gena thing day and night. I can just picture the lads below deck of a night after hauling the warp, Fuck lads, did anyone see the fucking Neuter Gena.

His laughter is infectious. He stands with the small wheel held lightly in one hand and his woollen cap pulled down over his ears, and his laugh comes straight from his belly. Where's the fucking hand cream lads, he chuckles, I can just see it.

I know that once we get into the lee of the island, things will settle down.

Now he tells me about how he had to sell the *Susan Deane*.

Broke me heart, he says, but the knees were going on me. And the daughter had no interest, Sure 'tis no life for a woman anyway. She has a good job in Apple. She makes more in a day than I'd make in a week's fishing. I sold the *Susan* into England would you believe? Some fella wanted her for a yacht.

The old timber boats are in demand again.

Not for the bastarding fishing they're not. The high polloi might want them for the fancy yacht clubs but it's all super trawlers now. It's all distant grounds now. You'd need to sell your own fish to make a living from the inshore. Your man sent me a few photos afterwards. You wouldn't recognise the old *Susan*. Fair dues to him he kept the name the same as I did. And I knew the real *Susan Deane*. She was a right good thing I can tell you. A beauty in her day. When my Alison was born the wife said I should change her name but there's bad luck in changing a name, hah? And besides, *Susan Deane* has a ring to it. Alison Morrish is only in the ha'penny place. I'd say your man the Englishman was all right. He wasn't the worst. I wonder if he got the smell of fish out of her?

The boat changes direction slightly and now the waves are coming over the starboard bow, the gunwales only fending half of it. I have to shift my place to avoid a drenching. The sea brake in upon us, as Pepys' diary had it.

Will I tell you what I miss out of the old *Susan*? This will give you a laugh now. Sometimes I dream I'm sitting at the table below with sheets of the *Cork Examiner* spread out for a tablecloth, and one of the lads is handing me a mighty feed of rashers and sausages and a few cuts of fried bread. The banter, hah? A feed of sausages after a good haul. You can't bate it.

It seems a strange memory after a life at sea. It reminds me of a man I met once who had been a pilot in Lancaster bombers during the war. His abiding memory was coming back from a raid on Germany, following a river, and seeing a fisherman in a boat in the middle of the river looking up as the waves of planes passed overhead.

Not too long now. We'll be getting a lee from the Maoil Rock. I'll land you at the pier. You know where the house is?

Is it the hippy's house down at *Tráigh an Tí*?

The very place, hah? She done it up grand. I had me tea there more than once. Comfortable out and not a drop down.

And now that the boat is steadying I look over the starboard side and see the island passing like a great ship outlined against the sun. The Maoil Rock, Trá na Maoile, Tráigh na Muc, Pier Strand coming into view and then the old pier, built by the Congested Districts Board sometime in the late nineteenth century when ten or fifteen families lived on this inhospitable piece of rock and made a living from fishing and whatever planting they could save from the salt wind and the ferocious rain. I remember being anchored here in the doctor's boat and foam from the breakers on the other side of the island blowing over our heads like thistledown.

Willy slows the engine and begins to nudge towards the pier.

I'll come back for you about six. As long as the wind doesn't shift.

He laughs. If it does you'll be marooned.

If I don't show up, send for air sea rescue and the guards.

That is nothing got to do with me. I seen nothing. I heard nothing. I never seen a shotgun, your honour. Here's herself. She seen us coming in.

I look up to where he's pointing and see the outline of a woman coming along the pathway past the old tower.

No shotgun anyway as far as I can see hah? She might have it concealed. Put your hands up as soon as you land I'd say. I surrender, hah? Take me to your leader.

The boat edges alongside in the shelter and I climb onto the gunwale and step off. Immediately I hear the engine go into reverse and Willy calls out, A visitor for you, Ash. Old friend, hah?

By the time I get to the top of the steps, Ash Reck is leaning against the rusted windlass staring quizzically at me.

Search me, if it isn't Jimmy Winter, she says. The famous writer.

We walk together along the sunken road at the back of the island. Masses of sea-thrift in deep red and pale pink bloom on the drystone walls that protect us from the wind. Then up through the fields in the place where the road has fallen into the sea, through bracken and in gaps between acid-yellow furze. Sheep and rabbit droppings everywhere.

We are recalling old times. I'm thinking of her voice. In this case, definitely a hint of an English accent. I feel confident.

She remembers how shy I was when she first came to our school. She was the sophisticated one, the travelled one, and I was the country boy. She talks about Miriam and how much in love I was. We laugh about the hippies and the concerts and the anti-nuke protests. At one point she stops and waves her hand to indicate the sweep of the island scooping up towards the Maoil Rock at the western end. Look at this, she says, can you imagine a more beautiful place?

You'll have a cup of tea, she says. I can't offer much else unless you'd like a fried mackerel.

I laugh. Tea would be lovely.

We have not, I notice, mentioned Mattie once.

I enter a big ground-floor room, an old blackened Stanley range at one end, a scrubbed pine table and four chairs, a pair of easy chairs on either side of the stove. A door is open to what used to be the back kitchen but I can see some kind of machinery in there. She catches my glance.

I'm a potter, she says. That's my workshop.

She hands me a mug glazed in cobalt blue. That's one of mine.

It's beautiful. Like looking into a night sky.

Thank you.

She lights a ring of her gas cooker with a match and puts the kettle on. An armoured tube runs away from the cooker and out through a hole in the wall. I remember seeing a large gas bottle outside.

The water is sweet, she says. The best well water in Ireland I'm told.

How long have you been here, Ash?

She thinks for a minute.

I came about 2005, she says. I did a night course in Geology in London and as luck would have it one of my lecturers was the woman who owned this place. Jeannie Newman. Dr Newman to us. Did you ever meet her? When I told her where I was from we became friends. She was the one who told me about the clay. The clay here is unusual. Eventually I discovered that she wanted to sell the place. I had a mansion flat off London Fields and property was good at the time. I sold up and moved here. I had a tidy sum left over too. Good enough to set myself up with the kiln and the wheel and other stuff. It took me a long time. It's not easy to get a kiln and a potter's wheel onto an island that doesn't have a ferry service.

How much do you own? The whole island?

I only bought the house and the garden here.

And who owns the rest of it?

A chap called Sheehan. Art Sheehan, I think. Short for Arthur, I should imagine. Why? Are you thinking of buying an island? The publishing business must be going well.

Just curious. By the way, the Sheehans are cousins of Longy Long's. Old Art was anyway. A second cousin, I think. I assume we're talking about the son now. The old man would be a hundred or more at this stage. They had a bad reputation. I once heard my Uncle Peter say that in the days of the hiring fairs, Art and his father used to hire a labourer for a year. In those days you paid the labourer in room and board and only at the end of the year did he get the money agreed at the fair. That was to prevent him wandering off. But Art and his father would wait till a week before the end of the hire term and then beat him up so that he ran away. That was breaking the contract and they were not obliged to pay him a penny.

The kettle whines its readiness. I admire her stillness as she stands there. Whatever brought her to the island, it has been good for her. She looks very much in command of herself. She takes a box down from the shelf, stretching to reach it and revealing the same figure she had as a girl, not an ounce of surplus flesh, her breasts straining against her sweater. She pinches some loose tea into a pot and pours the hot water onto it. She sets it on the range to draw and puts two mugs and a jug of milk on the table.

Sugar?

No thanks.

You're sweet enough already.

We both smile.

What brings you out here, Jimmy?

She's pouring the tea now. And sitting opposite me.

I'm writing a memoir.

I haven't read any of your books. I'm sorry. I'm not much of a reader I'm afraid. My ex-husband read enough for both of us. The only thing he definitely wanted out of the divorce was his books.

Sounds like my kind of man.

Well he turned out not to be my kind anyway. We were only married four years. A confirmed bachelor. It's always fatal to marry a man of fifty who hasn't been married before.

And a woman of fifty?

He was my second marriage.

Sounds like an exciting life. What's it like out here in winter?

Snug enough inside as long as the slates don't blow off. But I can get cut off from the mainland sometimes. My longest was two weeks. Willy Morrish is a lovely man, if it's possible at all he'll get out here. I love this place. I spent twenty years living in London. You have no idea how I craved the smell of the sea. I used to go down to the Thames at high tide just to smell it, but a river, even a tidal one, is completely different.

Do you have a TV? The internet?

She shakes her head and smiles. I'm lucky to have electricity in winter. I have a generator for the pottery.

They say there are ghosts.

I've heard the stories. They have yet to reveal themselves to me, but there are times when I'd enjoy the company.

How do you sell your pots?

Willy ships them for me. There's a gallery that buys them. I call them up and tell them there's a consignment and the weather is fair and they send a van to pick them up. I think they like the whole isolated island thing. It's in the bumph they print about the pots. Pottery from the western edge of Europe et cetera. Castle Island Pottery has a ring to it. And in the arts and crafts world scarcity is added value. They can charge more because I make so few and it's so hard to deliver them. Willy comes out for them. The money is in my account a few days later. The gallery owner gets them cheap because I don't need much to live here. But I like him anyway. What about you? Married? Children?

I tell her about Aoife and Marcus. I say that Catherine is a philosophy lecturer. I tell her about some of my books. I'm conscious of a need to justify my presence here.

You did well then. Congratulations. Mattie used to call you Lonely Rock. He thought you'd always be alone. I used to say, But he's always with someone. And Mattie would say, But inside he's alone. He pitied you.

Well I'm not alone.

The shadow of a smile at the corners of her mouth. But she says nothing. My irritation is left to hang in the air like an exhibit. The thought occurs to me that she knows. Could she have heard it from Miriam? Bush telegraph? Jimmy Winter's wife had an affair. She left him.

So no emails? No computer?

That's the second time you asked me that. There's no internet here. I don't want it. I don't want the outside world. When I was in London I was always on some demonstration or other. I protested for Palestine, against the National Front, against the invasion of Iraq. You name the cause, I was there. I was batoned by the Met at the G7 protest, four stitches and a dead arm for a couple of weeks. In some ways I was doing it for Mattie. You remember he used to talk about kiss-me-arse capitalists? Every time I remember those words I smile. I think he got it from his grandad, who was an old commie. But that was then, a different me, a different world. When I came here I just wanted silence.

She laughs.

Although there's precious little of that. The isle is full of noises. The sea breaking, seabirds, sheep, grasses or bracken moving, distant boats, yachts changing tack, ships passing. It's never still. But it's the kind of noise I like. It soothes the spirit. No buses, no cars, no trains, no construction work.

I can understand that. We have a house not far from here and I love it there. No internet either. And no TV.

It's like when we were children. Of course there was television, but we had a lot of peace and quiet too. Now the world is full of babble, stupid, trivial chatter. And we're poisoning it, droplet by droplet, grain by grain. Even the silence is poisoned. I walk this island every day and I see the shit that washes up. Why should we have the right to take-away food in plastic containers with plastic forks and cups when it's choking the ocean? The ocean can't breathe for the millions of tons of plastic and microplastic we put into it just for our convenience. You know this pandemic is a symptom of a sick planet. The animals are under stress and creatures under stress get sick the same as humans. It's the perfect metaphor for the death of nature. It's as if the creatures of the world are sending us a warning: this is what's happening to us, let's see how you manage.

Mattie would be proud of her, I think. She's looking into her tea mug as if she can see the future in it. The inside is a deep blue flecked with white like the ocean from outer space.

You remember the year of the anti-nuclear protests?

A stiffening in her manner. A slight chill. She avoids catching my eye.

Tell me about this memoir.

I give her the same story I gave Harney and Miriam. She nods as I talk. Suddenly she says, We couldn't understand you.

What do you mean?

228

By day you were nice to us. Mattie thought you were his friend. But by night you hung around with Longy and Harney, drinking and smoking dope. We saw you a few times with him and whenever Longy started his bullying you just kept quiet. Or you joined in mocking Mattie. Poor Mattie talked about you a lot. Jimmy is my friend, he used to say, why is he with Longy?

Now it's my turn to avoid catching her eye.

I don't understand it myself, I say. I think I was a coward.

I am conscious of the relief. It's the first time I've told the truth.

I never told Mattie that you were there that night.

What night?

You know the night I'm talking about. I'm not going to say it.

I shook my head. What night? I don't remember.

She pushes her mug aside and leans across the table, her face pale. Suddenly I can see the girl in her again, the reckless Ash Reck as I used to think of her. Once I saw her tilting her head back and downing half a bottle of Bass. Laughing in my face. Rushing into the water in her clothes. Crazy Ash Reck.

The night Longy tried to rape me.

Fuck. I don't remember that.

Of course you do.

It was forty years ago, Ash. I was drunk or stoned half the time. The only time I was really sober was sailing or when I was out with Miriam.

Miriam wasn't there. She would never have let it happen. She'd have torn him apart limb from limb. Miriam was an Amazon.

I don't remember Miriam being an Amazon or capable of tearing Longy limb from limb. I wonder if Ash and I lived in parallel childhoods, contiguous universes that overlapped in certain ways and not in others. In hers Miriam was a ferocious guardian, in mine she was my quiet girlfriend, my first kiss, my hand in hers. Our memories are incompatible.

What happened? Remind me.

So you can put it in your memoir? Forget it.

Was it at one of the bonfires?

No. It was the night Mattie's grandad had a stroke. Well, a TIA, they call it. A transient ischaemic attack. My dad had several.

I shake my head. That was afterwards.

No. It wasn't. Mattie was still alive. It was Irene Pearse told him.

I don't remember her.

Old Jack's next-door neighbour. She came looking for him. We were down at the chipper because Mattie had just been paid by the yard. He was buying me fish and chips and we were going to take it down to the pier. Then Mrs Pearse arrived. She was red in the face from running. She said she'd looked in on Mr Lantry because he wasn't looking the best earlier and she found him sitting on his chair and very disorientated. Everybody said she was a bit off, but she had the wit to phone the doctor. She probably saved his life. Anyway, Mattie rushed off. I wanted to go with him but he said no. So I decided to go home. I met you and Longy and the gang on the way. You took me drinking in the old Ghost Train. Remember the place? The ghosts hanging up and the rusty old train? It always stank. The minute we were inside the shed Longy started on at me. He got into one of the ghost suits, remember? He liked that. Give us a kiss, Ash? Like the old days, Ash? I knew he wanted it because of Mattie, because he hated Mattie. If he could have me he'd get his revenge and he wouldn't have to face Mattie's fist. The thing to understand about Longy is that he was a terrible coward. He backed me against the wall but I wouldn't kiss him. He tried to get his hand inside my pants.

I don't remember any of that. I don't even remember Mrs Pearse.

What you remember and what you forget is quite convenient, isn't it?

And I don't remember Longy doing that to you.

Then he had me on the ground and he was lying on top of me trying to get my jeans off. It was that lad O'Neill who stopped him. I was screaming.

Nailer?

Nailer O'Neill. He pulled Longy off. Harney was laughing. I remember he shouted at Nailer that you can't touch a ghost. You were just watching. I think it turned you on. I remember your mouth was open. I don't know whether it was seeing me with my pants half off or seeing Longy on top of me, but something got you going. Maybe you wanted it too.

Fuck no. I don't remember that.

Convenient. As I said.

No, really. I don't remember it.

I was meant to belong to Longy. Remember? Because I kissed him one night, long before I started doing a line with Mattie. We used to call it doing a line, remember? Nowadays you'd get arrested for doing a line. Seeing me and Mattie together was poison in his blood. I think he could have killed Mattie and never thought twice about it.

I study her carefully. She's angry, the hurt of forty years burning in her. We used to slip into the old funfair through a hole in the fence at the back of a place that sold tourist tat. We would mess about in the amusements. It was like a scene from Fellini's *I Vitelloni*, all the losers in one place. But we weren't losers in the end. There was a shed, not a tent, that housed the dark part of the Ghost Train. Luminous skeletons on the walls and a small table where the ghosts used to have tea without having to change their outfits to come out. A railway ran through it that used to carry the train. Longy liked it in there. On nights when it rained that's where we went to drink. Sometimes Longy would dress up as a ghost or just put on the mask. Those times I was convinced there was something missing in him, like a disguise was all he needed to be himself.

But Ash is not telling the whole truth about that night. She came with us of her own accord. She drank with us. She really was reckless. She knew Longy had a thing for her. I remember she had a T-shirt and no bra. Longy had her T-shirt up. She's right, he would have raped her but for Nailer. And I would have done nothing, partly because I was afraid of Longy and partly, I think, because she's right: I wanted it too. But I'm not going to tell her that. She can think what she likes but she won't get anything from me.

That bastard Long and Dr Charlie Harney, Martin Curran headmaster, and you, Jim Winter, writer of novels.

She points a finger at me and I see red clay under the nails.

Guilty as sin the lot of you. Except Nailer O'Neill. He was the only one with any decency in him.

The ping of a text. I'm at the pier waiting for Willy to come back for me. I take the phone from my jacket pocket and see Danielle's name. Not good news. I know it even before I put my glasses on to read it. Mike is dead, she tells me, along with the information that it will be – can only be because of pandemic regulations – family at his funeral. The same text will have been sent to dozens of others. The coldness of group texts, like public notices. In these days of contagion there is no space for public mourning. I text my condolences and ask if there would be an appropriate time for me to phone. I don't want to intrude at this time, I say. The reply comes back. Thanks Jim, give me a few days, *le désespoir est un maître dur*.

Despair is a hard master.

The wind is settling and the water is no longer white over the Castle Grounds. A classic gaff-rigged boat is beating steadily to windward, a yawl like the poet Richard Wood of Tiraneering used to have. We would see him coming and going. He never deigned to mix with sailing club people. He was intent on the authentic experience, we assumed, communing with the stars and the seals. Once he ran her onto the Sharrav Rocks because he was convinced there was a gap there that would be a shortcut home. He was towed off by the lifeboat. His boat was built like a tank sometime in the nineteenth century. Apart from a leaking strake there was no damage done.

I watch admiringly as the yawl falls off a wave and spray explodes, glistening in the sunlight. Forty years before I would have expected to see the doctor at the helm, although his rig was a cutter.

I've finally come to a dead end, I think.

Ash is not Deirdre, I'm sure of it. There was nothing in her demeanour that suggested she was nervous of me or that she had something to hide. We walked the lanes together, she made me tea. The conversation was pleasant until she came to the events of the night in the Ghost Train. I can understand her anger about that, but aside from the fact that I was a witness, it has nothing to do with me. Longy is the real target of her resentment.

And there's no one else. Longy would certainly not want the whole story brought to light again – it has the potential to destroy his career. Charlie Harney has nothing to gain. Miriam is an unlikely writer and although she resents the fact that I abandoned her it's hardly motivation to write a whole novel. And a literate novel at that.

I see Willy coming towards me a little earlier than agreed. I watch his progress through the swell and then along the smoother water in the lee. When he nudges up against the steps I'm ready. I step onto the gunwale, surprising myself that the old skills are still there, and drop lightly onto the deck.

How did it go, hah?

She hunted me.

She didn't pepper you anyway, hah? I see no blood. The victim was alive when I last saw him, your honour.

We're reversing out in a cloud of blue smoke. He puts the helm over and the stern swings east. Then slow ahead and we're passing the pier. It's then I notice that she's there again, standing against the corner of the old tower. I wave. She does not wave back.

How does she not go mad out here, I ask.

The daughter does be back and forwards.

She has a daughter?

She keeps an eye on her.

Where does she live?

Haven't a clue. Watch out now, we're going to have the seas on the beam, hah?

We move out of the shelter of Maoil Rock and the seas are coming at us again, this time on the port side. The wind is stronger and the waves are higher than the boat's sides. The boat rises reluctantly to them and then heaves itself down into the trough and we're soaked to the skin. I move into the shelter of the cuddy. Willy, in oilskins and boots, laughing at my misfortune, throttles back a bit and brings the seas more onto the quarter. For a time he concentrates on the boat. He sways casually with the pitching and rolling, as at home on the water as he is on land, if not more so. His eyes are fixed ahead. I know he'll be watching the entrance, calculating how close he can go to Gun Point to shorten the run.

Then he says: I have her number though.

I'm not sure I heard him right. I cup my ear and make a sign indicating I didn't understand.

He leans forward and shouts: I have her number. The daughter's.

I slide along the leeward gunwale and sit closer to the wheel. He leans down to talk to me.

She gave it to me in case anything happened. Fair dues. There be times when I'm bringing out the supplies and I don't see sight nor sign of old Ash. First I used to just leave the stuff on the pier, hah? But then I decided I should check. Just in case. So now I goes east to the house if she doesn't put in a showing at the pier. Oftentimes she's just working at the pots and lost track of time. But one time she had the flu and didn't she get the pneumonia. I had to bring her out to see the doctor. That time I phoned the daughter.

Could you give me the number?

Sure why not. You're a friend of the family, hah Jimmy?

He takes his phone from an inside pocket of his oilskins, scans through his contacts and hands it to me.

I see the name Mattie and an Irish mobile number.

I'm nervous again. I've been thinking about my conversation with Ash Reck. All the different ways of telling this story. I don't remember things she remembers. She misses things I can recall with clarity. Memory is no more than a simple fiction we tell ourselves, a way of rationalising the random events that really constitute our lives. A set of signifiers, the meanings of which are not always apparent to us or whose meaning varies according to context, time and circumstances and people. This or that moment lives on in our imagination for entirely innocuous reasons while something else, which for the other participants is no more than a triviality, grows like a malignancy that cannot be healed.

I go back to Deirdre's Chapter Two, a part that I only scanned when I read it first. It seemed like a pointless piece of description at the time, not advancing the plot or telling us anything more about Mattie or any of the other characters. In my print-out I marked it with a line in the margin and the word *cut*.

He saw people of his own age hanging around the Donut Bar in the rain. They were too far away to recognise, it could be anybody, so he climbed over the fence beside the Gift Box, novelty lines, beach wear, playboy items, Rasta figures, frames, jokes and much more, and into the Amusements. Mrs Pearse went by on the other side of the fence, her white mac buttoned up to her white hair. She had her head down. She was moving fast mainly because she never moved slow. She was the only person in the world who walked more than Mattie. She too was out more than she was in. The graveyard and the funfair were her favourite places in the whole world. Mattie didn't know it but she was thinking of a line of a poem that they learned at school. We suffer in their coming and their going. It was true.

All the rides were off because the season hadn't started yet. Last summer anyway most of them didn't get turned on. He got under the tarpaulin at the corner of the Ghost Train tunnel. The train was parked on the first bend of the track. There were luminous ghosts and a couple of skeletons. A smell of oil and cat's piss. There were broken beer bottles and fish and chip papers. Longy and the others came here at night. It was a place to drink out of the rain. That was why Mattie only came by day.

He sat in the last carriage and pulled the curtain back so that he had the light from the window of the tunnel entrance. It wasn't warm in there, but it was out of the wind anyway. He had his old tin geometry set hidden under the seat in case of emergencies. He opened it and ate some of the chocolate. Then he ate the rest. He had *The South Pole*. He was allowing himself the footnotes now, which were quite interesting. [8] was particularly good. A vessel sailing continuously to the eastward puts the clock on every day, one hour for every fifteen degrees of longitude; one sailing westward puts it back in the same way. In long. 180 deg. one of them has gone twelve hours forward, the other twelve hours back; the difference is thus twenty-four hours. In changing the longitude, therefore, one has to change the date, so that, in passing from east to west longitude, one will have the same day twice over, and in passing from west to east longitude a day must be missed. Mattie liked the idea of having the same day twice over. And there were a few days that he would like to have missed.

Next he was going to read Butler's *Lives of the Saints*. It looked interesting, although from what he'd seen when he looked through it, it was possibly the most violent book in the house. It might have been a horror story. One bit caught his attention. It was about St Sebastian, who continued to labour at the post of danger until he was betrayed by a false disciple. Sebastian died twice. His favourite bit was: It was a question whether Polycarp the priest or St Sebastian should accompany the neophytes. He'd need a dictionary for that. But he wondered if St Sebastian died twice because he was following the instructions in *The South Pole*.

Next time he was on the lam from school he would come straight here with *Lives Of the Saints*. No one would ever find him.

I feel cold and my heart is racing again. I put my hand to my chest. I can't breathe. It takes me some time to slow down, to draw air in. I misjudged Ash Reck; Deirdre's description of the Ghost Train fits a little too closely with Ash's memory. Although there are mistakes in Deirdre's account. For a start, the Donut Bar is recent. It did not exist in 1980. The sign in the gift shop window is new too – there were no 'rasta figures' in Rally in my time. And I still don't remember Mrs Pearse. But then I didn't know Mattie's neighbours. I was never at his house and I only ever saw his grandfather around the town, usually around the bookie's or coming or going from the Harbour Bar. But that means that whoever Deirdre is knows Rally, then and now. She (or he) certainly knows Rally in its present incarnation, rasta figures and all. This writer is not far away. She may even be someone I see. Or someone who sees me. A stalker?

I'm sitting at the window in Gortnacarriga, looking down over the valley. Johnny Whelan's cows are moving steadily towards the gate. It's milking time and they know where to go. And as I watch I become aware that my hands are trembling. The simple fact is that I feel hunted. I have a sudden memory of my response to Emily's joke on our first meeting. The first step is to admit powerlessness.

My phone rings and I see Catherine's name on the screen.

Danielle is in bits, she tells me. She wasn't allowed in to see Jack until the very end and he was in a coma anyway. She feels she let him down, that he slipped away without her voice in his head. She thinks that if he knew anything he must have felt lost. She keeps going over the sequence of events from the day he started coughing. Why didn't she call the ambulance earlier? She was fooled by his fitness and by his insistence that it wasn't the virus, that he had caught a cold on the old Kenmare Road where he and his hillwalking buddies had been the week before. One of them must have had it, he said, serves me right for breaking the rules.

I recognise the compulsion to talk that comes of being with the bereaved.

I'm glad you're there with her, Catherine.

I'm not much use, to be honest, she says. She's desolate, Jim. Completely desolate. It's not just losing Jack, but the whole coronavirus thing. Not being able to see him while he could still respond. And she's all alone except for me. Jack had no siblings and hers are all stuck in France, unable to travel because of the restrictions. She's in absolute bits.

Listening to her I think about Defoe's account of the common burial of the plague victims: *and they fell quite naked among the rest; but the matter was not much to them, or the indecency much to any one else, seeing they were all dead, and were to be huddled together into the common grave of mankind.* Though each plague is different, its results are the same. Human suffering on the epic scale. Thousands mourning. Here is Danielle grieving because she could not say goodbye and this very minute thousands are doing the same all over the world. Hearts broken beyond mending by a tiny organism measured in nanometres. Catastrophe is upon us and it is invisible and everywhere and humankind is not well-equipped to understand an invisible enemy except in religious terms, which may be why so many people believe the strangest conspiracy theories. The world is in pain. Or at least the human part of it. Nature goes its merry way, confident in its power to wreck lives or nurture them. Or perhaps that is too much. Nature is indifferent even to the fact that we are poisoning it. The desolation. The hell we make of ourselves.

I've never loved her more than in this moment. I don't want to lose her.

Catherine, I say, you were right. I did have affairs.

Silence.

Catherine? I'm sorry.

Silence.

It hasn't happened in years.

The line goes dead.

From: der-driu101@hotmail.com
To: writers.anonymous2020@outlook.com
Subject: Lantry Novel

Dear WA,

I'm enclosing my new chapter but the real reason I'm writing is to tell you my exciting news. Encouraged by your positive comments some time ago I sent the first four chapters to four agents in London and a week ago I received a positive response from one of them – she asked for the whole book, or what I had completed of it to date – and I sent it all to her. This morning she called me to tell me that she would like to represent me and that she would send the book out immediately to publishers – just the first four chapters. She tells me she hopes for a bidding war.

So, I'm really writing to say thank you for helping me so much. I now feel that my book will be published. I'm so excited I can hardly sit still.

I also want to say that this will be the last chapter I send — I feel that because I have an agent now she should be my primary reader. Please don't feel I'm cutting you out, I will be proud to send you a copy of the finished book.

Once again, thank you ever so much for all your help and advice. I couldn't have done this without knowing you were there. A million thank yous.

Deirdre

I'm parked outside the tourist office again. And again I'm petrified. My face and hands are icy cold, a reaction I'm becoming too familiar with. My heart feels as if it will leap out of my chest. I'm shaking. I begin to read her chapter but can't concentrate. It comes to me in snatches of text. Results day.

I know exactly what happened that day.

Everyone is happy. All the characters have done well. Ash and Mattie meet mid-afternoon and head for Nicky Wherley's caravan. They are both excited by the prospect of university.

The bone moon above the houses. Mattie and Ash going home by the strand and up through the town. Mattie was thinking that his grandfather was probably dying. He had written it, that very morning on the back page of *The South Pole*, after the notices of forthcoming volumes. Grandad probably dying, Mattie afraid. It was a warm, windless night and from the gardens of Union Street came the sweet scent of stock and roses. Ash held his hand as he told her how worried he was.

You should get a doctor, Matt.

But there's nothing actually wrong. Nothing that's different anyway. He's just worse.

She said the doctor would find something.

Anyway you have to wait, he said, you can't just see a doctor.

We do.

That's probably private, we don't have private.

Your grandfather is like basically an amazing man.

He's old school.

How he took care of you all these years.

She hugged him. He made a good job of you, she said in a serious, very grown-up voice. Mattie thought it was like the results had made her an adult all of a sudden. He looked at her in amazement.

What?

You're amazing, he said. Frankly, you're just so beautiful.

She laughed. Mattie Lantry, you're a charmer.

For a while, not wanting to part, they sat under the big chestnut tree in front of her house. She didn't want to go home, she said, she wanted this day to go on forever. She had never been so happy. Mattie had trouble expressing things like that but he said he felt exactly the same. He told her that he was the luckiest boy in the world. They kissed again.

Mattie, my period is late.

Mattie nodded but he didn't know what it meant.

My period is late, she said again, this time leaning forward so she could see his face properly. Like very late. Are you going to say something?

Mattie blushed.

We haven't got the R but it might be in M. We got the M.

As stared at him for a few seconds. Then she worked out what the R and M referred to. She could hear Mrs Cleary using the words in Religion. She grinned. The encyclopaedia you mean? You don't know what a period is?

Mattie shrugged. It's reproduction anyway. I don't know the details.

Ash suddenly had an image of old Jack Lantry explaining periods and babies to Mattie and she burst out laughing.

What's so funny?

I'll explain it.

So she explained periods. Mattie had very little information about the question of reproduction. They didn't do it in Religion and he didn't have the R in *Britannica*. As far as he knew it was something girls did. He paid careful attention. He needed to understand if he was going to marry Ash.

So if a period is late, she concluded, it can mean something. Guess what?

Mattie shrugged again. He stared at her, bewildered.

It means I'm frightened. What if I'm pregnant?

He didn't know what to say. He held her hand tight.

My dad will kill me.

We'll just leg it, Mattie said, do a runner.

She laughed. We'll sail to America in your grandad's boat. But it might just be a false alarm. I've missed my time before.

Under the chestnut tree a small forest of saplings twisting out of the parent's way. The young grow against the shadow of the old until at last they have the same shape and end.

They could hear party music from several houses of the estate. All the happy boys and girls. Celebrating the interregnum between school and university. Their days of freedom.

My phone rings. It is Catherine again. She tells me that Danielle is calmer now that the funeral is over. The whole thing was brutal from start to finish. There was an autopsy because by law all cases of Covid have to have one. Then, because he was an atheist, there was no priest and Danielle and Catherine were the only mourners. The funeral directors simply rolled the coffin to the grave and lowered it in. There was no ceremony. Another funeral was taking place in a different part of the graveyard at the same time and they had to orchestrate everything so the mourners didn't meet or at least kept the legal social distance apart.

It seemed pointless for me to deliver a eulogy when it would only have been heard by Danielle and the gravediggers, all of us masked up like bandits. But we each brought a poem to recite. Danielle's was 'Farewell Thou Art Too Dear for My Possessing' and I had Hardy's 'During Wind and Rain', but when I came to the lines about the raindrops running down their carved names I just burst out crying so it ended up with Danielle consoling me.

It sounds horrific. I'm sorry I couldn't be there.

You wouldn't have been able to come because of the restrictions. Can you talk?

I can.

I switch from the hands-free speaker to the phone. Too often in the past I have overheard people's private

247

conversations relayed through the car's sound system to be heard by an entire car park and every passer-by.

I miss you, she says.

I don't know what to say so I say nothing. The three or four seconds before she realises there won't be a response are agony.

Look, she says, it comes down to this. Is our relationship determined by our past mistakes, or is there something we want to hold onto that's important to us?

Even in my state of anxiety that sounds far too much like amateur psychology, agony aunt stuff, but I can recognise an olive branch when I see one.

I suppose, I say, we're even-stevens. We've both fucked up.

Silence.

That sounded worse than I meant it to be, I say.

It did.

I miss you too, Catherine. I've been stupid. But I love you and I don't want to lose you.

A car pulls in beside me and two Americans get out. I can hear their soft New England accents. They go into the tourist office.

Are you still there?

I'm here, she says. I'm thinking.

Before either of us knew about this we were happy.

We were.

We could be happy again. If we can put this behind us.

I want to try.

Me too.

I'm sorry, Jim.

I'm sorry too.

I'm out shopping and I'm just coming to the super-market. I need to hang up, Jim. I'll call you again this evening.

I love you.

I love you too.

From: writers.anonymous2020@outlook.com
To: der-driu101@hotmail.com
Subject: Lantry Novel

Dear Deirdre,

I'm absolutely delighted to hear that you have secured an agent. It's a first step but it's probably the most important one. However I absolutely insist that you keep sending your work to me. I'm hooked. I need to find out what happens next.

WA

Although I doubt her story about the agent, I'm terrified that it might be true. If she cuts me off now I won't find out how much she knows until it's too late. I'll read about it in the first review. I read on, even though I sense that this chapter won't reveal her hand, that she's making me wait.

In the springtime the buds on the chestnut tree had broken and the husks glued themselves to people's feet like pale brown, sticky beetles. But now it was late in the summer and the tree was tired. Mattie didn't think the children of this estate played here. He thought they watched television. Did trees get lonely? He had seen Longy and his friends and frankly he wasn't happy, although to judge by the bags they were carrying they were going to a party. He could hear the bottles. He could hear music. Mattie used to hear them talking in school about the night before. Mattie didn't understand a lot of the things they talked about. Half a bottle of Buckie, rolled a joint, dropped the pills, the slabs, smoking the green. Head-a-ball. Alkie. Mad. Mad cunt. Ash came to her window with the light on and looked out. She touched her stomach and smiled. In the easy darkness there was this recognition. Between them a filament of longing. He waved even though he knew she couldn't see because it was dark.

The houses wound around each other like a wheel. Somewhere deeper in the estate was the hub but Ash's house was close to the rim. Mattie thought you could spin through these circles forever and never see anyone looking out, all the eyes turned inwards on worlds they had not the power to imagine. He thought that this was a rich estate because of the circles. Poor estates were rectangles. Still, someone had written in Tippex on the Hillcrest Close sign the words, *Sarah = a dirty smelly whore.* It must have taken hours. Unless whoever did it had one of those Tippex pens, which Mattie didn't. He guessed the Sarah in question was Sarah Driscoll, father an engineer with the Council. She was in fifth year, one year behind him. She was nice to him sometimes. She wore glasses.

He went down the hill.

Jack Lantry was dreaming. In his dream his chum Westy West came to stand beside his bed. In the dream Jack knew that Westy was dead. His face was the colour of limestone. His eyes were the colour of lichen. His teeth were the colour of the sea. He sat with his back against the wall. Jack could hear his breathing, mechanical and fast, like turbines going full ahead. Together they looked at the grey light. I've had me innings, chum, Jack said. Westy said nothing.

Don't you give me the silent treatment, Jack said. You were always a ruddy fool.

This had been agreed between them since childhood. It did not require comment.

Aye aye, Jack?

Aye aye, Westy old chum.

You done for me in that fucking *Britomart*, Jack.

We couldn't stop, could we, Jack said. If I had the wheel I'd have turned her round, but I didn't have it, did I? Orders are orders.

The order was to sink the *Navarino* by gunfire. Fourth of July 1942. About nine o'clock in the evening and broad bally daylight. Old Westy's stone above in the graveyard says *Lost at Sea*. But Westy was never lost. He knew where he was all right, on his way to Davy Jones. Jack was thinking of that old *Navarino* slowly swinging in a cold grey sea up where the seas of the world swirl around the top. The way up is the same as the way down. Westy was an engine-room artificer on that ghost of a ship. The ruddy Heinkels got her, no steerage way. Knock her out, the old man said, and they opened up with the forward gun.

He had a bad feeling something was going to happen. The last time Westy came to him was the night Mattie's mother died. It seemed to him that steaming through the survivors of the *Navarino* was the worst thing that ever happened. Every man Jack of them knew it was a terrible thing to do, but they couldn't stop to receive survivors, could they? The place was crawling with U-boats. A few lads caught at the trailing nets and were hauled aboard, and some were churned up by the screws. The rest were left to die in the icy water. PQ17. The navy's shame.

Orders are orders, he said.

Westy shrugged.

We just got to grin and bear it, Jack said.

I find the number for Ash's daughter. I text her. *I'm a friend of your mother's from years ago. I'm researching the death of a friend of hers, a boy called Lantry. I was wondering if we could meet. I'm staying not far from Rally.*

Almost immediately the reply comes back. *Sure, I'm on furlough because of the pandemic so any time suits.*

No questions asked. As if she were expecting me.

It's as if I'm looking at a grown-up Mattie Lantry. She's sitting at the outermost table in front of Billy Regan's. The same facial structure. Mattie was tall and dark-eyed, broad-shouldered, his hands hardened by the boatyard work. His face was pale as stone, with pronounced cheekbones and full lips. It was almost girlish. He had a ratty Fair Isle sweater that he wore, seemingly without washing, and his cords were too flared for the fashion, a leftover from the early seventies, no one knew where he got them. A shock of black hair that she has too. But there's something else I can't quite work out. She's wearing jeans and a T-shirt, a light windcheater thrown on the seat beside her. The day is bright and sunny and the water is sparkling but there's a breeze coming down the harbour. A huge bank of sea-fog waits offshore for the tide to turn. It will come in on the rise and the day will turn cold and clammy. I remember being caught in it on the doctor's boat, a blank so dense we could hardly see the bow from the cockpit. I was employed at blowing a foghorn and listening for a reply.

There are boats coming and going, dinghy sailors calling to each other, a Moody 33 making sail, a group of sea-anglers noisily transferring from pier to boat. The bar is not open – it opens around eleven – so we have the place to ourselves apart from an elderly man strolling by, towed by a Jack Russell. I introduce myself and we shake hands.

Did you say Jim Winter? Mum talked about you. You were a friend of hers.

Those dark eyes. The memory is intense. I'm back in 1980, just as lost as I was then, as uncertain.

I was, I say. She and my then-girlfriend, Miriam Healy, and ...

I look at her carefully.

... Mattie Lantry.

My dad, she says.

I nod slowly as if I had only now understood. But the scene in the graveyard from Deirdre's opening is suddenly there in memory as sharp as a piece of broken glass on a sunlit road. The boy lying in the grave, the woman with the roses, the priest not understanding, the workers collecting the dustbins of the world in her beautiful phrase. I remember that he was found with his arms thrown out, almost as if he welcomed his end. Crucified, as Deirdre wrote.

I wondered when I saw your name.

How did you get my number?

Willy Morrish.

I see. I imagine Willy hasn't brushed up on his GDPR. Sharing data and all that.

I smile. I used to know Willy too, when I was living in Rally. There's not many around here I don't know. From the old days anyway. A lot of new people of course.

Can we get a cup of coffee here?

They won't open for another hour.

So what are you looking for?

Tell me what you know about your dad.

I know all about him. Mum told me the whole story several times. I think she wanted me to know that the reason he wasn't around was not that he didn't want to be. When we came here first she brought me to his grave to make sure there was no doubt. If that makes sense. I know all about how brilliant he was, and how eccentric. I know about the caravan where they used to go for privacy. I know Mum was pregnant when she went to uni. I know he was murdered.

We are silent for a time. The word 'murder' has fallen into the morning like a bomb. I am conscious of faint shivering of my skin, like a nano-earthquake spreading from my chest to my hands. I'm trying to think of a way of mentioning the book.

So you lived on the island for a time?

Not really. I was at uni in England when she moved here. I spent the summer on the island and Christmas with my stepdad. The following Christmas I was here. I got a job here to be near Mum. Brexit will interfere with all that, I expect. People won't be able to come and go so easily.

I think the common travel area will continue, I say.

She nods. Maybe. I have a feeling things will get complicated once we … once they leave. Anyway, the year I spent Christmas on the island there was a hurricane. It was incredible. We thought the sea was going to come in on top of us or the roof was going to blow off. It didn't happen.

That must have made a change from London.

She rolls her eyes and shakes her head.

Billy Regan is opening the pub door. He sees me and comes over.

Great day, thanks be to God.

Great day, Billy.

The forecast is shite though.

Rain?

Rain and wind. I could manage a coffee if ye'd fancy it.

We'd love one, she says.

Black?

Milk no sugar, she says.

Same for me.

He goes off at his lumbering pace. We both watch him.

I never yet heard him say something good was going to happen tomorrow, I tell her. Billy can always find the lead behind the silver lining. He has an unerring instinct for it. The lead is always brighter than the silver for him.

You're a writer, aren't you?

Guilty as charged.

Are you writing a book about my dad?

I was wondering if you're doing that, I said.

You're the writer, not me.

I'm watching her closely, but I don't know what I expect to see. She is watching me too. I have the feeling my question about the book took her by surprise, but I'm not good at reading people's expressions. Neither of us says anything for a time. I'm trying to wait her out, but I suspect she's doing the same to me. Whoever makes the first move loses.

Billy Regan is back, carrying a tray with two mugs and a milk jug.

Crab is on, he says, in case you'll be here.

I doubt I will be, Billy.

Fair enough.

The coffee is hot and bitter.

I notice the still, dark head of a seal drifting between the moorings. They are curious creatures. I wonder what they make of coffee-drinking.

Look Mattie, I say, someone sent me a book they're writing on the events around the death of your father. It's anonymous. I've been trying to think who it could be and I've eliminated everyone. You're the last chance.

Don't look at me. I'm not writing a book. But what kind of a book is it?

It's supposed to be fiction, but the details are mostly correct. Whoever is writing it, they know an awful lot about what happened.

I wasn't even born then. How would I know? All I know is what Mum told me.

It's a long time since I was so nervous. I'm not thinking straight.

And what does your mum know? Does she know who the killer was?

Don't you think if she knew she'd have gone to the police?

It is only now, when she says police, that I notice her English intonation. Close to but not the same as Deirdre's Zoom voice. But then, everybody's voice is a little distorted online.

I mean, why would she just write a book about it? She gets angry every time she thinks about it.

I went to see her.

On the island?

Yes. She's still very angry. She thinks I let your dad down.

Funnily enough, she never mentioned that to me. So tell me, why does Mum *think* you let my dad down?

A curious half smile. Maybe she's amused by my embarrassment.

Your mum claims I was Mattie's friend by day and Jason Long's by night. You know how Long hated your dad.

Longy Long, she snorts, the minister.

259

Junior minister. He lost out in the last reshuffle.

So you were part of the gang that tormented my dad. And this woman writing this book knows all about it?

I never tormented him.

She finishes her coffee in one gulp.

Thanks for the coffee.

She's on her feet now.

One thing I'd like to say, she says. You look scared to me. What are you afraid of? Do you have some dirty secret that this woman knows about?

She stands for a moment looking down at me, and then a wave of the hand.

Ta-ra, Jim Winter. See you around.

And she's walking to her car. She stops with the door open and looks back.

Stay away from my mum, she says. She's had a hard life. I don't want anyone messing things up for her again. Leave her alone.

Driving back to Gortnacarriga the thought occurs to me that she knew the writer was a woman. I try to remember if I gave that information away. I had planned to refer to the writer as 'they' throughout and I'm reasonably sure I stuck to that plan throughout our brief conversation. I pull over at a point above Cannavee Strand and send her a text: *How did you know the writer was a woman?* This time she does not reply immediately. I call Catherine. Danielle is slightly better, she tells me, but still anguished. I notice these technical terms – anguish is very existentialism *à la* Jean-Paul Sartre. For Catherine her philosophy permeates her everyday life in a way I have never seen with others of her calling. She doesn't turn up flashy phrases or quotations as I've seen others do, but it's part of how she sees the world. It often occurs to me that this is how philosophy is meant to be, but rarely is – a way of experiencing reality.

And how are you?

I'm OK, she says. You?

I miss you.

That's a good start.

I can hear her smile over the phone and I smile too.

When are you coming back down?

I was thinking maybe tomorrow, she says.

The sooner the better. Remember the day we decided to buy the house?

I have been thinking of that morning of transcendent sunshine, the intensity of spring, more than just a season, an affirmation, a promissory note, a force. It was a moment of abandon, a single decisive action. And from where I sit now it was a time of innocence.

No regrets? Catherine says.

No regrets.

What brought it to mind today?

I'm just sitting here over Cannavee Strand and I can see the house up the valley. I was remembering the day we came down to see it and we stopped here and tried to pick it out.

I remember.

It was exhilarating, the crazy drive west to see the place, thunderous downpours followed by intense sunshine. As we went west the weather changed and just before Rally we broke into clear blue skies. I had last been in the house as a teenager when Uncle Peter's wife Margaret served hot potatoes and boiled bacon and cabbage to the harvesters. Peter and Margaret are both gone now. Time swept them away as it will sweep us away. Mattie lies in his grave and something of him survives in his daughter. Motion towards, motion away from. Time is motion. Suddenly I am flushed with shame at what is to come. What this cursed book will reveal.

From: der-driu101@hotmail.com
To: writers.anonymous2020@outlook.com
Subject: Lantry Novel

Dear WA,

Tomorrow morning, La Galerie in Rally. I'll talk to you — The attached is just a first draft — Maybe you can help me finish it?

D

Mattie looked up at the empty cold distance between stars. Cancer is a constellation in the Northern sky with an area of 506 square degrees. Mattie didn't know what a square degree was. Its brightest star, Beta Cancri, has a magnitude of three point five. He didn't know what magnitude was either, at least not in relation to the light of a star. He would need to look it up. They had the M of *Britannica* at home. Cancer is the crab. He moves sideways and never forwards and he is both the most protected and isolated of all. A crab has its sexual organ on its legs. Nobody has ever said that crabs have a good family life. He was born under the sign of Cancer. The water form of Cancer is the torrent. Cancer people are sensitive, self-contained, home-lovers, sentimental; they can also be touchy and clingy. The moon rules. He didn't know what clingy meant and he didn't think it would be in the *Britannica*. Unless barnacles. They were hard to shift. There are jellyfish that glow in moonlight. *Pelagia noctiluca* is one. A large gathering of jellyfish is called a bloom. Sometimes covering ten square miles, the expert said, and up to ten metres deep. It glows purple or mauve.

No more school. Mattie was frankly relieved.

One time, by mistake, his grandad used a homework copy to get the fire going. Where's your homework, Lantry? My grandfather burned it, sir. Tittering. God give me patience.

Comic Morrish was standing outside the graveyard quivering. Mattie went up to him.

Willie must have been at sea again. Comic was always lost when Willie was on the boats.

What you doing here, Comic? You should be at home.

The dog did not respond.

That dog is interested in bones, Mattie thought. Lot of bones in a graveyard.

He tried to pick the dog up but Comic wriggled free and bolted through the gate. Mattie followed him and was surprised to find him tugging at something in one of the graves. Whatever he was tugging at kicked him.

Oi, Mattie said. You can't kick a dog.

It was a boy and a girl and when he got closer he saw that it was Jimmy Winter and Miriam Healy and there was some sort of how's your father. Miriam was crying. They were lying on the smooth place between two graves and as soon they heard Mattie they both jumped up and Miriam ran away.

Fuck you, Lantry, Jimmy Winter said. Why don't you mind your own business?

Why was Miriam crying?

Fuck off.

Mattie shrugged and turned to go but the minute he turned his back Jimmy Winter jumped him. Mattie tried to shake him off but Jimmy had his arms around him. He threw Mattie to the ground. That was the last thing Mattie remembered.

No. That's not true. It didn't happen like that. It's guesswork and bad guesswork. Even as a piece of fiction it's forced.

But I have to be careful. She's on the right track.

I didn't sleep last night. I spent the hours turning versions of my story in my head, trying to isolate what was true and what was fiction, trying to patch it all together so that it made sense.

But it has never made sense to me. None of it. The boy I was then. When I heard that my father had been transferred, that coming down for mid-term break it would be to the city, that I would never have to go back to Rally, I almost burst into tears. Because in the weeks of college I had invented a new me. I stopped using drugs. I drank more moderately. I applied myself to my study. But it was tentative, experimental, I wasn't sure it would work, that I could sustain it. The moment I saw my parents in the new house it suddenly was a reality. I could be this new person. I gave myself permission to begin to forget. To forget Rally and Mattie and Miriam and Ash. To forget Longy and his twisted pleasures.

And this morning as I drive down to Rally an overnight wind has blown out and the air is crisp and the sky is a powdery blue. Pure white clouds over the sea. A freckling of white sails, a trawler trailing a confetti of gulls. I tell myself I am that new person. I am not that I was, to paraphrase Iago.

I leave the car at O'Neill's garage, where they tell me they have the window glass in spares. Nailer, 'The Boss' as the repairs manager calls him, has heard I'm coming in. I have to call to his office in the sales section. I walk between the shiny new Toyotas, all hybrid efficiency and ecological boasting, and see a masked Nailer O'Neill in a tweed jacket in a shiny office, rising to greet me with the salesman's all-inclusive, How are we Jimmy? I feel like telling him that I can only speak for myself. Long time no see, he says. He offers me a coffee. We talk for a few minutes and then to my surprise he takes a copy of my last novel out of a drawer and asks me to dedicate it to his wife, Monica. Monica, it turns out, is only a massive fan. He himself doesn't have time for reading, as I can imagine. A busy man. When he gets home in the evening all he wants to do is watch the telly. The wife wouldn't let him bring all my books in. You'll embarrass the poor man, she said. But she has all of them though. Every last one. A massive fan altogether.

Next time I'm passing, I tell him, bring them all. I'll sign everything for her. Anything for a fan.

Nailer the hanger-on, never any harm in him. A big soft lad, lean as a sheet of glass. Now, my guess is that he's six foot two.

Monica would be over the moon, he tells me. Monica is a great reader. She has a path worn to the library and the bookshop. Do I remember Monica? She was three years behind us at school. He gestures at a photo on his desk. I see a Nailer O'Neill at twenty-two or so, still recognisably the boy I knew, and a slim, blonde, blue-eyed beauty in an elaborate wedding dress, the veil thrown back. I don't remember her. He's a grandfather now, it seems. One of his sons is at a sales desk in the open area among the shiny new Toyotas. He's on the phone when Nailer shows me out. I recall, somewhat surprisedly, that Nailer's real first name is Emmet.

I walk down to La Galerie. The sign on the door says *Closed Monday Lunchtime.* I push the door in. To my surprise I see Miriam, Ash and Mattie sitting at a table with a large cafetière of coffee in front of them. I feel the shock hit my system, the cold in my veins, the return of the hammering heart. This book is poisoning my metabolism.

They beckon me over. They're laughing.

You should see your face, Miriam says.

I sit down. A cup is pushed in front of me and Mattie offers coffee.

My heart is fast enough already, I say stupidly.

It's decaf, she says, and pours it anyway.

I add milk with a shaking hand. How much do they know? What do they suspect? I look at Miriam. I realise now they have been in control from the start. That is why she told me about Ash. First she froze me out then, a big concession, she reluctantly told me where Ash was. But from the start she was leading me on. If you see her, tell her to get in touch with me. Did they get Willie Morrish to give me the number? They intended to be found. This confrontation was planned. And that last chapter was intended to provoke me to react, a bait. I took it. But now I'll spit it out.

Which one of you is the writer?

You can take your mask off, Miriam says. You're legally entitled not to wear it if you're consuming food or a beverage on an appropriately licensed premises, which this is.

Yes, take the mask off, Jimmy, Ash says, and laughs.

After Mattie's death Ash called to see old Jack Lantry, she tells me. She was terrified, full of dread and sadness and anger. She cried all the way there. The old man was confused and tearful, but ever the gentleman charmer. How do you do, young lady? She could barely understand the words. There was something wrong with one side of his face. I'm fine, Mr Lantry, and you? Very well I'm sure. Then tears. Hers first, then his. Oh lassie, they did for poor Mattie. He told her Mattie was sweet on her, that he was forever talking about her. He held her hand for a long time while they talked. At one point he said, I'm for the high road, lassie, but they should never have done that to our Mattie. She remembered his exact words. Our Mattie. Then he sent her up to Mattie's room. Take any keepsake you like, dear, he said, it'll all go to the breaker's yard in the end.

I threw myself down on the bed, Ash says, and cried for ten minutes. I could smell him on the pillow. He always used some weird old-fashioned soap like carbolic or something.

She tried to memorise every detail of the room. Nowadays she would have used her phone to photograph it.

At that point I notice her phone – an iPhone 6 – on the table in front of her. So she wasn't entirely disconnected from the world or from email out there on her island.

When she stopped crying she took Mattie's copy of *The South Pole* with his marks and notes in the margin. She saw his note on the back page – *Grandad probably dying, Mattie afraid.* There were other notes scattered throughout. *Kissed Ash today* followed by a drawing of a wire figure leaping into the air with his arms raised. She burst into tears again. Then she was about to leave when she saw an old ledger. She opened it and saw that it was a diary. The first thing she saw was: *Mother of pearl inside razor shell reminds Mattie of Ash's eyes.* More tears. She took the diary too. She showed them to old Jack and he waved his hand. Take them, lassie, the peepers are going on me, I can hardly read the paper these days. He shook her hand again. You're a good girl, he said, as if she were a child.

So that's how you could write as Mattie? Because you had his diary.

I'm trying to think if Mattie could have seen anything. Longy and me. He could appear in the most unexpected places, always with something strange to tell, ideas tumbling out of him, stories about what he'd seen, where he'd been, to whom he'd spoken. And he liked hiding, or at least he felt he had to hide to avoid the gang. He could be lurking in the shadows of the Ghost Train or sitting among the boats at the pier. Suddenly he'd step out. *Jimmy, did you know that we're on the same latitude as Cape Bauld, Newfoundland? Jimmy, do you know the word for a big group of jellyfish is a bloom?* What did he see? And did he write it down?

Ash: It wasn't me. didn't write it.

Mattie: That would be me. Thank you for the advice.

Her smile is her father's. I can't take my eyes off her lips. That's why it was so episodic, because she was working off his impressions. She couldn't fill in the connecting narrative because she wasn't there, she didn't know the connections.

Me: I see. And how did you know it was me?

Mattie: From the start we had an idea because of the way you phrased the ad.

Ash: I was the one who saw it.

Me: I thought you didn't have the internet?

Ash: I'm on Facebook. But I was only guessing. Just something about it that set me thinking.

Mattie: It was just, Wouldn't it be funny if …

Ash: And Mattie was writing anyway, so what harm.

Mattie: Then when you advised me to change the names, that rang a bell, because you gave your own name and Miriam's even though neither was mentioned in any newspaper. We know because we did the same research. A bit more thoroughly, maybe. Then you said Mattie never made speeches in public. At that point we got serious and started looking for clues to your identity. They weren't hard to find. In your ad you couldn't resist boasting about your five novels and your one book of non-fiction. A study of Italian film, if I recall correctly. They call it a monograph, don't they? I never understood why. Anyway, it wasn't hard. Google Irish writers and count their publications. Wikipedia has most of them. We couldn't believe our luck. When you came to see my mum on the island we knew we had you on the run. We all laughed about the way you tried to play the innocent. We went back over the emails and there you were saying you had the feeling that all of this is based on real events. Remember that? I thought I'd split my sides.

Me: And you all decided between you to stitch me up? This draws laughter.

Ash: We know you did it, we just don't know exactly how or why. It's the reason you disappeared without trace. You couldn't get away fast enough.

Miriam: You went into voluntary exile. Not just that. After the murder you hardly came out of the house. And when you did you were jumpy, nervous. I couldn't understand what had happened to you. You were all over me and then you hardly wanted to see me. It wasn't until I talked to Ash and Mattie a few years ago that I started to figure it out. I had a diary too, though it was a pretty childish one by comparison with Mattie's, and there was one entry that really jumped out at me when I looked back over it. It was shortly after the murder. *J very strange since M died.* That's all it said, but it said enough.

Ash: That's what made the connection for us. As simple as that.

Mattie: That night, the night of the results, you were thrown out of the disco for fighting with Miriam. Right Miriam?

Miriam: (Nodding) Right. You were pissed out of your mind and I was annoyed about it.

Mattie: The graveyard was on your way home. You had to pass it. Why didn't you come forward as a witness? You were never interviewed by the guards. That was dodgy too. We all came forward, told our stories. They didn't have to look for us.

Miriam: You were supposedly his best friend. The rest of us came forward but you didn't. What were you scared of?

Ash: You were guilty.

Miriam: You were afraid you'd give something away.

Mattie: You slipped up when you told me you recognised all the names in the book from the newspapers. You weren't in the newspapers because the police never went near you.

Ash: The bank manager's son.

Mattie: Class is not really visible in Ireland, but it's always there.

I say: You're like the three weird sisters in *Macbeth*. Or a Greek chorus.

Laughter again. Sarcastic laughter.

Me: So you had Mattie's diary?

Mattie: And I had my mum's memories and Miriam's and Miriam's diary.

Me: So that's how you pieced it together. Nice work. But you're wrong about me.

Mattie: My agent is pleased with how it's shaping up.

I lift the coffee cup to my mouth with a flourish and drink from it. I am conscious that my hand has steadied. I swallow my coffee and put the cup down calmly on the saucer. Uppermost in my mind is the thought that I didn't see any changes in style between the excerpts. The two older women may be contributing memories and even diary entries, but Mattie is the writer. And Mattie may actually want to write a book. This may not be solely about revenge. She was writing it before she signed up for my workshop. She has a natural talent. I wonder if she has published other stuff – stories, or bits of memoir.

Me: I don't believe you.

Mattie: About what?

Me: The agent shit. It's too easy.

I notice an exchange of glances between the three women.

Me: Your book is not ready to go to an agent, Mattie. Credit me with some knowledge of how the business works. And no agent would send it out in its present state.

Mattie: You murdered my father.

Me: Why would I have done that?

She looks first at her mother then at Miriam. Then she lowers her eyes. She looks so much like Mattie it is unnerving. I'm reminded of a poem by Seán Ó Ríordáin in which he talks about seeing the eyes of a woman he loved in the head of her son. I remember how Mattie would look at me, at Ash, at the sea, at birds – he had a way of looking that was intense beyond mere interest. He saw things in their essence. Facts were like a scaffolding that he assembled to see through to the inner perfection. Like his obsession with the Gulf Stream and with the Pole – years before we started to think about the climate as a single organism, he saw it that way. I recall him talking to me once about what would happen if the Gulf Stream shifted, and he described the ocean we were looking at so vividly as a frozen waste that I could see it before my eyes. I see it still.

Ash: We were hoping you'd tell us. We're prepared to make you an offer.

Me: What kind of an offer?

Ash: We'll change the names and the details so as to protect everyone if you tell us what really happened.

Me: And if I don't?

Ash: We publish it.

Mattie: You're thinking about it. That means you have something to tell.

Me: Everyone has something to tell. I've made a living from that.

I lean back in my chair and take my mask from my pocket. The now universal signal that someone is leaving.

Me: No one will publish your book. Anyone who did would be sued out of existence. I'll certainly sue. So will Junior Minister Longy Long and quite possibly Dr Charlie Harney too. And I'd like to remind you that the guards failed to turn up even a viable suspect for the murder at the time. There is no evidence to link anyone to Mattie's death. Certainly not me. Because I didn't do it.

Mattie: Liar.

Ash: You're a cold bastard, Jimmy Winter.

Me: Everyone here has a mobile phone, I say. Please put them on the table.

They know exactly what I mean – I can see the excitement in their faces. Miriam takes hers from the pocket of her canvas smock. Mattie has hers in her handbag. She watches me carefully as she takes it out. Ash's is already on the table face up. Now all three phones are on the table. I touch them all individually so that their screens light up. Nobody is recording me.

Paranoid much, Mattie says.

You have no idea what happened. I let Mattie down, that's true. The truth is I would have done anything to be accepted into Longy's gang and I did. I'm not proud of it. In fact it's my abiding shame. They were the cool boys and I was an outsider. Being friends with Mattie actually made everything worse, because Mattie was even further out than me and I know, that's pretty spineless, before you even say it. But when they took notice of me I felt good. I had a place. I didn't like what I had to do, but at least I was in. But I would never have hurt Mattie. Never. And I can tell you why.

Ash: What *did* you do to be accepted?

Miriam: Tell us why, Jimmy, do. We'd love to know.

I put my mask on.

I was in love with him, I say.

I walk up to the corner of Union Street and knock on the door of Jason Long's constituency office. His face looks out from a poster completely covering the only window in the building. Jason Long, An Ireland for All, Your Local TD, serving you always.

What kind of a revelation have I just made? All the stupid stuff about checking the phones and then what? I was in love with him. They will be laughing at me now.

I hear keys being turned and bolts drawn, and then the door opens.

Come in quick before anyone sees, Longy Long says, I'm not meant to be here at all at all today. If they see me I'll be plagued for the rest of the morning.

He bolts the door hurriedly behind me. So much for serving us always, I think. He is not wearing a mask.

The room is bare as an army barracks, painted in civil-service green, the walls lined with plastic chairs, a rack of leaflets of some kind on one wall, a photograph of Longy's father standing beside Jackie Kennedy on another, a coffee table in the middle of the room with stacks of *Golf* and *Hello* magazines. It looks like a doctor's waiting room. I know politicians call these rooms 'clinics', but I didn't think they went in for this level of sterility.

He leads me into his office, which is equally bare, though painted magnolia. A Formica-topped desk, a filing cabinet, two grey plastic chairs on my side of the desk and again, a line of plastic chairs against the wall. For meetings, I assume. The constituency *cumann* gathering to plot election campaigns, fix contracts, rezone farming land, plan council strategies. On his side I note a very attractive Eames office chair in leather and chrome. Seven or eight hundred euro's-worth is my best guess. The junior minister is entitled to his comfort.

I won't shake hands, Jimmy, he says, if you don't mind. As the good Dr Holohan advises.

I keep my mask on. I have calculated that we are almost the requisite two metres apart. Good enough. I never really wanted to be any closer anyway. And considering how many politicians have developed Covid, from Trump to Bolsonaro to Boris Johnson, I think it circumspect to treat him as unclean. Besides, being masked feels a little clandestine in the context. I feel the same way every time I enter a bank now. There was a time when you'd have been arrested for going into a bank with a mask on. And there is comfort in knowing that he can only see part of my face.

So this is the nerve centre, I say.

He laughs. There's a fair amount of nerves around here all right. Time of a by-election you could say we're a club for nervous wrecks.

We sit down facing each other. He wears a toupee, I can see, that anomalous shock of brown hair on an ageing face. It reminds me of Silvio Berlusconi's hair job, though not as professional-looking – or as expensive. He's much heavier than he appears in the photograph in his election poster, a jowly neck settling downwards into a double chin, a heavy belly suspended in a white shirt, the buttons straining under the burden. No tie, the neck open to the first button signals that the minister is at home. He is wearing a tweed jacket, but a photograph hanging behind his head shows him shaking hands with Barack Obama in a well-tailored black suit. A transatlantic vibe. It's clear where the Long family looks for validation. The photograph is intended to show a politician with international connections, not just a local party man the height of whose achievements is a junior ministry, but someone with reach and power. In fact he was a full minister in a previous administration but backed the wrong horse in the leadership contest and was lucky to get the junior post – the conventional wisdom *pace* the *Irish Times* editor who wrote his political obituary. The photographs are telling the loyal membership that Jason Long TD would be back.

Congratulations on your distinguished literary career, Jimmy. We follow you here, you know.

And congratulations to yourself on your political career.

The call to serve, don't you know. It's a vocation frankly, runs in the family. Like your own good self, except there's little enough creative in what I do. It's all hard facts. Numbers. Data. You know the way. That's where the hard left have it wrong. It's all ideology for them, but we deal in facts, facts, facts.

I can imagine.

I will say this now, going forward I would be suggesting to the Development Committee here that we might think about a festival in your name. I would be proposing that. What would you say to it? Your good self and your good wife would be the guests of honour of course. The Jimmy Winter Literary Weekend. Or would it be James Michael Winter? Michael would have been the middle name if I'm not mistaken? After your late father, God rest him.

I write as Jim.

Maybe a three-day gig with music and Irish dancing and a few writers to give speeches or public interviews, that kind of thing. You'd be able to suggest a few names, I'd say. I'm going to say September when the tourism is dying down a bit. I'd be delighted to open it myself. If you'll give it your blessing Jason Long will not be found wanting. It'd be good for the town. When all this is over, of course. There will be no public gatherings for the foreseeable future I may tell you. You should hear the meetings we have with the science crowd. Jaze, it would stand your hair on end. The public don't know the half of it. PowerPoint things that would put the shite crossways in you. Modelling is all the go now. They have a mathematics professor doing the modelling for them. He gives me nightmares altogether, that's when I understand what he's saying. This virus is a total plague.

Well, I say, I'd be honoured of course, but to be honest I don't think it would work. You know, I'm not that famous or anything.

Longy laughs. A humble writer, now that would be a first.

Honestly, I don't think it would be worth it.

Well, Jimmy, we'll see. Jason Long would be a massive supporter of local talent. It is people like you that allow this country to punch above our weight on the international stage. Us politicians are only standing on the shoulders of giants. I don't have the time for reading myself, as you can imagine. It's all I can do to keep on top of my brief. You have no idea, Jim. The mountains of shite I have to wade through. But I would be a massive supporter of Irish creativity.

That's very kind of you to say that.

Sure it's pure true. And they tell me you have a house out at Gortnacarriga?

I don't know if you remember my Uncle Peter? I used to pick spuds for him in the summertime. It was his place.

I don't think I do remember him. Was he a Peter Winter? Let me think now. I would've been out that way canvassing often and often but I don't remember a Peter Winter.

He'd have been the other crowd.

Hah! A Blueshirt? Well that explains it. I wouldn't darken the man's door.

Well, he wasn't exactly a Blueshirt, but he was of that persuasion.

I would have known a lot of his neighbours though. Johnny Whelan there in Cannavee is a great supporter. A fine old trooper. You know him of course.

I know Johnny. A good neighbour.

Johnny is all that, he says. A gentleman. Can I offer you a coffee? We have one of these things that your man Clooney is always advertising. Margaret, the secretary, usually makes it, but I could take a hand to it myself. It's not rocket science she tells me, although it makes a very small coffee in my opinion. It is well known Jason Long is not technically minded, but I'd have a shot at it.

I shake my head.

Fair enough. I'm not gone on it myself, I prefer the tea, but sure we're in Europe now. It's all coffee in Europe. So tell me this now, what brings you down to Rally after all these years?

I'm sure Charlie told you I was writing a memoir.

A memoir? He said something all right. But that didn't register with me.

Really?

I smile behind my mask. If Charlie hadn't told him I was writing a memoir I'm certain I would never have heard from him. Junior minister contacts writer of his own free will? An event that has never been heard of in the long sad history of Ireland and its even sadder writers. And why bother to threaten me with a solicitor if he didn't know? I would have thought politicians had to be good liars, but Jason Long is as obvious as Pinocchio's nose. Then again, maybe that explains why he's a junior and not a minister.

Well, that's why I'm here, I say.

A memoir about your time down here in Rally?

Exactly.

Now why would people be interested in all that? Sure nothing ever happens here. A sleepy little town. Except in the summer time of course. It's mad altogether in summer. Friendly, mind you. We're very welcoming down here. The kind of place where people would know if you didn't come out of the house for a bit. They'd be keeping an eye on their neighbours. You know what I mean? It's a very safe place to live.

But something did happen, Jason.

He leans back in his chair and joins the tips of his fingers in front of him. It is a studied, deliberate gesture slightly undermined by the creaking of the leather, which sounds like subdued farting. The slow joining of fingers indicates self-control, power. I can see him doing it at a party meeting. I wonder if other people are more impressed than I am. I doubt it. But it means that he knows exactly what I'm talking about. Otherwise I would have got another string of vacuousness.

Would you care to be more precise, Jimmy?

No.

I think I sense panic. There's something fragile, unsettled, mobile about his features. He looks at me with big eyes, his mouth open. I notice the hand on the desk is clenched into a fist.

Jimmy, he says.

Longy.

You're a married man. I'm a married man. A hundred to one your good lady knows sweet fuck all about your teenage antics.

I'm talking about the murder of Mattie Lantry.

I know what you're talking about. And you know what I'm talking about and it's a different thing altogether.

We stare at each other in silence for a time. Then that dead smile that I was so familiar with as a boy.

You always were a snivelling little prick, he says.

He leans forward suddenly, his hands making a glassy sound as they slap down on the plastic surface of the desk. All the uncertainty is gone.

I'll make sure you come down too, Jimmy Winter. Full disclosure is the best defence. I'll tell them everything. Do you take my meaning? I mean everything.

His phone starts to ring. He takes it from a drawer and clicks it silent.

I hope you have a good lawyer, he says. Because the first thing I'll do is I'll sue you and I'll sue whoever is stupid enough to publish it too. Jason Long won't have his good name dragged through the mud just so you can make a bit of a sensation. A bestseller. You'll settle out of court and there will be a non-disclosure agreement. Am I right?

He thinks he's won.

You won't go to court, Jimmy boy, because you know what'll come out. They'll – what's that they say? They'll pulp the book.

I lean forward, closing the sacred two-metre distance a little. What if it wasn't me writing the book? What if it was someone else?

I can see him calculating and I can see the moment he comes to the conclusion that I'm bluffing, that it's too unlikely to be true. And I can see that he hates me for baiting him.

He shrugs and raises his hands palm up.

Kids of course. Experimenting. We all did things. Didn't we, Jimmy? Sure nowadays it's a thing of nothing. Ireland is a different place now. Gay marriage and abortion and what have you. You see kids holding hands walking down the street. Boys and boys. In our day someone would have bate the shite out of them.

His eyes still hold mine. I feel my gorge rising, bile burning somewhere just above my heart. There is something coiled in him, a tension ready to explode. It has been there a long time. This is the Longy I remember. As a boy he could lash out without giving any indication it was coming, just that sense of a spring wound up and ready for action. We were all afraid of him, except maybe Mattie Lantry. I half expect it now, a punch from across the desk. But instead he tilts back again. His cool is even more unnerving than his earlier smile. It reminds me of the face of a dead gecko, big dead eyes and a wide mouth. In Rome the landlady had a cat who enjoyed catching them. He would drop them at the balcony door of my flat and disappear. Come hunting geckos, Irish boy, was the message.

The beast has returned. Yesterday they announced one thousand two hundred and eighty-three new cases and we're back in quarantine. No travel beyond five kilometres of home, no meeting friends, no gatherings. I'm not sleeping. At night I slip out of the bed and go downstairs. I try to read. I put milk in a saucepan and heat it. Sometimes I drink it. I try to avoid alcohol but sometimes I pour myself a brandy. I read until my eyes tire. I check the newspapers online but quickly stop because the news is uniformly bad. The virus is everywhere. In the USA an unstoppable tsunami of infections is sweeping through the major cities and spreading into the states – more than eight million cases now. Trump seems to have recovered from his dose, to the disappointment of much of the world, and thirteen fascists have been charged with an attempt to kidnap the governor of Michigan. Johnson, Modi and Bolsonaro seem to be leading their people to the same oxygen tent as Trump occupies, and their countries are deep wells of infection that will surely lead to mutations of the virus.

Emily wrote to tell me that she had found a local publisher – Moosehead Books – to publish her Italian story. They wanted it called *Salter Lost in Rome* and she had agreed. She thanked me for my help. Tom told me he had sent the first four chapters of *The Bought Woman* to several agents and was awaiting a response. I have begun to receive emails from Judy again. She has sent nothing but has told me that she is working on a book based on her mother's life. Her mother was sent to England on the *Kindertransport*, a little Jewish girl who never saw her parents again. Her letters become increasingly interesting, and I have encouraged her to keep working and not to worry about sending me stuff until she's happy. Walter has disappeared.

So too has Deirdre. Her silence terrifies me, even though I don't think the book can be published for the reasons I told her – no publisher would touch it for fear of being sued. But she might edit it to remove the real names, to anonymise it. Or she might self-publish it and face the consequences. Either way, she never guessed my real reason for running away.

Before we closed up the house in late August, Catherine and I visited Mattie Lantry's grave. He and old Jack are buried in the hills above Rally in the ruins of Kylmoe, a very ancient but very poor church, first mentioned in papal chancery documents in 1199. The last remnant of that period is a beautifully constructed and off-centre Hiberno-Romanesque eastern window. The papal bureaucracy must have been extensive to reach this far into the poverty and desolation of the edge of the world. This was the part of Ireland most devastated by the Great Famine, and like all the burial grounds around contains its fair share of the imperial oversight – a sizeable mass-grave at one corner, a Famine pit.

Kylmoe is perched on the side of a broken hill littered with rocks and stunted briar. The banks of the enclosure are alive with angelica and loosestrife. Fuchsia grows wild and foxglove peppers the ditches with its purple fingernails this sultry late August afternoon. The vast majority of memorials in the graveyard are what are called footstones – simple chunks of uncut stone set up to mark a grave without any inscription. It is the perfect correlative of the poverty of this area, the bad land scarred everywhere with outcrops of blackening sandstone, the fields littered with the broken crust of the earth. The few properly cut and inscribed headstones stand out as the exception, so we found the Lantry grave easily. Someone was keeping it clean and there were faded red rosebuds that had never opened. By my calculation we were only eight days past his anniversary.

> *Here lies William Lantry departed this life 24th March*
> *1874*
> *his wife Sarah Lantry died 1915*
> *his son Thomas Lantry lost at sea June 1916*
> *His loving wife Mary Lantry died 1937*
> *their son William Lantry died January 1st 1954*
> *Matthew 'Mattie' Lantry died August 16th 1980 aged*
> *17 years*
> *his grandfather James 'Jack' Lantry died August 20th*
> *1980 aged 91 years*

Thomas was killed at the Battle of Jutland, I told Catherine. His ship, the *HMS Indefatigable*, blew up when a German shell penetrated to the magazine. There were three survivors out of a crew of over a thousand and Thomas was not among them. Old Jack Lantry followed him into the Royal Navy. Mattie told me the story.

It's such a sad place, she said. Did you see where they've marked out the location of the Famine pit? And those child graves.

She wandered off to photograph the church and I knelt down to pull some of the creeping buttercup that was invading his grave.

Under my breath I whispered, I'm sorry, Mattie.

I remember that night of crazy drinking, driven as much by some kind of unconscious despair as by the good news of the exam results, and the argument with Miriam, which led to me being thrown out of the disco. The two of us shouting at each other, surrounded by shocked or bemused dancers, and then, after the arrival of a pair of bouncers and the owner of the hall, her hissed dismissal: *How dare you touch me*. Now, I don't even remember what we fought about or what I had touched, if anything. Miriam says I was drunk and she's probably right. One thing I do know, whatever Ash and Mattie did – and they seem to have done everything – none of the rest of us were getting even close. When Miriam said, How dare you touch me, it can't have referred to anything very intimate. I was two years in college before I had sex and even then it seemed a miracle. Miriam reacted like an electric shock whenever a hand of mine strayed near a breast or a waistline, never mind her thighs. I don't think Longy, loud braggart that he was, had any more success than me. And I have good reason for thinking that. So I don't know why I remember her words so clearly, or why she said them.

I went out into the night. Rain was threatened but it was warm even for August. I saw Longy standing at the back corner of the Harbour Bar, a line of empty Bass bottles in front of him on the ground ranged like an armed guard. I tried to turn away before he saw me, but I was too slow. Drink and hurt slowed me.

Come here, Jimmy boy.

He was with an older man, someone I didn't know. Not a local. There was an exchange of looks between them. I may remember a snigger.

I'll see ya, Longy said.

See ya Longy.

Come on Jimmy, he called to me. He set off up the hill and I followed like the drunken fool that I was. I can still remember the sense of belonging whenever he noticed me. It makes my skin crawl now. I was craven and I knew it even at the time. How terrible had my life been that his callous ministry was like a balm to me? I can't imagine that my childhood had been so unhappy that it prepared me for this serfdom. He turned in at the kissing gate to the graveyard and flitted between the monuments. He stopped with his back to a Celtic cross, his legs spread.

In an essay about the relationship between fiction and lies, Mario Vargas Llosa said that we write books so that people can lead other lives than the ones they live, because human beings cannot accept that they are constrained to experience only one single life. But what if the purpose of fiction is the opposite: to determine one's singular life, to surround the reader or writer with a swarm of alternative lives that are not hers or his and which she or he cannot lead, in other words to refine over and over again, by a continuous process of elimination, a definition of what exactly one's life is? The precise existential inescapability of it. If that is the case then each of my books has told the story of a life that is not mine. The opposite of the autobiographical fallacy. Read my books and know that I am someone different. I am that darkness that lies beyond the dark of my books, the darkness of the edge of what's knowable. None of the sins of my characters is mine, mine is different but partakes of the same essence of transgression. Though each of the characters is potentially a part of me, none is, and by observing what I am not you may come to what I am. That line of Polonius the doctor loved to quote whenever we had to change tack comes back to mind: 'by windlasses and assay of bias, by indirections find directions out'.

This morning I told Catherine about the dread I had suffered that it was me who was really writing Deirdre's book and that I had somehow repressed all knowledge of it, and she gave me a look that said: *I knew you'd lose it completely sooner or later.*

I think she's heading towards Longy being the murderer, I said.

I had deleted the email that implicated me. Catherine had already snooped once and could do it again. I couldn't take the risk of that happening. If Deirdre put the thought in her mind …

What makes you think no one would publish this book, she said. All names have been changed, any resemblance to actual persons, living or dead, is purely coincidental – that's the usual disclaimer isn't it? I think a publisher would smell a bestseller. Nineteen eighties murder mystery solved in work of fiction. Prominent politician implicated. Too good to pass up.

Except it's not coincidental and changing the names won't change the relationships and it'll all be obvious to anyone who does five minutes' research on Google. And Minister Long would bring all the big guns to court. He could bury a publisher under a mountain of shit.

Tell me something, Jim, tell me honestly – why have you never written this story? As you explained it to me, it's your style. This is something that has really bugged me. Not so much as a passing reference in any of your books. All the elements are there in your published work – the setting, some of the characters, the sense of guilt and dread. But the story itself? Not a word. Just tell me now, honestly. The past is the past.

It was my chance for absolution, to tell everything, to match the things she told me about her early experiences of love in her convent school with a sordid tale of my own coming of age. But there is no equivalence. Hers were early, tentative moves into the world of love and sensuality, full of innocence and the excitement of transgression. Mine is about submission and betrayal, a tale of abjection. There is no question of love between me and Longy.

You think I killed him.

She looked at me in shock and I realised the thought had never entered her head.

What?

I don't know if my confusion showed, but I tried to cover my tracks anyway.

I almost feel I did kill him, I said too quickly. I've always felt that I let him down.

She could smell a lie now.

You know something you're not telling.

No no, I know what everyone else knows, that's all.

She stared at me angrily, her lips whitening, her eyes fierce, penetrating. In such moments I knew I loved her and I could not bear to lose her despite all my lies.

I don't believe you, she said.

It was one of those times when the possibility of catharsis presents itself, the chance once given never to be repeated to purge my conscience, straighten my life out, seek to win her forgiveness, take off the mask of deceit that has become a second skin. I have made much of such moments in my writing, agonising over how to resolve them. But the world of fiction is not that of life. Instead the phone rang and it was a call about one of her doctoral students who was collapsing under the strain of the pandemic and health issues, and thus the moment passed.

But the truth is I panicked. I saw the possibility and I was paralysed by the thought of the consequences. Dear Catherine, everything I told you about this story is founded on a lie. The truth is I made a silent bargain with Longy Long that he would leave me alone as long as I whored myself for him. This is my secret that I have never told you because I couldn't bear to face it. This is my shame – as much why I did it as what I did. This is the nuclear bomb in my heart. You with your clear-eyed courage and your philosopher's determination to look reality in the face could never understand the motivation of a coward. Because a coward is what I was. What I am.

What ails you, Winter, Mattie called. How did he get there? He seemed to emerge from the graves like a ghost. He could see me on my knees but I don't think he could see Longy or what I was doing. Are you sick or what?

Jesus fucking Christ, Longy said, stepping out from the shadow of the cross.

Mattie paused, shocked. I imagine he thought it was a fight or that Longy was hurting me in some way, because in a matter of seconds he was coming at us fast, fists clenched.

Longy pulled away and lunged. I rose to my feet and turned quickly, and my shoulder caught Mattie in the chest and then Longy swung hard. His fist connected with Mattie's cheek but he was already on his way down, tripping backwards over the kerb of the grave behind him. I can still hear the sound of skull on stone, in my memory it's like an egg cracking though I know that can't be real. He did not get up. Longy stood over him, fists ready. He was wearing basketball boots and bell-bottoms and a loose floral shirt and I could see that even in the fright and the blow he had not lost his erection. I vomited sharply and forcefully into the nearest grave.

Fuck, Longy said, he saw us. The fucking cunt saw us.

I ran then. Longy could have beaten me to a pulp. He was up for it. I could hear his breathing even as I was vomiting. His natural response to adrenaline was to hit someone. But he was too drunk to follow me.

I don't remember which grave Mattie fell at, and even at the time I was too drunk to have any clear idea of where we were in the graveyard other than that it can't have been far from the kissing gate. When I went back next morning I couldn't be sure that the Garda forensics tent was in the same place. He tripped and fell backwards and I was gone almost before Longy could turn back to me. What I remember most clearly is the shame. Do I remember Mattie groaning after the fall or did I invent it? It's possible that we were further in than I remember, further from the gate and more hidden from the road. It seemed to me that the coroner's report suggested more than one bruise to his face. There was something about an injury to his leg. My memory is anything but perfect. In some ways I have purged it of that night so that only the bare facts remain. Or what I think of as facts.

And speculation. There is more speculation than I care to admit. Was he dead when I ran? Did I see the cracked skull or did I imagine it? The most I could have seen was blood. How much did he see before Longy hit him? Was the sight of me on my knees in front of his worst enemy the last thing he ever saw? Did he understand what Longy and I were doing? Suddenly I recall with precision the words of a newspaper report: The court heard that the victim had inhaled blood from his nose and mouth and died by asphyxiation. His nose and mouth? Not just a blow to the head then.

I remember the light from Fastnet glowing against a capstone of low cloud. I ran all the way home. The faint throb of the disco and drinking parties in various secluded spots. All the boys and girls celebrating their results while I had suddenly and irrevocably entered the world of the unforgiven. But I never thought he was dead. Not in that moment of flight. I thought merely that he was hurt and I dreaded what he would tell people tomorrow, because whatever he thought he said. What he saw between the graves in the shadow of the cross. I don't know what I would have done had I known he was lying dead in the grave of Mrs Pearse's son. And the light coming and going like something from a bad film. And waking late to hear the news reporting a death in Rally, suspected murder in a graveyard. Vomiting again, into the toilet bowl this time. Disbelief. Shock. And a hangover to beat all hangovers. The racing heart that didn't settle for weeks. I was breathless and woke at night from dreams of drowning. If I could have undone that night, the things I did, that blow. Love of a kind turned into murder of a kind. The cliché that we all kill the thing we love – every time I hear it quoted I feel sick.

Since then it has always been with me, a shifting darkness that lies under everything I do, an infection waiting below the skin to overwhelm my resistance, the return of the repressed. I have never felt clean since that moment. Though what I was leaving was no Eden, still it was the end of a kind of innocence. Or at least ignorance.

The truth is, I don't know whether or not he was dead when I ran. And once I turned to run I turned my back on knowing. There is no recovering the past. I will never know the truth. But mixed up in all the shame of Mattie's death is the knowledge of the sordid bargain I made with Longy. He would stop tormenting me and I would service his needs. A hundred to one your good lady knows nothing about your past. *You were always a snivelling little prick.* He had the precise measure of me.

Here in this beautiful place among the stony hills and the wordless dead I make my confession: Whoever else was there, whatever else they did, it was I who killed Mattie Lantry. I know it now. I killed him by not taking his side, by wanting him, by serving Longy, by watching him fall, by running away, by lying, by hiding, by keeping my secret. I have never told anyone what I did. Now I never will. I am certain that Jason Long won't either. As for young Mattie Lantry, who knows what she'll do, but whatever it is I have it coming.

The breeze coming down the hillside whispers through the long grass and the bloody fuchsia. It does not whisper of forgiveness.

Acknowledgements

I want to say thank you to Illan, Bríd, Ruán and Odhran, in whose house the bulk of this book was written, at their window overlooking the 'Bawn of Cannavee' and the ocean; to Liz, as always, for her love, support and critical eye; to my agent, translator, friend and fellow Genoa supporter, Stefano Tettamanti, whose faith in my work inspires me. I am grateful to the team at New Island for their continued belief in my work and, in particular, to my brilliant editor Cassia Gaden Gilmartin and Djinn von Noorden of the eagle eye.